CHEYENNE GUN

THE ADVENTURES OF
FOX RUNNING & JOHN DOOLEY

CHEYENNE GUN

RUSTY DAVIS

FIVE STAR
A part of Gale, a Cengage Company

LIBRARY OF CONGRESS CATALOGING-IN-PUBLICATION DATA

Names: Davis, Rusty, author.
Title: Cheyenne gun / Rusty Davis.
Description: First edition. | Waterville, Maine : Five Star, [2020]
Series: The adventures of Fox Running & John Dooley |
Identifiers: LCCN 2019031063 | ISBN 9781432868840 (hardcover)
Subjects: GSAFD: Western stories.
Classification: LCC PS3604.A9755 C48 2020 | DDC 813/.6—dc23
LC record available at https://lccn.loc.gov/2019031063

First Edition. First Printing: April 2020
Find us on Facebook—https://www.facebook.com/FiveStarCengage
Visit our website—http://www.gale.cengage.com/fivestar
Contact Five Star Publishing at FiveStar@cengage.com

Printed in Mexico
Print Number: 02   Print Year: 2020

CHEYENNE GUN

Chapter One

September 1882, Brittle Canyon, Wyoming-Dakota-Nebraska Border
The late afternoon sun warmed Fox Running as he squinted westward across the flatlands from the peak of the flat-topped canyon wall. An unbidden grim smile emerged as he saw the riders.

By habit, the slightly built Northern Cheyenne warrior's hands rested on the butts of the two guns he wore at his hips, even though the men below were far out of range. He wanted to make sure they saw; they felt the challenge; they knew he was not afraid. Of them. Of death. Of anything.

The wind gusted; the north wind that foretold the hard nights to come when the creeks would freeze. His hair, finally long again as a warrior's hair should be, streamed out from the back of his neck and across his bare shoulders, pulling at his temples against the band he wore around his head to keep the hair from his eyes. The cloth was marked with the blood of someone who would be avenged. Soon.

He snorted derisively as he watched the riders crane their necks and stare. It had taken them long enough. Perhaps Tallridge's men needed an Indian tracker! He should apply for the job, he thought mirthlessly, as they slowly walked their horses near the edge of the rock-strewn slope. Six. Eight. Fifteen men. Three packhorses he could count. They were looking. Planning. Let them come.

Fox Running rubbed the scar a white soldier gave him long

ago and wondered how many other men who had seen this as a place of play as a child had later stood on these hills as warriors amid the red-tinged, brutal, tumbledown rocks that gave the impression giants had strewn boulders. How many, like him, waited for those coming to kill them? How many heard the spirits setting them upon a path that brought them to the place of killing or being killed? How many went to their final home here? Were they watching now? He closed his eyes for a moment and invited their spirits to fill him.

A dust devil caught his attention as it swirled across the rocks toward the hallowed place beyond the canyon. There, far to the southeast in land he could only see in his mind, lay the ground that was sacred, where bones and bullets would mingle in the earth until the land was no more, where the dream remained alive even as the Northern Cheyenne sang their death songs. They had been with him even when he forgot them. They would be with him again in the fight to come. Perhaps he would be with them when it ended. Little matter. He was home. No one would drag him away again.

Another chill gust made him think of time. He had turned nineteen during the waning days of the Midsummer Moon. He felt many years older. Almost a third of his life had been spent in battles. Most men his age were beginning their lives. These men riding toward him, like the rest, wanted to end his. Only the spirits knew if these outlaws would succeed. He would give them their chance.

With his black vest snapping in the wind against his bare torso, he folded his sun-roughened arms across his chest and silently dared them to come.

He could leave if he wanted to continue the chase, or leave the work of justice to others. He had left his horse by the nearly sheer rock wall to the east. He had climbed his way up; he was certain no one would stop him from leaving. But he had no interest in that sort of game. All the pieces were coming together. It ended here.

Standing there in plain view was his way to taunt them. They needed to feel defiance. They needed to see there was one Indian they could not intimidate. He was waiting!

He thought of using the rifle at his feet, but there would be time for that later. Of that, he was certain.

The cowboys were not so patient. Three men pulled their rifles from their saddles. They aimed in his direction. Although the wind-distorted echoes of shots came to him, he heard no bullets pass. After a few rounds of desultory firing, they gave up, shouting insults that had no better range than their guns.

The spirits in the winds carried the threats away to the place where all the white man's empty words had gone. Talk! He had heard enough.

He could see them prepare to make camp. They were looking for wood now. He had already gathered most of what was easy to find. The colder they were, the more they would rush into action in the morning. He knew they would not sleep. His fangs bared at that thought.

The deep blue of the sky foreshadowed a clear night, but there would be no moon. Cowboys would not seek to scramble up the rocks in the dark. Moccasins might do that chore, but not boots. The outlaws would talk and plan, then come to kill him in the morning. He would be there, knowing that whatever happened, even if they all made it to the top, which they would not, they would never take him alive. Nor would those who deserved justice ride away from this place. He had no plan beyond giving the spirits the choice of who should live: the guilty or the innocent. The spirits flowed through him as never before, and they left no room for fear or doubt.

For days these men had hunted him as though he were prey. Now the prey was waiting and ready to see who would live and who would die. This was the moment for which he was born. No—the one for which, from the Little Bighorn to Boston to Hat Creek Bluffs to the Great Sioux Reservation, he had been honed.

CHAPTER TWO

June 25, 1876, Little Bighorn Creek, Montana

The camp stretched beyond anything the young Fox Running had ever seen, swelled by other tribes that had joined the Lakota for their annual hunt. It should have been welcome to once again hear the Cheyenne tongue and see faces he had not seen in many, many moons, but it was not.

No one ever told him the details, but he knew something very bad had happened last spring that made his family leave the camp of the Northern Cheyenne and live with a band of Lakota who were related to his mother, Doe Leaping, by marriage.

It had been sudden, for one moment other boys spoke to him as though he were their friend, and the next they glared in hate-filled silence. When he asked Red Eagle, his father, why the family had left under cover of darkness, he had received a reply that they would do what they must. When he was older he would know what he must, his father said, but until then, he was not to speak of it.

Yesterday, Red Eagle had argued with two of the Cheyenne who had come to the vast camp. Fox Running's mother was now tight lipped and tense. His younger sister even seemed shaken but would not speak of what had happened when he was away from the lodge. He had lately come to realize how much she, too, had changed, for despite being five years younger, she was as tall as he was.

If he had friends, Fox Running would have asked them what was taking place, but he had spent much of the last year as an undersized Cheyenne boy in various Lakota villages among people who measured worth by deeds and stature. He was looked upon as someone tolerated by the rules of hospitality. Those rules, however, did not require boys to make a stranger feel welcome. Most of the games he would play with Lakota boys ended up in a fight sooner or later. It had become simpler not to bother.

Although small, he had learned how to fight, and that the quickness within him often offset the fact that many boys his age were taller and heavier. One fight had left him with a cut across his cheek that had not yet healed, but it was the only scar on a face dominated by fast-moving, dark eyes that saw everything. "Cat face," one Lakota boy called him until he learned better. Unlike his father, who had a round face and prominent jaw, Fox Running had a thin, angular face with a strong Cheyenne nose.

One Lakota boy, meaning well, had once told him that a blood feud sent his family from the Northern Cheyenne people, but the boy knew nothing more. Fox Running knew that a blood feud started when one man killed a member of another family, but he did not understand how this could have happened. Red Eagle was taciturn, stern, and distant. Fox Running could not picture him killing another man for any reason, except when there was a war. The Lakota boy had stammered and seemed afraid to tell the full story.

Fox Running hoped his mother might this day tell him everything, for she seemed more worried and wet eyed than any time before. He was hanging near the camp in hopes of getting her alone, when she might speak freely.

But the camp was crowded. An edge of fear had rippled through the lodges. Yesterday there had been a scare that soldiers were near. Scouts reported that far off in the shimmering heat they were certain they had seen riders in a column, the way soldiers rode. When warriors rode out, they found nothing and blamed the sighting on the way smoke and haze made distant objects appear to be what they were not.

Fox Running was not so sure. The heavy air above the baking Plains had a feeling about it he could not name, as though a tremendous storm was about to break—yet there were no clouds. Even in the thin linen shirt he wore over the leggings that were a prize possession because he had won them in a fight, he was perspiring freely, long, black hair plastered to his forehead.

The land here rose and fell. Last night he had heard an older warrior urging vigilance, declaring that armies could pass one another and never know. A younger one then laughed and said no enemy would dare attack a camp so strong as the one they were in.

Fox Running looked up through the haze of the cooking fires. Perhaps he would climb the ridge that overlooked the camp and see for himself. It would be a better way to spend the day than being shunned everywhere he turned.

Then came the shots. A few. A volley. Soldiers! He saw his father run to find a loose pony and mount. Red Eagle was one of the first to stream out of the village to attack a small line of soldiers in the distance. They were trying to disperse the herd of ponies that was kept for the warriors. Fox Running saw other men call to their sons as they ran. Perhaps he was not even worthy in the eyes of his father. His eyes stung.

One of the old men pointed toward a bluff where more soldiers were gathering. The small flags they flew were visible in the wind. More warriors were mounting and riding.

Fox Running had a rifle and a pistol. He grabbed both and ran up the hill, trailing the mounted warriors. He did not know what would happen this day. He understood his father was trying to prove himself. Fox Running wanted to do the same. Although he would not turn thirteen for another moon, he would show the Lakota and all of them that there was more to being a warrior than being tall!

He reached the top of the slope and saw more warriors than he ever had seen at one time. The soldiers were never outnumbered, but they were this day. They must have been fools to attempt an attack. Perhaps they were all drunk, as so many often were when he saw them at the trading post.

There was Crazy Horse, who was Fox Running's hero, leading a wild charge that smashed into a line of soldiers caught out in the open. Gunfire crackled as Indians and soldiers clashed in a violent collision.

Other soldiers were digging in along a ridge. He kept running to reach them, for there were few Indians attacking these. As he ran, Crazy Horse's attack was slowing down. Fewer guns were firing. Fox Running looked back in fear that the soldiers had broken through, but there were warriors riding everywhere, and no soldiers! The warriors must have driven them away.

He kept on. The soldiers ahead of him had dug a line and were trying to shoot down his people. Buffalo Eye, one of the Northern Cheyenne men he had been told argued with his father, was riding toward the line, as though one man charging would send the soldiers scurrying home.

Cavalrymen who were dismounted fired at him. Fox Running dropped the pistol and picked up his rifle. It was old and shot poorly, and he had barely a handful of bullets, but he fired them all at the soldiers, who ducked from reflex as the bullets passed far overhead. Fox Running felt the burn of shame that he had missed. Soldiers rose again after he stopped and fired at Buffalo Eye, knocking him from his horse as he rode within fifty feet of the soldiers' line.

Fox Running dropped the empty rifle. It had been a great prize, but now it was useless. There would be more and better ones to take when this fight was through. The riderless horse had run on into the solders' line. One of the blue-clad soldiers came out to finish off Buffalo Eye as he thrashed on the grass.

Fox Running picked up the heavy pistol. Too heavy. He had to hold it with two hands. The barrel waggled and wavered, up and down, but then he gripped it harder and fired it. The soldier's hat flew off! Fox Running kept pulling back the heavy metal hammer and squeezing the trigger. The soldier fell as he tried to scramble back to the safety of the line they had dug. Other soldiers left the shelter of their line and came to get their comrade, dragging him away.

Their rifles now turned on Fox Running, but he was too quick a target for them to hit as he fired the last two bullets and turned to help the fallen Cheyenne warrior.

Buffalo Eye had been struck in the hip. Fox Running grabbed the larger man under the arms and tried to drag him off. The soldiers fired again, this time all at once. Fox Running heard one bullet whine as it went past. Something struck Buffalo Eye and made his right leg jerk into in the air and spray blood. Fox Running pulled harder and walked backward faster.

Guns fired from behind him. He could see the soldiers shift their rifles to another target. Some Cheyenne and Lakota warriors had emerged from somewhere in the swirling chaotic fight. They and the soldiers exchanged fire for a few moments as two warriors dismounted to quickly grab Buffalo Eye under the arms and drag him to safety. One grabbed Fox Running by the arms as well and tossed him upon a horse before he could protest. The warriors pulled back then, away from the soldiers' fire, as both sides settled down to a shooting contest.

"Who are you, child, that you come to do the work of a warrior?" said the Lakota warrior leading the group.

15

"I am Fox Running, son of Red Eagle," the boy said proudly. "I am of the Northern Cheyenne."

"Then let the Northern Cheyenne be proud of this name," the warrior said. "Go with these men. Take the wounded Cheyenne to the village, and let your name be known to the elders. These, we will handle."

Buffalo Eye was in pain, but stoic. His eyes met those of Fox Running. He nodded as a sign of respect, keeping silent lest he make noises that would be a sign of weakness.

As they rode to the village, they passed the place where Crazy Horse had charged. There were bodies everywhere. Fox Running's face reflected his reaction to the slaughter, which was greater than even the stories told at the fire. He could not believe the soldiers had all been killed, but the ground looked littered in blue.

"They came to kill us, Little Warrior," said one Lakota warrior. "They come to kill us all. They did not have to kill us. They have learned it will not be so easy. They will be back, but we will fight as long as the grass around us does grow. You will fight with us, for you are a true warrior. We will tell Crazy Horse of this, for he will be glad to know."

Buoyed by a rare compliment, Fox Running waited to tell his father. For once, his father would be proud.

November 25, 1876, Rosebud Creek, Montana

The Northern Cheyenne camp was strong, and they would spend the winter there. Fox Running felt content. There was food—the remnants of the feast ensured that no one went hungry for days. Best of all, he was home. He was no longer an interloper, but finally with his own people. Perhaps not welcome, but that would come in time.

He watched a young woman a few years older than he was as

she gathered berries by the creek. The sun reflected on the snow, sparkling like shiny stones. The creek rushed past the camp, as it had for generations of the People.

Home.

Then the bugle sounded. Guns. Red Eagle emerged from the lodge, rifle in hand. For just a moment, his eyes locked with those of his son as the other men of the Northern Cheyenne camp grabbed rifles and headed to form a line outside the village.

Fox Running could hear gunshots and see smoke as a line of blue-clad soldiers galloped into view, as though they could sweep away the vast collection of lodges where the Cheyenne were gathered.

"Defend these, my warrior son," his father said, pointing to the women leaving camp to hide.

Red Eagle ran off with the warriors. He looked back once at his son, to whom he had started to grow close in the weeks since the Custer fight, as they bounded from sight. Warriors did not wave.

Fox Running followed his father with his eyes until he was indistinguishable from the rest of the Cheyenne, some of whom vowed as they gathered weapons that this would be another victory. Red Eagle had not boasted or smiled. He had simply run to the fight.

They had only arrived at the camp after spending much of the past two years with the Lakota. He knew his father was anxious to show he would fight with the other warriors, and to end the blood feud that had sent him away. Fox Running's task was to uphold the honor of the family in case any soldiers came through into a camp that others had said was even stronger than the one at the Greasy Grass on the day Custer attacked.

Fox Running and his family had received a begrudging welcome when they arrived two days ago. Since the Custer battle, the Cheyenne, Lakota, and the rest had all dispersed from their joint camp. At first, Fox Running and his family had gone with the Lakota, but then the warriors—mostly young men without families—went with Crazy Horse. Red Eagle was not among those chosen.

His father had said that, because the day had come when all the Indian nations would be hard pressed to survive, it was time to go back to their own people, but they had gone slowly. They traveled with some other families, and Fox Running knew there were messengers going back and forth. None would tell him what was being said, although he asked each one often. Buffalo Eye, who limped badly but lived, had been one of them.

His father had said little of his son's exploits. Red Eagle had been with warriors who kept soldiers pinned down but could not defeat them. When he returned, he gave his son praise, but they were words with as little warmth as a January sun. Even the Lakota boys who ridiculed him for being small had offered more. But as the days wore on, and they journeyed back to their own people, Red Eagle walked often with his son. For a man who rarely spoke, it said much.

When he asked his father again when he would learn why there was a blood feud, Red Eagle had only admitted he had killed a man, made a cryptic remark about Doe Leaping, and told him that when the time was right, when it was time to end the blood feud, when he would be pledging the honor of the family, the boy would learn all that was necessary. That time would not be today.

Now, as much as he wanted to go with the warriors, and also believed that was his place, Fox Running knew that, today, his job was to stay behind to protect his mother and sister, and other women and children.

He went to the lodge for his gun, a pistol that came with a holster and belt, taken by his grandfather, Talking Pheasant, from a cowboy someplace. Unlike other boys, who could learn a rifle but not a pistol, the smaller gun had been easy for him to learn, and he was more accurate with the long-barreled .45 Colt than were many of the Lakota boys with their Winchesters. His skill ensured that the taunts he took for his small stature were muted when he was near, and that the rude jokes comparing his small size with the impressive height of his father were not said more than once when he was close by enough to hear them.

He looked over his shoulder. Doe Leaping had Yellow Bird by the hand. They were moving away. They would be safe until the soldiers were repulsed. He watched them go until the mist and smoke masked them from his view. Doe Leaping never looked back. Yellow Bird did once, to wave before she was swallowed up in the flood of non-combatants heading for safety.

Knowing they would be safe, Fox Running turned to face the noise of guns, which swelled and thundered like the day Custer had attacked. Even louder. He soon learned why.

Blue-clad riders surged into sight. Somehow, they had broken through.

Fox Running drew the pistol the way he had seen the cowboys do at the trading post two years ago, when he and his father witnessed a gunfight. It was heavy, and he still needed a second hand to brace it as he pointed it. He thumbed back the hammer, looked up startled at the horse that seemed ready to ride him down. He pulled the trigger as the horse galloped past, the soldier's saber swinging over his head.

Hammer. Trigger. Hammer. Trigger. On they came. He could not hear other guns.

Then a horseman leaning low pointed his saber to run Fox Running through. The .45 exploded in his hand. The rider recoiled, but the saber slammed into the boy's head. He reeled. His eyes barely saw the next rider. Something hit his head hard, and he fell into a deep pit of silence where the screams of the Cheyenne being slain around him could not be heard.

"Whoa, whoa, whoa."

The words came gently. Someone put a cold, damp cloth on his forehead.

"Easy, little man. Easy. Just about got your head taken off mixing up in that scrape. Thought you was a goner. Easy now, boy."

It was dark. There was a fire nearby. He could smell the smoke and feel the heat, but he could not see. A hand on his chest held him down, firmly but not aggressively.

"Blood in your eyes. Hold still."

It was a white voice. A soldier? His first thought was to run, but when he tried to move, the world spun.

"Not gonna hurt you, boy. Easy. Here. Clean your eyes yourself."

The wet cloth was placed in his left hand. He rubbed his eyes until he could finally see clearly. A young, white face looked back. Each shoulder of the man's blue coat sported one bar.

"You understand me?" the soldier asked. He spoke louder. "Speak English? Know white man talk?"

Fox Running tried to speak. A choking sound came out.

The soldier held a canteen to the boy's lips. Fox Running drank once deeply and handed it back, although he felt he could have drained it dry.

"I know your talk," he said at last. Indeed he did. His grandfather said learning the white language was one way to defeat them, and so he learned everything he could. It was one of the things the Lakota boys held against him.

"Good!" said the round face looking back at him. "You got hit on the head real bad, like to cut your face in two. Gonna be an awful scar, but you're awake today. That's a good sign. We were wonderin' what to do with you if you didn't. 'Fraid you'd be more wolf bait if we left you. Like the rest . . ."

The voice faded in obvious awkwardness.

Fox Running tried to look around, but it was dark, and his head reeled.

"Where is my family?"

The soldier took off his hat, scratched his head, and replaced the hat. He looked uncomfortable answering the question.

"Don't rightly know," he said. "Folks scattered about every which way, so I hear. A lot of 'em didn't make it. Way it is. You got hurt. Don't rightly know more. We were scouting south and got here last night. Went to water the horse and found you."

Fox Running had more questions, but he held his tongue.

"Got some bread," the soldier continued. "Meat's gone. Beans, too. Bread's only two days old. Want to try eatin'?"

He did, but he did not want the soldier to know. He looked around again. This time, his eyes did not blur, even though his head pounded on the inside.

Soldiers everywhere, even though this was the very same camp where the Cheyenne had been. He could see no sign of the many lodges that had been there. What had taken place? Perhaps it was the darkness. Or his eyes.

The soldier looked awkward. "You stay here. I mean right here. Maybe there's some corn or something. Stay right here."

Shoulder Bar walked away. Fox Running used the time to look around more closely. He only saw soldiers. One man gave him a long look that told Fox Running what the soldier wanted to do with him. He wanted to defy the soldier with a glare, but his head hurt just holding it upright. Shoulder Bar was back before he could decide if he could run away safely.

"How old are you?"

Fox Running kept silent. Was he a prisoner? No. Soldiers killed prisoners, especially boys who would grow to be warriors.

21

Everyone knew that.

"Thought you was dead when I saw you. Got me a brother back in Missouri about your size. About eight, he is. Something reminded me . . . um . . . I was about your size when the Jay-hawkers came. Before the war in Kansas. Kids shouldn't see this kind of thing. You was almost dead, I guess, but I guess that wasn't in the cards."

Fox Running started to tell the man his age, then realized that if they thought he was only a boy, they might let him go.

There was some dried corn on a tin plate. The soldier shoved it at him. Fox Running's hands did not grasp the plate.

"Not poison. Ain't gonna hurt you. Take it!"

Fox Running tried to rise above the pounding in his head. At the trading place, where he had gone with his grandfather since he was old enough to stand in silence while the old man bartered, he had come to know in both Indians and whites when men were honest and when they were not. This one was. At least for now. He took hold of the offered plate, scooped the corn from it, and began to eat. He wondered, if he threw the corn in the soldier's face, whether he could reach the safety of the darkness beyond.

"Not sure what's on your mind, boy, but there's about forty troopers with me, and since they missed the fun yesterday, they are ready to shoot any Indian they see. Don't get no ideas. If I wanted to leave you dead, you'd still be by the river. It's over, boy."

Fox Running chewed silently. He felt weak and knew any food was needed. This man was not a threat. Others—such as the one who stared at him with hate in his heart—might be. Death to no purpose was not bravery. It was merely death.

"I will stay." The words scratched in his throat.

Shoulder Bar seemed surprised. "Good."

The soldier waited in silence. A man comfortable in silence was good.

"Not sure I can get you to your people," Shoulder Bar began. "Um . . . not sure, really, how to tell you, but by the time we got here there was this one big hole what was a grave for all of the folks . . . um . . . what got killed. All covered. Don't know how many, 'cept what the other soldiers were saying, and most of 'em were bragging. Dunno . . . um . . . your religion . . . um . . . you want to say a prayer or something . . . um . . . but no dancin' . . . um . . . you understand, like that."

Fox Running realized Shoulder Bar was trying to tell him that all the Cheyenne dead were buried in a common grave. He wondered if his family was there. No! After all they had endured, it could not be. However, his eyes told him that where the Cheyenne had a mighty village, now there were only soldiers. His mind grappled with the idea that his family had already made their journey to the long fork and were gone from him forever.

"I would like that," he said. He recalled the man's concerns. This was not the time to fight and tell the man that his notions of Indians were as absurd as every other white man Fox Running had ever met. "I will not dance."

"Good. Good. You ride with me, and we'll see what happens. Can't just let you go. Army won't like that. Maybe if they come in, you can find your family. Maybe they made it. Right now, nobody knows where your people went. We move out in a few hours. Might want to at least try to sleep. Don't try anything, son."

Fox Running understood. He was alone. The only one who might help him was Shoulder Bar. There was nothing to do but survive. A time to escape would come, sooner or later. A warrior learned to be patient.

He heard the urgent sound of hooves. Then shouts. "Lieutenant!!"

Shoulder Bar rose.

"Won't chain you, boy, but if you go wanderin' away from my fire here I can't help what happens. Sticks there to feed the fire. Use 'em." The lieutenant moved away from the fire. Urgent voices spoke in the dark. He came back a short time later.

"Moving out now. Be light in an hour or two anyhow. Heading south. Not against your people. Not the Cheyenne. Something down Crow country. Can't leave you all alone here. Against orders, even to leave a little kid behind. Look at me. No, not right. You still look pretty peaked. No. Get you back here when I can, if I can, but for now, orders is orders."

Fox Running's heart sank. As long as they were moving through the area of what the soldiers called Montana he might find his way home. He had been to the north and west and east. The south? Never.

"You said I could see this grave."

Shoulder Bar nodded and spoke to some other soldiers nearby. "Hopkins, Stedman, take this young fella where the Cheyenne are buried. Bring him when it's time to move out."

Fox Running walked through the camp. The way other soldiers looked at him made it clear they did not agree with their lieutenant's decision to bring him with them, or probably even to keep him alive. The two men walking with him said nothing.

When they reached the common grave, Fox Running looked at the dirt pile that covered it. He knelt in the dirt, ran his fingers through it, and felt empty of all things that he could think or say. He was still searching for words when one of the men tapped him, gently, on his left shoulder.

"Sorry, son, but it's time to go."

★ ★ ★ ★ ★

Fox Running felt the ground sway sideways the first time he tried to mount Shoulder Bar's horse. The man's hands gripped him, then lifted him up as though he were a child and not thirteen and nearly ready to be a man. It was humiliating!

As they rode, he came to understand that a small group of Crow Indians had been attacking trappers and others traveling the rugged country to the north of Fort Laramie. He wondered what anyone thought forty men would do against the Crows. It was too small a force to capture them, and too big to sneak up unseen on a wary enemy. He felt shame that these foolish soldiers, just like the ones he helped defeat at the Greasy Grass, had somehow defeated the Northern Cheyenne at the Rosebud. He wondered what had made the Cheyenne weak; what bad medicine could have hurt them.

Shoulder Bar talked little as they rode. When they camped, Fox Running noted that the man always seemed to watch him, as though he knew escape was the most important thing in Fox Running's mind. Fox Running knew, however, that he must be patient. To flee in Crow country and have both the army and the enemies of his people looking for him would be a mistake.

They were on the second day of their expedition when they came to a wooded area. The soldiers stopped. The trail they were following, little more than a beaten track where hooves had flattened the dead grass that lay under a smattering of snow, split in two directions. Part of the rough path led into the trees, part down a gully that seemed to lead to another gully. Flattened snow showed each trail had been used since the last snowfall, but it was hard to say how recently.

"We split up," Shoulder Bar told the soldiers, riding behind the much-smaller Fox Running as they shared the saddle. "If you see recent tracks, fire three shots. Wait for an answer. If neither trail has anything fresher than what we have been following, we give up the hunt and turn for the fort."

The men were pleased to hear that. The sky was starting to look like snow, and December could be a cruel month on the Plains.

Shoulder Bar led his men into the trees. Fox Running could sense the trap. There were no birds. There was nothing moving in the underbrush. Any deer or rabbits the soldiers should have scared had already taken cover. Yet the horses moved slowly at a walk as though the soldiers were unconcerned.

Fox Running tried to think of what he should do. If the Crow killed the soldiers and freed him, would he be safer? Would the Crow even do that, or would they kill him, too? If they were lying in wait, they knew the size of the group of soldiers they faced. There must be enough warriors that they were confident they could win.

If there was a fight, could he escape, or would the soldiers shoot him and think it was a trick of his? Could they not see the trap? He could see the gray-blue of the clouds through the thinning trees. They were almost through the woodland. It would be soon. Two of the men were joking now about something at the fort. Fools!

Something moved in a tree about twenty-five feet ahead, perhaps ten feet from the ground. The best ambushes used men to attack both ends of an army column. He had learned that. They must have already passed one of the attackers. There! He could see the man up high, taking aim at the soldiers. At Shoulder Bar!

With a loud exclamation, he jerked in the saddle, pushing back against Shoulder Bar, who yelled angrily at being struck. Fox Running grabbed the horse's reins and turned it to the right. He kicked hard against Shoulder Bar's legs to free them from the stirrups the soldiers used. The rifle in the tree barked.

The boy and the officer tumbled from the saddle as the horse stumbled. Shoulder Bar lay still as more shots rang out. Fox Running reached for the flap of the black leather holster holding the pistol Shoulder Bar wore at his waist. He dragged the man to the base of a pine, then drew the pistol. It was heavy, even heavier than his own now-lost gun, and it wobbled even when he held it with two thin, cold hands.

Around him, soldiers were firing blindly. Answering gunfire came from above them. Shoulder Bar groaned. Fox Running tried to hold the gun and check Shoulder Bar's coat for blood. It was damp from snow falling off the trees, but there was no red on the fingers Fox Running drew back.

Crack!

A branch snapped behind him. Fox Running held the gun in both hands again, with the hammer cocked.

The soldier he pointed it at blanched and held his hands out.

"No kill Injun," he said. "Corporal Kincaid. Want see lieutenant."

The trooper knelt by Shoulder Bar. Fox Running ignored him and turned his attention back to the woods, where sporadic shots were being fired. He sensed more than saw the Crow warrior standing ten feet behind Kincaid. The Crow warrior was as shocked to see a Cheyenne boy pointing a pistol at him as Fox Running was to see the warrior pointing the gun in his general direction. Voices were yelling. Soldier voices.

Fox Running locked eyes with the Crow warrior, who had a line of white paint under his left eye. He tried to tell the warrior to run while he could be free. This did not need to happen. He wanted it not to happen.

It did.

The Crow shouldered his rifle. Fox Running pulled the trigger.

Kincaid's howl was audible above the double explosions of the guns. Fox Running saw death in the trooper's eyes as Kincaid raised the rifle toward him. Four soldiers raced past them. One gave Kincaid a puzzled glance.

"Kincaid!" another voice called. "Look here."

The corporal kept his rifle fixed on Fox Running and his finger tight on the trigger as he cast a quick glance behind him. "What is it?"

"Crow fella here, corporal," said one trooper. "Dead as they get."

"Cover him. Cover the kid," Kincaid said, pointing at Fox Running. Two soldiers trained their guns on the boy, who had lowered the pistol. Kincaid got up and went to the dead Crow.

"Well I'll be," he muttered. "Boy killed him dead center. You do that on purpose, kid? You miss when you tried to get me?"

Fox Running took no joy in killing the Crow. He recalled his father telling him that in battle, nothing happened for the reasons men said after, because everything happened so fast. Now, he understood. He did not answer the man. *Soldiers never believe Indians,* his grandfather told him, *unless they are told that which they have decided to be true.*

Shoulder Bar struggled to sit up. Fox Running dropped the pistol and moved over to the soldier, who had struck his head on the hard ground when they fell off the horse. The snow provided little cushion against the frozen mud, but no blood showed. This was a good sign. Fox Running put his hands behind Shoulder Bar's neck to support the man's head.

"What . . . where's Gibson?" Shoulder Bar asked. "Boy, you all right?" Fox Running said that he was.

"You . . . you . . . what did you do?"

Fox Running didn't answer. The name Shoulder Bar had muttered was repeated by the soldiers. Then a man with three stripes on his arm came through the crowd. "Sir!"

With effort, Shoulder Bar stood. "Gibson, what happened?"

"We found the Crow bushwhackers sir, or rather, they found

us. We got four of 'em, might have wounded a couple more from the blood in the snow. Boys figure maybe three or four got away altogether. Private Nichols was cut in the face by a splinter. Private Harrow was hit by a ricochet from a rock, I believe. He'll have a fancy scar for the ladies. Sergeant Kirkpatrick's men came to join us and have gone in pursuit."

"Weather?"

"Fierce and soon, sir."

"Round up the column. Give me a few minutes, and we'll be on the move. I think we've done what we came to do."

Shoulder Bar gave Fox Running a long look and then walked off without speaking. Fox Running could see him talking with several of the soldiers. They talked for some time. The corporal was very animated.

Fox Running thought about how the village would have celebrated his first kill as a man. No one would do that now. There was no village. He had saved a soldier's life. By the time anyone heard the tale, it would be old. So might he.

Shoulder Bar returned. "You knew?" he asked. Fox Running nodded. "How? How could you know? Did you plan this with them? That's what my men want to know."

Fox Running did not want to say. If soldiers knew the ways of the land, they might use them to hurt his people, wherever they were.

"If you do not tell me, these men will believe you were part of them," Shoulder Bar urged gently. "Corporal Kincaid is still uncertain whom you wanted to kill."

"There were no birds," said Fox Running. "Wild things hide when men prowl. When the trees are silent, you should be afraid, Shoulder Bar."

"And the horse?"

"I could see the man in the tree. I did not want to be shot."

"And Corporal Kincaid?"

29

Fox Running almost smiled. Now it was funny. Then it was not.

"The Crow are terrible shots; if he missed him he would have hit me. I did not want to let that happen. If the Crow had run away I would not have shot him, because I did not want to kill anyone, but he did not do that. I did not have a choice."

Shoulder Bar made an obvious and unsuccessful effort to prevent himself from smiling. "You know the corporal almost killed you?"

Fox Running shrugged. "It will be as the spirit wishes it, Shoulder Bar."

"Shoulder . . . oh. I guess I never introduced myself. John Van Diver. I am sorry. There were . . . other things. What is your name?"

"I am called Fox Running."

"Where did you learn to shoot, Fox Running?"

"My grandfather found a pistol, and I practiced." Fox Running decided this was not the time to tell about fighting against Custer.

Van Diver shook his head. One shot. One kill. Few of his men could do that. And the boy was so young! In the light he looked older. Maybe eleven, from the size of him. Good thing he wasn't running wild with the hostiles!

"We are going to be riding as fast as we can for the fort. The storm that's approaching seems to be moving fast. Can you ride on your own all that distance? We can go faster that way."

"I am Cheyenne," Fox Running replied. "As far as the soldiers can go, I can go farther."

One Crow pony had been left behind. Fox Running took that one instead of one with the awkward saddle soldiers used. Snowflakes were starting to fall.

"Hey, kid."

Fox Running looked down. Kincaid stood near, holding a

soldier's heavy wool overcoat.

"Might want this."

Fox Running understood this was about more than a coat.

"I do," he said, slipping into it. The wool was scratchy in the places where there were holes in the buckskin shirt he wore, but it was warm against the north wind that made swirling circles of snow on the featureless land ahead.

"Stay close," Van Diver called to the men. "If you lose sight of the horse ahead of you, stop and fire in the air. We've got a long ride ahead. Let's go!"

31

CHAPTER THREE

Fort Morris, Kansas, April 1877

Lieutenant John Van Diver crumpled the telegram and threw it to the far side of his quarters. Surrender. Or so they said.

Dull Knife, Little Wolf, and a few hundred of the Northern Cheyenne whose camp along the Rosebud had been destroyed last fall had surrendered and were now camped near Fort Robinson in Nebraska while the government and the Indians talked over where they would go. Van Diver corrected himself. The government would make that decision. The Indians had lost. They would do as they were told.

He knew that Indians always believed what they wanted, but the lesson of war was that the winners dictated the terms. He wished the Indian Wars had not happened, as did many of the men with whom he served, but once the first shots were fired, there was no choice but to fight to win. In the long run, he was certain, the Indians would be better off than they were on their own without any of the benefits of civilization.

By rights, he should send Fox Running up to Nebraska, where the surrender had taken place. Undoubtedly members of his family were there—some relations, even if not his father, mother, or sister. Although Van Diver had been able to keep him around by labeling him a servant, the boy was more like a younger brother. He spent some time trying to teach the boy to read and write. A lot of time. It helped pass the winter, and he found it enjoyable. Fox Running was a fast learner with a quick mind.

Van Diver had assumed Indians could not ever read. Fox Running was proving many of his notions were false.

One thing he was certain about: the boy wanted to be with his people. Van Diver knew that having feet of snow around during the weeks they were in Wyoming, before he was transferred to Kansas, prevented Fox Running from just taking off. They had been in Kansas a few weeks now. The army was more worried these days about raids hitting cattle drives and immigrant trains than anything else, and both passed through Kansas with regularity.

Van Diver found it hard to believe that in the weeks to come, once the weather improved, the boy would not one day up and walk away while Van Diver was away from the post on long patrols. In time Fox Running would hear about his people and try to join them. It was the way life was.

Van Diver did not want the child to go. In time, the boy would grow into a man, and he would be one of those the army would have to hunt down, for while Fox Running would do anything when Van Diver asked, he had shown a strong willingness to defy any authority he did not choose to acknowledge, which was virtually everyone else but Van Diver.

The lieutenant looked again at the ball of thin yellow paper. Picked it up. Threw it in the fire.

"Do not lose that."

Fox Running was, Van Diver knew, barely listening. The camp of the Northern Cheyenne lay down the slope from Fort Robinson. They boy's eyes had barely left it, as though he could see his family at this distance. Van Diver had written a pass that would ensure the sentries would know that the boy, even if he was not on the rolls of the prisoners, had family members there and was being allowed to visit by Van Diver.

"If you lose it, when you come back, they may think you are

running away. They do not know you. I do not know the guards. I do not know if they will shoot before they ask. Are you listening to me?" Van Diver frowned as he stared at the boy.

For a moment, Fox Running's focus was back on him.

"You have been good to me, Shoulder Bar," he said, using the name he always used instead of Van Diver's real one. "I did not have a brother until we met."

Van Diver felt himself feeling the kind of emotion that made a man weak. They were there to fight Indians, not adopt them. Time for the boy to go.

"Back by dark. The rules. If your family is there, we can work it out for you, but you have to do what I am telling you. The soldiers here are afraid of something bad, and that means they will shoot before they think. Back by dark. Not later. Not for any reason. Do you understand?"

Impulsively, Fox Running embraced the soldier, then bolted out the door, clutching the piece of paper that would allow him to see his family.

It had been less than half a year, but it felt like much longer as Fox Running moved through the lodges of the Northern Cheyenne. Some glances he received were hostile. How could this be? Then he realized he was wearing a jacket Shoulder Bar had given him; it was not a soldier's jacket, but it looked much like one. It had belonged to a child at the fort who had died. He had on the pants soldiers wore with the yellow stripe on the outside of the leg. His buckskin leggings had been ripped too badly after the Rosebud to be saved. He was barefoot; the moccasins he had last autumn were now too small. Shoes hurt his feet, and he would not wear them. His hair had grown since it was cut where blood had dried in it after he was hurt. Shoulder Bar wanted to cut it like a white man. It was one of the few real arguments they had.

The long scar across his forehead that reached down over his right eye, between his eyebrows, and ended on the bridge of his nose was still livid. It had been pink for weeks and was just now turning white. The boy had picked at it endlessly as it itched all winter. He did not know that it changed his face, or that the thinness his face had in the fall had given way to a gaunt, hollow-cheeked boy who wore hostility like a coat.

The first five lodges he stopped at were pointless. They claimed not to know who he was seeking, that he existed, or anything at all.

In time, a man with an air of authority who was about ten years older than Fox Running materialized in his path.

"I am Stone Leg," said the man. "My father is among those charged with keeping order here. I help him and protect the People. Who do you seek, and who are you with? The army said we could camp in peace."

"I am not with the army," said the boy.

"You wear army clothes. Many who have turned away from us and joined the army dress as you do."

"My name is Fox Running," he replied, dismissing Stone Leg's words with an impatient wave of his left hand. "On the day the soldiers came and the camp by the Rosebud was destroyed, I was separated from my family. My father is Red Eagle. Doe Leaping is my mother. Yellow Bird is my smaller sister. My father's father was Talking Pheasant. He died the month before the fight on the Greasy Grass. What does it matter what clothes I have found to keep away the cold? I have come home to my people. Where is my family?"

Stone Leg looked at Fox Running with no enthusiasm. No welcome. Only suspicion.

"Who are the sisters and brothers of your parents?"

"There are none alive," said the boy. "My father had a brother who died of a fever as a child. He never spoke of him, for there was pain with the memory. My mother's family was killed by the soldiers when she was very young. They may have had cousins, but I do not know them." This was not the time to talk about a blood feud and being banished. He should have listened to his parents' talk. He should have remembered names they rattled off forever.

"This is a tale that could be told by a spy the soldiers have sent," Stone Leg scoffed.

"I have no time for this talk," Fox Running flared. "Out of my way."

The larger man moved to cut him off. Fox Running thought of trying one of the wrestling holds Van Diver had taught him, then decided he did not want the first day of his return to be marred by a fight. His mother would scold!

"You will wait. We are careful, Fox Running. The soldiers seek to learn the hiding places of those who did not surrender. They send spies to lurk among us. You must understand. I shall see if there is anyone who knows you. Wait here until I return."

Time stood still for what seemed like forever. Fox Running grew impatient. Just as he was about to go exploring on his own, Stone Leg approached quickly, with a youth behind him. Fox Running felt his heart leap. The youth was Horse Striking!

"Horse Striking! Do you not remember me? My family camped near you at the Greasy Grass. My mother and yours sheltered by the stream when the soldiers charged, before the men cut them off."

"My mother is dead," the young man said. "She was shot at the Rosebud, and she died after we fled."

"I am sorry to hear this," said Fox Running. "I am seeking my family." He reeled off the names.

Horse Striking looked back flatly.

"It is I who am sorry, Fox Running. They were all killed. The day of the soldiers' attack was the last anyone saw them. Red

Eagle had joined the men who tried to charge the soldiers but was killed then. This was seen by others. None of those who fought where he did survived. Your mother and sister did not leave the village. No one saw them die, but they were never seen after the attack. The soldiers either burned or buried the bodies of those who fell, so we do not know for sure how they died, but we looked for days after the soldiers left and found no one alive."

Fox Running's face twitched. Knowing it was so different from hearing it.

Horse Striking kept talking. "Many, many died. Crazy Horse's warriors took us in, or we all would have perished. We almost starved. Where have you been that you did not know this and are now in the clothes of the white soldiers?"

Fox Running told what he thought they needed to know of his story, from being injured in the attack to being taken by a soldier who showed pity on him and kept him alive.

"You are hiding something, I think," said Stone Leg. "There was talk that came from the country of the Crows of a Cheyenne warrior who fought with the soldiers against them. Did you think no one would know of your shame?"

"The Crows were shooting at me, Stone Leg! At me! I was not fighting with the soldiers. I was trying not to die so that I could come back to my family! I did not have a choice!"

"There is always a choice," said Stone Leg. He folded his arms across his chest and looked down at Fox Running.

"I shall talk of this with the elders," Stone Leg said at last. "Some of the People are turning away from the spirits and to the white men. Some work with the soldiers who rode down the People. Some have loyalty that shifts with the wind. Those may be welcome in the fort of the white soldiers, but they are not welcome here."

"Stone Leg, these are my people!"

"The People, Fox Running, are those who have survived what the soldiers did, not those who have crept into their forts and become their slaves. The elders will decide, but if you are what I believe you have become from what is known to me, it would be better for you not to enter this camp again."

Fox Running's eyes burned. "Horse Striking! You know me!"

Horse Striking glared. "I know you were the boy who talked to the whites at the trading place; who copied the whites with your gun you would fire; who learned their ways; who spoke their talk; who did not respect the elders when they scolded you for your waywardness; who seemed to not care about the traditions of the People. Perhaps you have only become what you always were. Your father was once with the Crazy Dogs, and you know what happened! Your father killed a clan brother because of . . . that which happened and was sent away lest the blood feud destroy us. This is not the behavior of a family that will be loyal to the People in our time of greatest need."

Horse Striking and Stone Leg turned away and walked back the way they had come, leaving Fox Running looking through misty eyes at the lodges of his people, knowing that all he ever held dear in the world was dead.

Van Diver had been prepared for a number of reactions. The stiff boy holding in hurt and anger was not among them. Fox Running answered questions with one word or let them pass unanswered.

As it came time for the visiting officers who shared the common room to go to sleep for the night, Fox Running went to the Shoshone boy even smaller than he was who had been sent to tend the fire overnight.

"I will do it," he said. "Sleep is not mine this night."

The boy did not argue but found a blanket and was asleep long before Van Diver closed his eyes on the sight of Fox Running staring into the fire as though it held urgent answers.

Dawn had barely broken when the boy was gone again. One of the officers from the post came to Van Diver with a tin cup of coffee as Van Diver stared out the window at the camp.

"Find a stray? I know some of them act as though they could be saved. They fool you because you fool yourself. Like trying to tame a wolf. They bite you in the end. Cut him loose now before you find you have to kill him when he comes for your scalp."

"A stray? I suppose you could call it that." Van Diver related how he and Fox Running came to be in Nebraska.

"You should have stayed at Fort Morris," the officer said. "Malvers. Bronson Malvers." They shook hands.

"Four years out here," Malvers said, once they had shared various postings and the names of officers and others they might have known. "The one thing I know? No matter how hard you try, an Indian is an Indian. Nothing more."

Van Diver remained silent.

Malvers moved toward the window. "The way I hear it, they've decided to send them down to the Darlington Agency in Indian Territory—the whole lot of them. They would have been walking right past you, and you could have gotten rid of him that way. Good riddance, I say. The chiefs keep saying they were told they could stay here. Who cares what they want? Savages. Guess maybe yours is a little better than some, if only because he's so small, but it comes out sooner or later. They look like kids, but they fight like wildcats, and it only gets worse as they get older. See? They can't even go a day without a fight," Malvers said.

Van Diver glanced out the window and saw it was true. Sentries were moving into the camp. Some Cheyenne were also running toward what could only be some kind of incident.

Malvers had stayed at the window. "Isn't that one yours?"

It was. A large Cheyenne man was holding the boy's legs while two soldiers held his arms. Van Diver set down the coffee.

"Not worth it, you know," Malvers said. "Not worth it. Let them deal with him. Go back to Kansas. No good comes of not letting nature take its course. As long as they don't kill us or the settlers, who cares if they kill each other?"

Van Diver gave Malvers a look of contempt. He rushed out to intervene, hoping to convince the sentries to release the boy to him.

"I want an explanation," Van Diver said when they reached the relative privacy of the officers' quarters.

"They said I was not Cheyenne."

"What?"

"My family is dead. They said I have gone to work for the army. They said they only want Cheyenne who will be part of the People." Fox Running looked at Van Diver with tears in his eyes. "They have told me to leave them and never come back, because I am no longer welcome among my people! My father had a fight with a warrior, one of the Crazy Dogs. He killed him and was banned for a time until the blood feud was over. It was about my mother, I think. That was why we camped with the Lakota. Now none will know me. There was never forgiveness; there was never atonement. The family of Red Eagle remains banned, and since I am all that is left, I am not allowed to be with the People!"

The irony of the situation was not lost on Van Diver as he waited at the entrance to the Cheyenne camp. He had asked Malvers to watch Fox Running, something that was easy to do because the boy sat unmoving. Van Diver had not wanted to come here, because he had become attached to the boy, and now he was asking the Cheyenne to take him because the boy was so miserable.

The warrior Stone Leg, the only name Van Diver could squeeze out of Fox Running, came to the entrance of the camp after Van Diver had a messenger find him.

"I have done nothing wrong," Stone Leg said when he saw the soldier.

"You have," replied Van Diver. He related the story of Fox Running, from the time he found him until the time they reached the camp. "He wants to be with his people. He is much like my little brother, and perhaps I should have let him go home sooner. He has army clothes because I wanted to share, not because he works with the army. All he wants is to go home to his people. If there is fault, it is with me."

"Did you chain him?" asked Stone Leg.

"Of course not."

"A Cheyenne who could have come to his people when they were wounded and did not is one who did not want to come to his people," Stone Leg said. "In the trials my people are facing, many who walked the road when it was easy with fat buffalo turn their backs on us. We turn our backs on them. Did the boy tell you of the death his family caused, a warrior of the People? His family was banned for the crime."

"You are making a mistake," Van Diver said. "Whatever his father may have done, the crime should not affect Fox Running. You are wrong."

"This is possible," Stone Leg answered gravely. "There are some who say the man Red Eagle killed was this one's true father; others claim he taunted Red Eagle that he was. We know the boy did not look like the sire. The truth is now known only by the dead. The blood feud remains, and the boy—whatever he has become—cannot return to divide the People."

"All he wants is to have a home."

"These are dark times, and in dark times even the spirits of the best men see darkness where it is not. Yet I ask you: why is

41

it that when we asked about this boy, throughout all of this camp, none vouched for him from the People, only a soldier? If he is a true Cheyenne, the spirits will make it known in their own way and in their own time, but he is not welcome in the camp today."

Van Diver watched the retreating figure of Stone Leg. He understood.

During the War Between the States, when the soldiers were under attack, they only trusted those who were suffering right there with them. Everyone else—no matter who they were, even family back home—was just, well, everyone else.

The boy had lost his family and his place. There was no reason to stay. They would leave for Kansas today and camp tonight on the Plains. He had no idea what to do with Fox Running. He would need an answer soon before the boy did something that would end up making everything even worse than it already was.

He was too late.

Van Diver was not surprised when he reached the officers' quarters and the common room was empty. On a chair, folded neatly, were the jacket and trousers the boy had been wearing. The message was clear: Fox Running was going to live as an Indian. Malvers said he had gone to retrieve a newspaper from his sleeping quarters, and when he came out, the boy was gone.

"I know you meant well, but I think it is all for the best," Malvers said. "His problem is that he's an Indian. There's only one solution for that problem." He mocked squeezing the trigger of a gun. Then he walked out, puffing on his pipe, and slammed the door behind him.

Van Diver thought of going back to the camp to warn Stone Leg: they had wanted to see if Fox Running was a Cheyenne and he was ready to show them. Then he thought better of the impulse. What started as an act of Christian charity had become far more complicated than a junior officer in the U.S. army wanted or needed. He left the clothes on the chair and headed for the stable. He had done all he could. It was high time to get back to the work of being a soldier.

Fox Running watched Van Diver as he left the officers' quarters. The man had meant well. He had saved Fox Running's life. Regardless of whether Fox Running paid the debt on the day of the Crow ambush, it was debt he would always have. Although he knew he could prove to Stone Leg which side he was on by attacking some soldiers, that would mean Van Diver would be smeared with Fox Running's actions. That would be wrong.

For now, there were other things to focus on. He had on nothing but a long wool shirt and needed to find something to wear against the chill of the weather that would not label him an outsider in the camp.

Enough dirt and enough darkness were the only friends he needed to enter the Northern Cheyenne camp undetected. Soldiers watched the side of the camp toward the fort; the rest of it, they left unguarded. No one looked at another grimy child.

Fox Running realized his earlier mistake. He had been, indeed, thinking as a white man of going through the gate and asking by the rules to be accepted by his people. He had learned a lesson never to do that again.

Having infiltrated the camp, on the first day there he kept to its fringes, watching how it was separated by clans and families. He looked for familiar faces, both fearing they might know him and wishing they would. After a time, he ruefully admitted that his habit of preferring his own company to that of others— coupled with the ban on his family—meant there was no one he could walk up to who would welcome him.

There was a path from the camp to a place set apart. He soon learned why. This was the place for those sick and dying. Piles of shirts, leggings, and moccasins were building, cast aside by those who would no longer need them or were too sick to care. He watched and watched, then sauntered to the pile, trying to guess the sizes of things in the dimness. He was not alone. In a time when there was little, it was no sin to take what others would never again use.

The extra shirt was good. When he reached the trees, he realized the leggings were too long. He would cut them when he found a knife. Soon it would be warm enough to go without. His hair was too short for him to braid, so he tied it back with a loop of rawhide he had found on the ground. The piece of leather was cold, muddy, and wet, but at least he now looked nothing like a white man. In time, he would find food. For the time being, he could pass as a boy separated from his family. It would not last long, but it could get him some food for now.

Chapter Four

Fox Running soon learned that the camp had its own way of life. Men like Stone Leg kept order, to ensure that all were fed. Others tended to healing; still others cooked for multiple families. With a thousand people camped, not everything or everyone could be overseen.

At the edges of the camp were others like him, who either had no home or were in some form of disfavor. Some were shirkers who did little work. Some white men prowled; these the soldiers would shoo away when they found them. A few were traders trying to wheedle things from the Cheyenne. Some others seemed to have no purpose but were watchful like mountain lions eyeing prey. Those Fox Running soon came to watch, for they appeared to be waiting for something.

One man stood out. Blue Feather was a trader who seemed to know everyone, whether Indian or white. Men came to his lodge at all times of the day and night. One young man told Fox Running that Blue Feather could get anything, including guns, but that the price could be steep. He watched the trader, realizing after a while that Blue Feather took items from the discards of those who were sick or dying and traded with white men for them. He thought the man was profiting from the dead until he also realized that Blue Feather always had extra food to share with those who had none. It was all probably illegal, but Fox Running could not help admiring a man who found a way to do well for himself and do good for others. The man limped from an old injury, yet went through every day with a smile to the world. Once, his shrewd eyes rested on Fox Running and stayed overlong, as though seeing the predatory animal in a pack. Then Blue Feather moved on, and Fox Running could hear him telling a white man he was buying an ancient Cheyenne war bonnet, when Fox Running knew for certain two women had been making it for the past week.

Soon, the underlying layer of tension in the camp became almost tangible. Some bit of news or rumor was filtering through, but Fox Running did not know what it was. All news provoked fear, for having surrendered to the soldiers the Northern Cheyenne expected treachery. If he could not forgive Stone Leg's attitude, he came to understand it. The Cheyenne were vulnerable. They could not run. They could not fight back. They were surrounded by men who were their enemies, and talk of exiling them to some distant place was making things even worse.

Fox Running had acquired a knife lost by someone. It was not new or very sharp, but it was something to put in his belt. He felt comfortable now moving about the camp and joined in the tasks to be done—from distributing food, to helping the healers care for those with fevers, to hauling water. For now, blending in without notice was an end in itself, and he thought not at all about what might happen next. He was among his people; he ate; he existed. That was enough.

For days, soldiers around the camp had been working in a field at the far edge of the fort that was being prepared as though a vast multitude would be arriving. Soldiers had mowed down the tall grass with scythes. More sentries were patrolling, and these were not simply marking time as others had before them. They were watchful and were changed often. Riders came and went, always with secrecy and urgency.

Some spread rumors the Great White Father would come to see the Cheyenne. Others said some of the generals from the army were coming; while others insisted Sitting Bull was coming back from the far north where he had gone with his people after the Greasy Grass fight—beyond the reach of the soldiers.

On one sunny morning, Fox Running was certain someone important was arriving. The leaders of the Cheyenne were donning ceremonial clothes too old and precious to be worn except on the most important occasions. There was a buzz of expectation.

Then the cavalcade of proud horses arrived, escorted by dozens of soldiers. Some looked ready to kill, others watched the crowd to protect the man they were guarding.

It was Crazy Horse, the legend who had made the soldiers abandon a fort in the Powder River country and who had helped defeat Custer at the Greasy Grass. Fox Running got a glimpse of the man he had last seen briefly at the Custer fight. He looked older, gritty, but proud. His head was held high.

Behind the proud warrior, hundreds of men and women and children streamed. Some were in rags. Some had cheeks caved from famine. Most walked with a pride the Cheyenne knew from hard experience was a shell covering the gnawing pain of hungry bellies and the deeper despair of surrender.

Fox Running could hear music—a military band. Crazy Horse and his guards rode toward the fort for a formal greeting with the soldiers as Fox Running and most of the Cheyenne waited for another glimpse of the Lakota leader. The wait seemed endless, but at last, in time, Crazy Horse came to visit Dull Knife and Little Wolf. Soldiers, who rarely entered the camp of the Cheyenne, entered with him. Fox Running wondered whether this was to protect Crazy Horse or prevent him from leaving.

Fox Running strained to see his former hero. He finally

climbed a tree, because he was too small to see more than legs and backs from the ground.

From the tree, he could see everything: the Cheyenne camp, and far outside its limits. He noted again a white man who looked familiar to him. This man had been walking in the same small meadow for more than two weeks. He was rough-hewn, bearded, and exuded danger. On this day, he was once again waiting in the meadow, but this time he was more animated, walking faster as he moved between two trees, without the languid movements that had made Fox Running think he was marking time. Whatever he was waiting for, the time had come.

The bearded man finally settled on a place to stand near one tree. Behind it, Fox Running could see a rifle. Rifles were not uncommon near the camp, but men carried them openly—from the guards to those Cheyenne men allowed to use broken old guns to hunt small game under the close supervision of the soldiers.

This man was hiding his rifle behind the tree. As time passed, he joined his weapon and looked out from behind the trunk often—always toward the place where Crazy Horse was meeting with the Cheyenne chiefs. Fox Running wondered at the man's strange behavior.

Noise erupted from the crowd. Crazy Horse was walking away; no, he was walking toward a place in the neighboring meadow where a black stallion had been tied to a tree. Of course! As poor as they were, the Cheyenne would still have a gift to honor Crazy Horse.

The man with the rifle had ducked out of sight. Fox Running finally understood. The man's hiding place was not accidental. He had been waiting for Crazy Horse with a rifle. That could only mean one thing.

Fox Running scrambled down. Legs barred his way to Crazy Horse. He gave up trying to push his way through the pack and ran for the edge of the crowd, which had become a wall between the Lakota war leader and the place where he was being taken.

Perhaps! Crazy Horse could not move fast in the crowd, while Fox could run fast now that he was free from the throng. No! Not that way; this way! He reached the meadow. There was no bearded man in sight, no rifle. For a moment, he thought he had imagined his fears. Then he remembered the man with the rifle was hiding. All he would need was a clear line of sight to the horse.

Fox Running could see the image in his mind as though it had already happened. Crazy Horse would mount, and the man would shoot.

Unless there was no horse. If Fox Running could reach the animal in time, he could take it, and there would be no chance for the man to shoot Crazy Horse. He had outpaced the crowd. All he needed was to run fast. He took two deep breaths and then ran as fast as he could.

There was the horse! No! He had startled three bored-looking soldiers. One put his rifle to his shoulder, as though one boy was a threat.

Fox Running tried to spread his arms wide to show he had no weapons and took his eye off the broken ground. His left foot hit the edge of a rock. White pain. He landed hard and rolled.

One of the soldiers had run forward. Both of the others had their rifles trained on him. Fools. He needed to warn them. He blinked to get his bearings. The crowd was to his right. The bearded man with the rifle must be to his left. He pointed and tried to explain, unaware he was speaking a mixture of Cheyenne, Lakota, and English. The stupid soldiers were yelling at him instead of doing what he was telling them.

Crazy Horse's entourage was just emerging from the trees.

A soldier told the trooper nearest Fox Running to watch the

49

boy as Fox Running got up, limping. The man who spoke and the other soldier put their rifles to their shoulders, as though on parade, and moved over to greet Crazy Horse.

Fox Running tried to explain to the remaining soldier and pointed again when the man did not seem to understand.

"Calm down, son," the man said. "Simmer down. Simmer down. Talk slower and speak white talk. I can't understand you!"

Fox Running was sure he saw movement behind the soldier. He shoved the surprised soldier to the ground. The man kept a firm grip on his rifle. Fox Running grabbed for the holster at the man's waist, as he had done with Van Diver once before. He swatted away a hand that sought to pull at his right arm. The revolver tumbled out and landed in the dirt.

Fox Running picked it up, but the soldier grabbed him around the thighs and brought him to the ground. The impact broke the man's grip. Fox Running still held the pistol as he lay on the ground. He got up on both knees. Holding the pistol tight with both hands, he took a moment to guess which tree the man had chosen. Hammer. Trigger. Nothing. Another tree target. Hammer. Trigger. Another. Again nothing. Hammer. Trigger. There were angry voices yelling. Men pointing. One man with a black beard had his mouth open so wide Fox Running wondered if a bird could fly in.

Fox Running had time for one more shot. He was certain this must be the right tree. The gun fired as a soldier hit him from behind with a rifle butt, knocking him flat.

He had missed. The man who had been waiting for Crazy Horse fired at the soldiers. One soldier fired back. Two more. Then the man fired again in a different direction, before running toward his waiting horse. Fox Running had failed.

"Squad, fire!"

A small volley exploded behind Fox Running. Another. Another.

"Cease fire!"

Dazed from the glancing rifle blow to his head, Fox Running watched soldiers run toward where the bearded man was last seen. Three other soldiers pointed rifles at him. He dropped the revolver and moved his hands away from his sides to show he meant to do nothing further. He smiled. Crazy Horse was not dead!

"Captain!" One trooper was motioning to an officer to join him.

Fox Running started to get up. A cavalryman slammed him in the ribs with the butt of his rifle, making him double over in pain. "You stay there, Injun. Move and I kill you." The face of hate looked upon him.

Gasping and in pain, only one thought filled Fox Running's mind: *Let them tell me now I am not a true Cheyenne.*

Soldiers were moving to and fro. Fox Running dimly heard loud, fast talking amid the thunder that throbbed in his head. A bloody, swollen lump on the bottom of his foot made it impossible to stand, so he sat. He would save his strength for when he had to walk with the soldiers watching for weakness. The bruise on his ribs hurt, as did his head, but he would not touch the injuries and let the soldiers know he was in pain. He heard a commotion behind him but was not going to allow a soldier to hit him again. He kept his gaze fixed forward, steeling himself not to react to what was said.

"Look at what you have done!" came a deep Cheyenne voice speaking in his native tongue. "Why is it you have done this?"

Fox Running stared straight ahead.

"You will talk to me!" A powerful hand grabbed his left shoulder and spun him around. Fox Running looked up at the angry, startled face of Stone Leg. "You!"

"Greetings, Stone Leg. Did any shots hit Crazy Horse?"

"What have you done?" the Cheyenne repeated. "Why are you here?"

"I am Cheyenne. These are my people."

"The soldier I spoke with left many weeks ago. You did not?"

"I did not. He was a good man, Stone Leg. He feared what would happen if I returned to the People; that I would fight in a war and be killed. He taught me much that was good, but it was time that I left him to return to the People."

"Did he tell you to shoot Crazy Horse?"

"Ask any who saw. A white man was here to kill Crazy Horse. He had waited many days," Fox Running said, before explaining what had taken place. "I do not know if he escaped, but I know he did not succeed."

"How do you know?"

"If he had, there would be pain and mourning. There is anger, and there are questions. Crazy Horse is alive. I am content."

"What is he to you?"

"You spoke true. When my father left to avoid the blood feud, hoping time would cure tempers, we took refuge with the Lakota, with Crazy Horse, for my mother was the granddaughter of a Lakota man and a Cheyenne woman. We were mostly welcome there. Crazy Horse was a leader I could respect, for he cared not about the past, only about surviving. He had time for children."

He could recall being too shy to get close to Crazy Horse then and hung about at the very edge of the children when the great warrior spoke with them.

"When the warriors went north after the Greasy Grass, my father hoped to come back to the People. He did not know we had been declared dead to the People. We arrived at the camp on the Rosebud two days before it was attacked. He believed he could set everything to rights, but then came the attack, and he died with those who scorned him, for they were all Cheyenne."

Stone Leg was silent a moment. Then he bent down and spoke softly to Fox Running. "I and others who keep order in the camp will speak with the soldiers. If what you say is true, you may come and camp with my family for the night until we can decide . . ."

He straightened as new footsteps approached. It was Crazy Horse himself.

"Tell me, boy who blazes fire, do the Cheyenne welcome all in this manner?" the great warrior asked Fox Running, speaking in Lakota.

Fox Running sat straighter, ignoring the pain in his head. "I am Fox Running, the son of Red Eagle, who rode with you at the Greasy Grass, and Doe Leaping, whose grandmother was related to your wife's family. There was a man who wanted you dead . . ."

"And *he* is now dead," finished Crazy Horse. "As you might have been, Blazing Fire. Your father . . . I recall there was a blood feud." He frowned as he subjected Fox Running to a thorough inspection. "You are the boy with the pistol who charged the soldiers at the Greasy Grass and saved the Cheyenne warrior! I saw you at a distance on the day of the battle. I was told of you and sought your family, but after the fight there was much chaos."

Crazy Horse turned to Stone Leg. "I heard some of what was said between you. If the Cheyenne do not want this warrior, send him to the camp of the Lakota, for as long as the grass shall grow we will honor those who are brave. From this day forward, he will be treated among the Lakota as my ward."

He lowered his head toward the boy. "And now, Blazing Fire, may I ride my horse?"

Fox Running's confusion at how to respond to his new name

was so clear on his face that the Lakota war leader laughed loudly.

"We will speak another day, Blazing Fire," he said. "For the days of our people may be numbered, but they are not over."

Crazy Horse and his men moved onward. The warrior mounted the horse, rode it around the meadow to show how well he could control a strange animal during his first time on its back, and then rode proudly to the land set aside for the Lakota.

Stone Leg had been speaking to the soldiers. They followed the crowd after Crazy Horse left. He approached Fox Running.

"The soldiers tell us that the man they killed had a Sharps rifle used by men who hunt men. Others have reported seeing him, but no one knows who he was or why he was here. That he fired at them makes them believe he was doing wrong, but they do not know. They are not certain if they believe you, but they have not found anything you said that was a lie."

Stone Leg looked intently at Fox Running.

"When Dull Knife and Little Wolf agreed to come to this place, it was promised we would work with the soldiers to stop fights and bad feelings. We do not know if we can live in peace, but no one will say the Cheyenne did not try to do so. I and others keep order. I have told the soldiers I am responsible for you, and they will let you come with me. If you run away, it is a breach of trust. The white soldiers will seek you. I will seek you. You may feel you have been judged harshly, but these are harsh times, and we must live as the spirits would have us. Are you ready to come to the lodge of my family? There you can decide if you wish to live as Fox Running of the Cheyenne or Blazing Fire of the Lakota, or if you wish to live as a white man with the army."

There was only one choice. The home he wanted with the

family that was dead would never be. He would take what there was.

CHAPTER FIVE

September 1877, Fort Robinson, Nebraska

Crazy Horse was dead. There had been an argument. Threats. Defiance. Then a soldier stabbed Crazy Horse with his bayonet one day, while others held his arms to render him defenseless, leaving the warrior to linger for hours before his death.

Fox Running had been among those to see the warrior. Crazy Horse had asked to see him, which surprised the boy.

"Blazing Fire," Crazy Horse said. "Do not trust their promises. They have lied from the first. Stand tall for our peoples. Do not ever surrender." The war leader was gasping at this point. "Do not surrender in your body, but above all do not surrender in your spirit, for that is what they will try to kill first. You do not understand the world of the spirits, Blazing Fire. This is what I must tell you that is urgent. Only when you serve the spirits can a warrior be great. Listen for their voices, and do as they ask. A warrior who serves the spirits can be killed but can never be defeated, for the spirits will rise up new warriors in their turn."

Crazy Horse had taken time to say good-bye to many before the pain grew so great that his family asked to have his final hours alone. After he died, the warrior's parents would take his body and first put it on a scaffold, where his spirit would be freed before he was buried. The war leader's body was then taken by his family and buried in a place they would not reveal, so that no one could disturb its rest.

Fox Running was heartsick, for even with all of Crazy Horse's fame and all those who wanted to see him, Crazy Horse had always found time for him, and had been the only adult—Lakota or Cheyenne—who made him feel truly welcome. Now he was gone, and Fox Running was again bereft.

He could not return to the camp of the Northern Cheyenne, because there was none.

In the summer, the Northern Cheyenne who had surrendered and were on the rolls of the soldiers were corralled and marched at the point of a gun to the south, where the soldiers said they would live with their cousins, the Southern Cheyenne, instead of in the north, where they expected that the treaty they had signed would let them live.

The soldiers went down a list of names to determine who would go. There was no one named Fox Running on the list. He had asked Stone Leg what he should do, for he did not want to leave his people, but he also did not wish to leave Crazy Horse.

"I fear we march to our deaths," Stone Leg had told him. "Stay with Crazy Horse. Learn the ways of a warrior, for if the white man will send us far from home when he promised to let us stay, there will be more war. If they kill all of us, someone must be left here to carry forward our fight."

Now, as Blazing Fire, he was on the rolls of the Lakota at Fort Robinson as a ward of Crazy Horse. The soldiers had counted them all time after time, in case one Lakota should start a war that a thousand soldiers could not win.

However, Crazy Horse's death had reverberated through the Lakota. There were fears and accusations that some within the Lakota themselves plotted with the soldiers. Division and dissension followed in a time of bitter realization that the Lakota had fallen and might never rise, so wounded were they in spirit.

Few had much interest in a Cheyenne boy with no Lakota

family. Day by day he found himself less welcome with those who were Crazy Horse's closest friends. He also saw more and more young men drifting away. Yet he remained. None asked him to join them. He was now fourteen but still far smaller than anyone else his age. He did not have the build of a warrior. He thought of Shoulder Bar once. That was a place he had been welcome, but it was a place he did not belong. He did not belong here, either. Not any longer. Did he belong anywhere?

October 1877, Nebraska
It had finally become the turn of the Lakota. The soldiers had told the rudderless people they would be moving to a new agency, for with Red Cloud's people who were already at the fort and the ones who had arrived with Crazy Horse, the land would not support them all.

There was some truth to this, for the hills had been hunted bare. Some of the camps were in places that would flood when the snows melted in the spring. There was no clear leader to fight, and so the Lakota acquiesced, demanding to return in the spring and making plain to the soldiers that this was not an idle threat. The spirit of the Lakota seemed to flare back to life with this latest demand. The soldiers agreed that the Lakota would spend the winter on the Missouri River, but no longer.

Fox Running slipped away in the night, alone. The stallion they had given Crazy Horse had been left largely unattended since his death. Fox Running hoped the spirit of the warrior would not be affronted if he took him. He had no clear goal, but with the South the place where the soldiers wanted the Indians to go, there was only one choice: he rode north.

No one was following him. Fox Running was certain. Living wild with the gang of outcasts—all that would take him—had sharpened his senses. Too wild. For too long. Everything had come to a head when they tried to rob that pay wagon. Now he had more dead men to his name and both red warriors and white soldiers who would have happily killed him.

Ever since he left Fort Keogh back in Montana he had stopped and waited for any possible pursuers, lying in ambush more than once when he was certain he was being followed. He was not. He had followed the Yellowstone River for a time, then cut across hills he did not know. All that mattered was putting distance between himself and Fort Keogh.

That he did. He could not distance himself from guilt that he had failed to live up to Crazy Horse's dying words. But what was he to do? He would not leave the land, and all that roamed free were young warriors and rootless young men who knew only that they did not want to die as old, shuffling men who were afraid to meet the eyes of the young. He had stolen; he had killed. And now, he could not run far enough to run away from what he was.

Riding with the Black Canyon Gang had been a mistake. He may well have had little choice, but it remained a mistake. He could not have more fully ignored Crazy Horse's advice. Owl Wing had been a good friend when he first left the reservation, but as they drifted west, they met more drifting youths and drifted into trouble. It had been one thing to take a shirt when he had none; to steal food from those with plenty of it. It was another to wait and rob wagons.

Those who steal are thieves. Those who kill are killers. He was both. Two of the gang's members were dead from his gun—both Little Cub, the Shoshone who led it, and Buff Walker, a white tough who also rode with the motley collection of mixed breeds and lost souls. The soldier they wanted to kill had been wounded, and for all Fox Running knew, he might recall the gang member who saved him as his assailant!

Every day he put distance between himself and Fort Keogh, the better. Two Moon, who oversaw the small collection of Northern Cheyenne who had been allowed to stay behind near the fort, had been clear that all Cheyenne who lived with him must abide by the laws of both peoples, and that anyone who broke any laws would be punished. Although most had known him as Blazing Fire of the Lakota, some knew him as Fox Running of the Cheyenne. If he stayed, he would have been found, sooner or later. He would not have been taken alive.

He knew what happened to Indians when their names were on "Wanted" posters. White men would kill in hopes they found the right man and keep killing anyone who looked like the right man until the bounty was withdrawn.

He was safe, but lost. He was somewhere near what the white men called Nebraska, or maybe Wyoming. The caves and crevices here in this rough country would serve for a few days. He had plenty of food. He thought again about trying to find the Northern Cheyenne he was told had escaped from the Darlington Agency in the south. Anything would be better than being on the run on his own at age fifteen, but sometimes, the only way to be safe was to be alone. It was a hard world, and only the hardest survived.

The volley of gunfire made him start. Single shots, or even the multiple shots of a hunter desperate to hit what he missed, were not uncommon. Only soldiers fired in volleys, and then only when fighting an enemy that was more than one man.

Almost one moon had passed since he started camping along the Hat Creek bluffs. It would be late into the month the soldiers called January of the year they called 1879. The escaped

Cheyenne were in their winter camp, if the stories he had heard were true. When he first arrived, he had seen patrols and wondered if they were scouting for the escapees. The Lakota had returned from the south but were at the Pine Ridge Agency in the place the soldiers called Dakota. They would be far from this place. Bandits? No. Soldiers at war meant Indians.

He made sure both of the .45 pistols he kept were fully loaded, as was his Winchester rifle, although it only had a few rounds of ammunition. He wore a broad-brimmed hat and a dirty brown jacket over a once-white shirt, and black trousers that flopped above moccasins. He kept his hair long, as did most who roamed the far reaches of the hills that broke apart the Plains into sections of rock and grass. The scar that trailed down his face was pink against the biting fury of the cold north wind. He usually wrapped cloth around the hands that held the reins of Crazy Horse's gift stallion, but this day he kept them unwrapped in case they were needed quickly.

He had been hiding in a small cave, but if the army was near, he needed to scout the land. A refuge could easily become a trap.

As he rode along the northern edge of the flat land, he spotted a group of perhaps forty figures moving in the broken hill country about a quarter mile to the south. They were moving through hills on the far side of the flatter ground. They then vanished. He scanned the hills behind them. They had to be out there somewhere. There was the flag, which meant soldiers. From the size of the snow kicked into the air by their horses, they outnumbered those they pursued. They might have been a mile behind, but with the broken trails of the hills, they could be half a day from catching their prey.

It must be a party of Indians being hunted. Cheyenne? Probably. Did it matter? He had been a boy without a people this past year, after spending the months before that more Lakota than Cheyenne. Would he be welcome? Would anyone even know who he was or care? Probably not. But something primordial within him said these were his people, and they were pursued. It was enough.

The flatlands had no shelter. He waited until much of the short day's light was gone to cross to the south side, where he saw those being hunted. He knew the trail to take, because it was the only route through rocks and treacherous footing. He waited, listening, chilled by more than the weather. Whatever was taking place in the hills was a deadly game. He was fifteen and alone. No, not in spirit. At a level he did not understand, there were moments he dimly felt the spirit of Crazy Horse, calling him forward. He knew he should not interfere. He knew it was right to do so. He gave the horse a pat on the rump and clucked it into motion. He would take his chances.

He had spent enough nights with all his senses alert to know when he was nearing those doing likewise, even when the world around him was blue-black with darkness above the gray-white of the snow.

"I am Fox Running," he called. "Son of Red Eagle of the Northern Cheyenne, and one-time ward of Crazy Horse with the Lakota name of Blazing Fire. I have guns but they are not in my hands. You may show yourselves."

A hammer was cocked.

"Those behind me need not fear. I do not have guns that shoot backward. Come closer and see for yourselves. I have food."

"Did they send you?" asked a familiar voice.

"Greetings, Stone Leg," he said with no expression, as if meeting a man he had not seen in almost a year was expected. "No one sent me. I travel south from Fort Keogh and am bound for the Pine Ridge Agency." This last was only partially true, but he did not want to admit that he was hiding from everyone.

The dimly seen man touched the horse.

"Is it you, boy? You look more like a white man's outlaw than a Cheyenne."

Fox Running let that pass. "What do you do here, and why do the soldiers chase you?"

Stone Leg recounted their escape from Indian Territory, and the decision by some of the Northern Cheyenne to see Red Cloud, learning too late he was not where they sought him. Instead, soldiers captured them. At first, there was peace, but then soldiers told the Cheyenne they would be forced back south, which led to an attempt to escape. Some did, but many never made it out of the fort alive.

"I do not know how many died, but we are heading for Fort Keogh, for we will be safe with Two Moon," he said, explaining that about thirty were with him, mostly women and children.

As they talked, a man with a horribly scarred face passed, bearing the look of one who walks with the spirits even as he goes to a place he would rather not travel. He stopped and looked Fox Running up and down, then gazed as if looking within. He nodded in the gesture of respect warriors used for one another and kept walking. Fox Running returned the gesture, for he knew this man was different. He was the last of the group—the place where the boldest fighter would walk to protect all who came before.

"That was Dead Face, one of our leaders," said Stone Leg. "His face was ruined by soldiers as a boy. He came to join us on our escape, even though he was already free. He has given all he has for the People but said the spirits will walk him where he belongs."

Fox Running looked at the man's retreating figure. He had heard the old speak of those who walked with death glowing about them. This was such a man.

"If you have come from Fort Keogh, you must know the best way," Stone Leg said, interrupting his thoughts.

Fox Running considered that.

It was a long journey, and they could not hope to outpace well-fed soldiers the entire way. Once they reached the far hills, they would again be in broken country where they might have a chance. But they would have to cross the flat lands to get there, and do so soon before they reached creeks that could not be forded if the weather turned warmer, leaving them trapped.

"The army is only hours behind you," he said. "I could see you and them from the far hills."

He explained that the best crossing was about a mile ahead, but even that would be a risk, for it was more than a mile wide and the Cheyenne would be exposed and could be wiped out if the army caught them on the flat lands. Stone Leg did not seem concerned.

"We will die before going south again," Stone Leg said.

"Let me help."

"In what way?"

Fox Running knew he could stall the army by making them fear an ambush. If they stopped often enough—and he was certain there were places where he could hide and fire upon them—there might be a chance for Stone Leg's group to cross the flatlands. He explained the plan.

"The soldiers are not like those you see at forts, Fox Running. They have pursued us for many days. They have become hardened like warriors. They only want to kill."

Fox Running looked back with no expression.

"Since the camp at the Rosebud was destroyed, Stone Leg, I have been without a place and without a people. These past days, my spirit has been wearied by my failure to be whatever it is that I was given life and air to be. If I die as a Cheyenne, doing that which is right, for once, perhaps my spirit will have the

64

home that I do not."

"Whatever has happened, this is wisdom the boy I met at the fort did not have," replied Stone Leg. "Those with me need rest. We will begin to march when they eat."

Fox Running gave them all the food he had. It was not much, but he was not worried about where his next meal might come from. He felt happier than he had in days. He had a purpose, and for once he could be a warrior.

"Take the horse," he said to Stone Leg as the escapees prepared to go. "He is too big to hide, and it may help some of you get away."

Stone Leg ordered several children put on the horse. "The spirits sent you, Fox Running."

"Go with them, Stone Leg."

Dead Face was the last to leave, taking the position of honor by being closest to the danger they faced.

"The spirits will guide you on your journey," he told Fox Running.

Fox Running could almost touch the aura of death around Dead Face. He wanted to tell the warrior that his life was too precious to spend, yet to Dead Face, death was his gift to the People.

"I will not forget," Fox Running promised. "I will never forget."

"Then it is well."

For a moment, Dead Face looked as though he was deciding whether or not to speak.

"When the Spirit Walker meets you, tell her of this. Tell her that I have done what I have done so we will have a place of honor in the day that is to come. If you witness that which is to happen, tell her all that has happened so she knows it was not in vain. The spirits could never be that cruel to the People. Some must die so others can live." He stared into Fox Running's soul. "Be not afraid."

Then Dead Face was gone.

Fox Running, pondering what this valediction might mean and who the Spirit Walker might be, walked along the trail the Cheyenne had taken. He found several places to fire at the soldiers, then run away. He would have enough bullets that he might be able to slow them down three or four times. When the light dawned and they approached, he would earn his place as a warrior, even if it was the last thing he did.

But the soldiers had fooled him. The snow-covered ground showed the trail as a dark line amid white. It had been easy to follow, even in the dimness. Troopers on the move almost surprised Fox Running. He found some rocks. There was little time to find a better place.

They were probably too far away for anything but a chance shot, but he opened fire. He was not trying to kill them, but to buy time for those trying to escape. The flame of the pistol's barrel gave the soldiers a perfect target. Fox Running was pinned down by the fire. He fired back, using more ammunition than he expected. He would need a moment to pull back to a new position, but they would not give him that chance.

He did not know that the soldiers, honed by two weeks of fighting the same delaying tactics Fox Running was now using, had learned how to deal with ambushes triggered by one or two warriors. Their fire intensified. He scrambled over rocks that were uphill from his position, feeling bits of rock fly into his legs as the soldiers, now that daylight was breaking, could see him abandon his position.

Finally, gasping, he had reached the last place he could hope to make them delay even for a moment. As he waited alone, he could not deny to himself that fear was with him behind the boulders. This was where he would end his fight. He had nineteen bullets and his knife. He would have to conserve his fire. They would have to dismount and rush him to reach him, for this spot was above the trail. The longer he waited, the more he told himself he could still escape, and the more he scolded himself for doing so. He wished he could know if warriors felt this way, or if they were as brave with death around them as the songs said that would chant the names of those who fell in battle.

He waited uneasily. And waited. They must have moved more cautiously than he expected.

Two distant shots echoed. Two answered it. For a moment he was sure they had seen him, but the only noises he could hear were his heart pounding as the wind moaned a death song.

He cautiously looked over the top of the rocks. There was the tip of a flag moving closer. No! It was moving down toward the flat lands. They outsmarted him. The soldiers had divided. He only fought some of the pursuers. One group took the valley floor; the group Fox Running had fought was just now coming down from the rocks.

He looked to the valley and wanted to scream. His people had not made their way to safety. Not even close.

In a depression that in spring and in floods would be filled with water, a pitiful remnant of the Northern Cheyenne was waiting. Perhaps some had escaped on the horse?

No. The animal given to Crazy Horse that had carried him so long was wandering aimlessly. They had let it go. They would not be chased and killed with their backs to the enemy. They would sing their death songs with their faces to those who came to kill them and die as Cheyenne. They were not planning to leave the tiny gully alive!

He saw one young man who was not dressed as a soldier walking back from the pit. He could tell from the man's posture that he had tried to talk the Cheyenne into surrender. He had failed.

Fox Running clambered over rocks. Perhaps as the soldiers closed in on the warriors, women, and children, he could still be in time to join Stone Leg! But the soldiers who were still in the rock foothills blocked his way.

He stood on the rocks, all thoughts driven from his mind of anything except anger at his failure and pain at the deaths he could not prevent.

He emptied his pistols at the soldiers, who were far too distant for him to hit anything. An officer with two bars on his shoulder pointed. Several men left the group and slowly rode in his direction. The rest began a slow trot toward the depression. He could faintly hear a voice from the soldiers below. There was no answer. Then the guns began.

Fox Running was mutely watching the charge of the cavalry against the few remaining Cheyenne when seven troopers surrounded him.

"Drop the guns, boy," said one.

"Or we will shoot you," snarled another. "Give you what you deserve."

"It is a boy, Reynolds," said the first man sternly. He followed Fox Running's eyes as the one-sided contest below came to its end. In their final charge, troopers were firing point-blank into the rifle pit where the Northern Cheyenne had made their stand. Fox Running was numb, wet eyed but too proud to show more emotion.

The first trooper, gray hairs showing brightly against the black that dominated his bristly mustache, dismounted as others kept their rifles pointed at Fox Running. He touched Fox Running on the arm.

"Come along now, son. This is over. You don't want to see that any more. Come along, lad."

He lifted the pistol from Fox Running's unresisting right hand. He took the second from the holster on the boy's left hip.

"Empty," he told his fellow troopers.

He looked at the knife in the boy's waistband. Disarming Indians was tricky when it came to their knives. If this one showed resistance, they would take the knife. Until then, he was no threat. There had been enough killing, and it was over.

"What is the name of this place?" Fox Running asked the soldier.

"Hat Creek down by the Pit there," he said. "Hat Creek Bluffs here where we're standing."

Hat Creek. Fox Running promised that if he lived a hundred summers, he would never forget this place. Or this day.

Fox Running and a few Cheyenne escapees who had been captured were put in a barracks that had been used by the Cheyenne before they broke out of Fort Robinson. On their way back to the fort, the same soldiers who had hunted down the Indians without mercy shared food and overcoats with the survivors. Some talked of adopting the smallest children. One white woman, who he understood was a writer, cradled tiny ones in her arms with the help of a white man in civilian clothes who looked horrified at the wagons of the dead, stiff Cheyenne that followed the horses.

A few days after their return, a burly officer entered the quarters and summoned Fox Running. "Come with me, Scar On Face," he said brusquely. "No shackles," he told the guard. "The boy is not going anywhere. I can always kill him if I must."

They reached the officer's rooms, which were much warmer than the barracks where the Cheyenne were confined.

"Do you call yourself Fox Running now or Blazing Fire?" the man asked after stuffing a pipe full of tobacco and then lighting the pipe with a piece of wood from the fire. He clearly enjoyed the sight of the boy's slack-jawed response.

"The scar. Never seen a face with one like it. A couple of

years back, you were here with Jim Van Diver when he was a lieutenant. You probably don't recall; you were all-fired on living with the Cheyenne and getting away. Did well for yourself, just like all you savages when you go off on your own."

Shoulder Bar, thought Fox Running. He vaguely recalled this man. "Malvers," Shoulder Bar had called him. If it was the same man, a short time on the Plains had eroded his youthful air and replaced it with puffy-faced cynicism that grew from loneliness and disappointment and was nurtured by alcohol.

"He asked me to keep an eye out, if I could, while you were in their camp. Hard to miss you after that stunt with Crazy Horse. Then you snuck out. When the Cheyenne came back north, Jim—he's a captain now at Fort Riley—asked me to see if you showed up. Bad penny and all that, I guess. Funny thing. Notice from up Fort Keogh way said thugs were robbing wagons, but that this Lakota kid they called Blazing Fire managed to shoot some of the gang when they tried to kill a soldier who was trying to protect a Teamster. They said to arrest him anyway because he was part of the gang. Description could be anybody, except for the part about that scar. No one is looking, because you are too unimportant when we all have better things to do, but in time someone would find you. I think there would be justice done, but Jim would blame himself for not saving you, as if anyone can save you from yourself!"

Fox Running waited. The man was coming to the reason for his talk. All he wanted to do now was get Fox Running to say or do something stupid. Fox Running was learning to wait out the ways of men like this. If he had planned to arrest him, he would already have done so. There was no escape from this place. He had to wait.

"Me and Jim have been in touch by telegraph. You're being sent to Fort Riley, under guard for certain and chained if you want, and Jim is going to figure out what to do with you. Jim's a good man, boy. Better man than me. Better man than you. Far better than you. Jim's going to probably stick his neck out for you again, even now that he's married. I'm here to tell you that when he does, you do anything that hurts that man and I will find you, because good men like Jim don't come along much. Might just be a better world if all you hotheads and hostiles were removed from it, because none of you are ever going to change. You ought to know, boy, that the army wants these Plains peaceful. Way I see it, you have done nothing but disturb the peace the past two years. You just saw what happens when the army gets mad. Not pretty. Your people asked for what they got by refusing to listen. The old ways of your people, all of that, is going away. Change, boy, and you got a long life ahead. Don't, and you won't never see another year. Don't take that as a threat; understand that I am making you a promise. You leave in the morning. Sergeant!"

A man entered.

"Take the prisoner back. Any trouble, chains and shackles until he reaches Kansas."

Malvers gave him one last look. "Change or die, boy. Don't matter to me which." He motioned with his head for Fox Running to be taken away.

CHAPTER SIX

Fort Riley, Kansas, August 1879

Fox Running swept the broom across the grime- and filth-covered floor as the flies around him droned the endless music of summer in a cowboy town. The customers who in the spring had stared at him as though he had two heads now nodded drowsily in the sunshine that filtered through the hazy windows.

Shoulder Bar had made it clear that with a wife and baby, the need for frequent patrols to protect immigrant wagon trains, and feelings running high in Kansas over the men killed in the flight of the Cheyenne to the north, Fox Running could not stay with him at the fort. He was going to have him work with someone who would give him a chance, but it would be the last time Shoulder Bar could do anything, now that Fox Running was getting older and would soon be an adult and be treated like one.

"Michael O'Malley is a good man," he had said when Fox Running had arrived from Fort Robinson. "Irish, I know, but he keeps his word. He will give you work, food, wages, and a place to stay. He does not care what you are. It is about time you stopped wearing being an Indian like a chip on your shoulder. Give me your word you will not run off. This is the last chance I can give you. I do not mean to be hard, but these are hard times. Your choices are dwindling."

Fox Running had agreed. He had no place to go. There had been one band of Cheyenne still free, but with hundreds of soldiers looking for them, he assumed it was only a matter of time until what happened to Dead Face, Stone Leg, and the rest happened to them. If he thought he could die with them, he would have taken the risk, but he had no idea where to go.

He might have been able to live with Red Cloud, but he had been a prisoner on a reservation before. Never again.

Sometimes he regretted his choice. Being an Indian in a town filled with soldiers and cowboys meant endless insults for which he wanted to hit a customer over the head with the axe handle O'Malley kept under the bar. But the grandfatherly old Irishman had been kind.

"Nothin' they say, laddie, compares with what the English say about the Irish," he would say.

Fort Riley was busy. There were others his age, but they worked on farms or in stores. And they were white. Most seemed to him as children, as perhaps he might have been if the attack on the Rosebud so long ago had not changed his life. Perhaps if his father had been content to stay with Crazy Horse, they might have been together on the Pine Ridge Agency. The spirits had decided otherwise.

He had turned sixteen over the summer, but if he had grown it was not by much. He was still the height of many white children years younger. However, O'Malley let him dress as he pleased, and wear his hair long as he liked. He ate every day, slept indoors, and did not need to look over his shoulder. The faces of Hat Creek lived in his dreams and nightmares, but life could be—and had been—worse.

"Dinna spit in their beer or their faces, laddie, and the rest comes out in the wash," O'Malley would say. "This is Amerikay, and if they let in the Irish, there is no telling what a man can become!"

He was a man of endless songs and stories in the eternal war on silence that he waged—usually with mirth, sometimes with deep, weepy sadness for the loss of his wife and children to a fever.

Fox Running had started as an employee but soon wandered into a quasi-world of being, if not family, one of two people with no one else in the world who could find refuge in the other.

O'Malley tried to limit how much the wild cowboys drank, for although the more he sold the more money he made, when too many drinks turned common words into insults and brawls, flat broke cowboys never paid for the damage they caused. On this day, as the afternoon slowly ticked past, two Texans who had reached Fort Riley two days ahead of their trail driving comrades refused to hear any hints that they had had enough.

One of them finally noticed Fox Running was an Indian. "Irish, you got an Injun in here! You tryin' to scalp us?"

The Texan and his friend found this intensely humorous. Fox Running ignored them and moved away, sweeping grit and clumps of dried mud toward the door.

One Texan stood up and tottered over to Fox Running, looming above him. "You speak-um real talk, boy?"

"Let the boy be," intoned O'Malley in the bored tone reserved for drunks who needed coddling.

"Don' think it's right, Injun kid like that. You scalp-um white men, boy?"

O'Malley, who had seen more than one flash of the temper Fox Running tried to contain, spoke up again. "Boy's got his work to do, friend. Let the lad do what needs doing. Want him working for the wages I pay him."

But the cowboy, with the ability of the truly drunk to focus on only one subject, would not let the matter go. "You scalp Custer, Injun kid? Maybe you want me to cut your hair? Hoo-hee, Carter. Think we should give this red savage a haircut? Shave him bald?"

Carter hooted his agreement.

"I'm game, Roberts," he said. "Cut it all off! Ha-hee!"

O'Malley motioned to Fox Running to move away from the cowboys and into the back. But Roberts was quicker and grabbed the boy's arm with his left hand while pulling a large knife from its sheath with his right.

"Boys, boys, boys," O'Malley called out, stepping out from behind the bar, with his trusty axe handle in hand.

"Set it down, old man," said Carter, pulling a gun from his holster. "Whiskey had as much water as whiskey. Men just up from Texas deserve a little fun. Just set that hunk of wood on the bar. Not gonna hurt nobody. Just havin' fun. Injun kid ought to know his place. Cowboy deserves fun."

"All it is, Irish," Roberts called. "A little fun. Bet he don't bleed much unless we miss. Now hold still, Chief Gonna-Scalp-Ya!"

He pulled Fox Running toward a table. The boy pushed back, almost breaking the cowboy's grip. Carter stepped in closer. O'Malley used the moment to reach for the axe handle, but Carter, less drunk than Roberts, saw the motion and turned to fire his pistol.

The shot missed and sailed into the ceiling. Roberts, wrestling with Fox Running, turned to see what was taking place.

O'Malley, long inured to the sudden explosions of violence that were endemic to the frontier, had dropped to the floor as soon as he saw Carter turning. Three more shots came in succession, but O'Malley could see nothing, only hear the sounds. He looked up after a brief pause to see one more shot from Carter, and that one as the man was on both knees on the floor with the jittery shakes. The bullet kicked splinters into O'Malley's arms but otherwise left him unharmed.

The Irishman leaned against an upturned table and pulled himself to his feet.

Roberts was a lump by the door, inert as a sack of potatoes, with a stain growing around him. Carter had stopped shaking and was flat on his back, spasming weakly with two red holes in his torso. And by the doorway, with a still-smoking pistol in his two very steady hands, was Fox Running.

"Oh laddie, laddie, what is it ye have gone and done?" wailed O'Malley. Carter was dead before O'Malley could finish checking whether there was any breath in the man. Roberts had clearly been killed instantly. O'Malley didn't even bother looking closer.

O'Malley could move fast when he needed to. He put the *Closed* sign on the door, ordered Fox Running to help him drag the dead men behind the saloon, and then to set to cleaning the floor with a vengeance.

"Clean it, all the blood, me lad. Then toss dirt and mud upon it, for if you clean it proper and it is the only clean space, it will be noticed. We bury the lads after darkness."

"He was going to kill you!" Fox Running said. "I had to stop him. I pulled a gun from the man who held me and shot the other man, twice. The first man went for his other pistol, so I shot him, too. He was so close that I could not miss."

"Ye saved me life, laddie," O'Malley said. "Now to see what we can do about saving yours."

O'Malley was grateful that only four men were in the saloon at the time; all were either regulars or habitually drank so much that their word alone would count for little. One Kansas gunfight blurred into the next. With any luck, this one would be blotted out by a new fight within days, if not hours.

Fox Running was by turns defiant and glum. The Texans were trying to kill him and a man who was kind to him. He felt fully justified. O'Malley said no jury would convict a white man of murder for the crime. But Fox Running was not a white man. He was a sixteen-year-old Indian with a history of violence.

A couple of weeks ago, Fox Running had heard from a cowboy that some Cheyenne made it to Fort Keogh. The thought of running away to the Tongue River Valley and risking a run-in with the Black Canyon Gang had flitted in and out of his mind since then, but he liked O'Malley, and he had given his word to Shoulder Bar. Now he wondered again about running off, for he knew, as did O'Malley, that when the rest of the Texas trail crew arrived, if he was in town there would be a reckoning.

O'Malley thought of the boy's choices. Turning him in to the law was never an option, any more than was turning him loose, to be hunted until he was caught. The boy might be skilled at evading pursuit, and apparently skilled with using a pistol, but he was still a boy. He was no match for those who would come after him, and the truth of the boy's whereabouts would surface sooner or later.

He thought through the night. O'Malley was all the family Fox Running had. Some place had to want an Indian boy who had no one and needed to be somewhere no one could find him—and needed it fast.

Then he recalled the man—the funny Eastern man—who had passed through Fort Riley recently and stopped at the saloon for a drink and a chat.

Some group in Boston was starting a school for Indian children. The man had been to the fort looking for stray children no one wanted, not realizing most Indian families looked upon their children as prizes, not burdens. He had made a circuit of central Kansas, come up empty, and was staying at the fort.

Peter Petengill was unhappy to see the Irish saloon owner. As if there were not enough Irish in Boston! His interest grew as O'Malley explained that he was seeking help for a boy, about eleven, who had been living rough. An orphan, who was part

Cheyenne and part Sioux.

Petengill and Maurice Darby, the educator waiting in Boston for Petengill to round up pupils from the far dregs of the frontier, believed that, despite their primitive habits, Indians could be manufactured into hard-working Americans if all of their superstitions and ways were removed through harsh discipline that broke them of their habits of sloth and indolence.

The school had secured backing from churches and reformers who thought the Indians should be saved and not slaughtered. The fall term would start in late September, and several students were already living in the school's dormitory in downtown Boston, but Darby had practically demanded Petengill find Cheyenne and Sioux students. The man wanted to boast that the warriors who had killed Custer had been transformed into janitors and factory workers of proper habits for the 19th century. He believed it would increase donations, and refused to allow Petengill to return empty-handed.

Petengill stroked the waxed, upturned mustache he sported as O'Malley talked about the need to save the boy from himself. He'd been considering taking the next train East, no matter what Darby wanted. The stunt the fool Northern Cheyenne pulled in escaping from Indian Territory and then the slaughter that followed before some made it to Montana had all the Plains Indians thinking more about going back to their old ways than about embracing the future. They wanted to become extinct, as he saw it.

He had also spent far too much time on beds that were like rocks, and speaking to frontier settlers who lacked the education and breeding to offer anyone a proper model of society. Although he knew some religious societies wanted to open Indian boarding schools on the reservations out West, it was his opinion that having settlers who were primitive in their own way try to educate Indians was a futile pursuit.

"One hundred what?" he said, emerging from the place he'd mentally wandered to while O'Malley was running on about something, as if the opinion of an Irishman who operated a tavern in a dust-pit like this was of worth.

O'Malley wanted to thump the pompous fool with the affected cane the man used as a walking stick, but there was a life in the balance. "The boy is heading for perdition, sir, and some of us who hope to save him raised a fund for his transport. We would pay it to you, of course."

Petengill was quick to read between the lines. There must be a reason they wanted the boy sent East. A problem? Well, they were all problems. Stiff-necked. Rebellious. Discipline properly applied would remedy that! But $100? That was a tidy bonus for whatever trouble the boy might cause.

"Let us see this boy," Petengill replied. "The Indian School of Boston is always ready to help those in need."

The meeting was more of an inspection than anything else.

"Eleven, he is, you say?" Petengill said, clearly concerned that the maturity Fox Running radiated was at variance with his small size and alleged age. The age was a lie, but with a big enough bounty, what could it really matter if the boy was twelve or thirteen? They could pound him into submission once he was away from this wild, lawless frontier.

"That is what the army told me," O'Malley lied glibly.

"How came he by that scar? It gives a frightful cast to his features."

O'Malley was warning Fox Running into silence as he answered. "I believe it was a youthful misadventure while hunting with companions," he replied. "Terrible injuries these lads get for lack of civilized care."

"Speak English?" Petengill asked the boy at length. "Know my talk?"

"Yes, sir. I understand every word you say," Fox Running said in a tone that O'Malley knew meant the boy's temper was starting to bubble.

"Well, what do you think?" O'Malley said, gripping Fox Running on the shoulder far harder than was necessary. "There is that matter we discussed."

"I believe you are out of date on the costs of transportation," Petengill replied. "I believe the amount would be closer to $150."

"Ahh," replied O'Malley. "Then give me the day to take up a collection among those who want well for the lad, and I shall meet you this evening to conclude our business."

"What liquor was he drinking that he smelled like that?" Fox Running asked O'Malley when they were alone. "I do not like him."

"Laddie, he's English and that says it all," said O'Malley with a deep sigh. "Some men from the East put something on their hair to make it smell oddly. They claim ladies like it. Not being a lady, I am not able to offer an opinion."

He and Fox Running shared a snicker at the expense of the affected Petengill and his Eastern ways.

"I canna see the future, boyo. I do not know if this fine school of his is all smoke and talk. But I can tell you this, laddie: if you keep living the way you have, you will be dead with a gun in your hand within a year or hung from a tree. I dinna like the man, but there will be Texas cowboys in town who will not stop hunting you if they think you are nearby. These are the cards, lad. Try it. It canna be worse than living on the run. I will na chain you and force you to go, but I have no idea how else to help you live long enough to grow up."

Fox Running could feel the edge of wisdom in what O'Malley was saying. He nodded to the old man, less because he agreed than because he knew of no other option, and he trusted that if O'Malley said this was his best choice, and perhaps his only choice, it was.

O'Malley tried to keep the ache from his voice, for if the boy was not his blood, their spirits had shared a common root somewhere.

"Then let us be done with this, laddie. And when ye come back, ye can tell me all the ways of fancy people with fancy manners!"

CHAPTER SEVEN

Boston, October 1880

"Andrew!"

The harsh, nasal voice of Colin Price cut through the classroom like the vicious swing of a whip.

He was addressing a small young man in the front row with the only head of unkempt hair in the room, a tie so askew as to be barely tied at all, and a suit that looked as though it had spent the night balled up in a corner.

If this young man—so different from the others sitting in rows with their clean, attentive faces turned toward Price—heard the teacher, his face did not show it. He seemed to be inspecting his hands with intense interest.

A barely audible buzz filled the classroom. The boy the school called Andrew had only been back in classes for a day. To the newest students he was both a legend and all but a stranger; he spent more time in the darkness of the detention rooms in the cellar of the musty old building than he did in class.

Fox Running had tolerated the school for the first weeks. He cared little that they gave him a white man's name. He already had two names; what was a third when it was only for the school? As for their rules about speaking in Indian languages, his speech had evolved into such a mix of Cheyenne, Lakota, and English that he had learned to police it when he was around one kind or another, except in rages when all three were likely to emerge at the same time. Unlike those who came from their home reservation, talking the talk of whites came easily to him, even if during his days in the detention dungeon he spoke any language he pleased, including the rude Irish phrases O'Malley instilled.

His initial acceptance of his situation had not lasted long. He kicked and fought when they cut his hair in the short style of white men and broke the nose of a barber who applied lilac water to his hair without asking. He refused to wear shoes on all but the coldest days. When he realized that rules were to be enforced by physical discipline, he met the challenge head on in a series of battles that often left him in the infirmary and sent more than one so-called attendant looking for a job that carried less risk. Two of them went to a local hospital.

Once he had been unconscious for several days when an attendant cracked his skull with a club, after the collective efforts of five men could not subdue him. That eruption had been triggered by a guest speaker who was telling them about the city's Columbus Day ceremony, which the school was planning to require its Indian students to attend so as to give thanks for the discovery of America by the enlightened Europeans. The plan was abandoned after Fox Running charged the speaker and was in the act of throwing him out a window when guards stepped in, triggering a school-wide brawl.

When he returned, he was not in the least reformed. One of the school's main features was a series of lectures on the wonders of Anglo-Saxon civilization and the woeful shortcomings of everything that there was about the Indian way of life, from its religion to its customs. When one lecturer said the Cheyenne were savages lacking any knowledge at all, Fox Running demanded the man explain how to survive for a year on the internal organs of a buffalo, which he described in great detail to the discomfiture of the man and the amusement of the class. He was said to have smiled during his beating afterward.

Those beatings, however, declined after one of the school's disciplinarians went too far and made a disparaging comment about the slaughter of the Cheyenne at Hat Creek. Fox Running fought back with brutal efficiency that showed he had mastered the art of planning surprise attacks. The target of the ambush was taken away on a stretcher and never seen again. The staff regarded the boy with horror amid its contempt.

Faced with the fact that he would give as good as he got, no matter what damage he received, the only resort left was detention in the dank cellar of the sagging building, located in an old industrial area of the city. His time in the detention rooms was measured in weeks. Other students would come back after a few days and show a change in attitude. Fox Running would return after being away for two weeks and barely last three days before making a return visit.

During classes, he projected an impassive façade that would suddenly crack without warning. When a class he was in was told it must write a poem about Custer's heroics in the War Between the States, he threw an inkwell through a window.

Yet there were times when he showed another side. During an apartment house fire near the school, he broke curfew and worked side by side with the firefighters throughout the night. Most were stunned when dawn revealed that the one passing buckets and carrying children from the building was an Indian.

When a Baptist minister and Old Testament scholar visited the school, he and Fox Running wound up in an animated discussion that ended only when the minister realized he was going to miss his evening service. The man hugged Darby on his way out the door and blessed him. Fox Running later explained that the two were discussing creation stories from the Bible and those from the Lakota and Cheyenne. After the child of the school's cook took sick, Fox Running had all the students gather around her mother, each praying silently in their own language so as to avoid getting in trouble. The girl was very sick at the time but soon after recovered.

But hostility was never far from the surface, even when the violence was restrained. A math teacher who barely lasted a month tried to give his pupils a lesson using what he thought were appropriate examples. "If Sitting Bull has forty horses and Crazy Horse has thirty horses, how many horses do all the Indians have?" Mr. Palmer had asked.

"None," Fox Running replied.

"How can that be?" the teacher thundered.

"The soldiers stole them," Fox Running deadpanned as the class erupted behind him.

Petengill had been admonished more than once for bringing the boy to the school. To Darby, it was clear the boy was far older than O'Malley had said. Fox Running himself had not denied it and was honest when asked his age. When asked why he allowed O'Malley to lie about his age, he told the school's clerk that no one ever asked him, and that he thought white men enjoyed lying to each other because they did it so often.

He was undeniably smarter than many of his fellow students. He could read better than almost all of them, thanks to the time Shoulder Bar had taken with him. He had seen maps at various army forts and understood geography. He understood arithmetic and would write well if he was in the mood, which was not often.

He flatly refused to sing in their choir, but when the alderman from the neighborhood dropped by, joined him in an Irish song, leaving the alderman beaming at a school that made Indians into Irishmen. When they made him draw, he produced nothing more than stick-like figures featured in Indian attacks on soldiers, who were always bleeding more profusely than anything possible in life.

Above all, he made it clear that he cooperated when he chose and if he chose. In history classes, he would contradict and interject to the point where no teacher wanted to face him, because the boy's questions reflected an understanding that went far beyond that expected of a savage.

Over the school's first year, amid the chaos of plugging the leaks in the roof, weeding out teachers who could not teach, and learning how to control children in such a way that balanced the necessary brutality of the punishment with the benefits it was supposed to confer, his constant fighting and rebelling had been one part of a larger picture. Now, as the school began its second year and its funders were beginning to ask about results, Darby had pushed the teachers and staff to stop coddling the few hard cases that had bent but were not yet broken.

Fox Running was at the top of that list.

Price, who was new, made it clear he was going to try.

"Andrew!" Price now stood directly in front of Fox Running. The boy's eyes finally moved. Looking at Price from under his eyebrows, moving nothing else, he stared the teacher dead in the face.

The man shivered a moment, then responded to the tremor of fear with a determination to show this boy who was the master here! He slammed down on the desk the wooden stick he used to point to examples on the chalkboard and to swat hands when students needed to be reminded of their place. If it made the boy blink, Price was not aware.

"I asked you to give me the sum of 743 and 629," Price repeated shrilly, waving his stick at the numbers on the board and then again at the boy, all but poking him in the nose.

Fox Running grabbed the stick from the startled teacher and snapped it in two. He snapped the broken pieces in half and then in half again.

Price saw the wild, savage spirit of the Indian in the eyes that stared back at him with hate. He recoiled as the student stood up.

"Everyone who is not a fool knows that 1,372 is the exact number of scalps taken at the Little Bighorn by the Lakota and the Cheyenne on the day Custer learned how to count, something other whites should learn," Fox Running said amid the dead silence of all the other students. "Especially those with hair they spend as much time plastering with byproducts of buffalo urine as you do."

A titter of laughter filtered through the room, for Price was one of the vainest and youngest of the teachers. He wore his hair cut in a way that made it seem puffy and was always preening himself when he caught his reflection.

Price turned purple and took one step forward.

"Please do try," the boy said mildly.

Whatever he saw in the Indian's eyes made Price stop dead, afraid. With the teacher frozen in place, Fox Running walked out from behind the row of desks, turned away, and walked to the door of the room, throwing the pieces of the shattered stick over his left shoulder. He turned as Price took a step toward the door behind him.

"Do not trouble yourself on my account," he said. "Perhaps this is the day that someone in this school will learn something." His tone made clear whom Fox Running considered the teacher.

"I will find my own way to detention," he added as he turned away from the shaking teacher and opened the door. He let it close behind him as his unshod feet padded down the wooden floor of the hallway.

John Dooley had been a police officer before he went off to fight in the War Between the States, but after the Wilderness he never walked again without a painful limp. The minié ball that ripped his left hip and groin to shreds had seen to that. It was almost three years before he could walk, and another two before he could finally move without a cane.

He had spent the years since the war as a watchman, often doing little more than watching the time go by in jobs his friends on the force would find for him out of kindness to a bluff, honest man who had been dealt a bad hand in life.

He had been a guard at the Indian School of Boston since it opened. He was never sure if his job was to keep the students from escaping or to guard the school from citizens who realized there were wild Indians in their midst, but it paid well, demanded little, and kept food on the table.

Dooley had nothing that resembled a family, having learned that gaping wounds that require frequent dressing were more than the young woman who promised to wait for him when he went to war could ever stand. By the time he could care for himself, he had come to expect a life on his own. The school, with its quirks and personalities, had become something like a dysfunctional family and less like a standard sort of employment.

Dooley was clean shaven, a big man with a full head of sandy hair, blue eyes that enjoyed the pleasure of simple things, and a firm jaw that could set hard when the men who ran the school were talking about students he knew far better than they ever would.

On this evening, he heard an Irish rebel song from a detention room and smiled. Unlike the teachers, who knew the best students the most, he knew the ones whose spirits resisted the bridle and were in the dank cellar more than they saw the daylight.

"I hear an Irish troublemaker pretending to be an Indian is again among us," Dooley called out with a grin. Talking to the students was forbidden, but so was his pipe and so was his flask; and when men tried to interfere in a man's right to some comforts, a man had a right to do as he saw proper.

"Mr. Dooley!" Fox Running called out from behind the wooden door of the detention room, clearly happy to hear the man's voice. "I think I need a softer pillow."

The game had begun several detentions ago, when Fox Running joked about using a slab of bread for a pillow if Dooley would only give him a few gallons of water to soften it.

"Foxy," Dooley began, using the name reserved for times when Fox Running was the only one in detention, since Dooley used the names the students preferred, " 'tis you know you need to think of changing your ways. Your company is grand, and ye have a charming voice for the old songs, but is there not a price to be paid for all your time down here?"

"Yes, I think there may be a contest to see who puts me here the most. You might want to place a wager. We can be in it together to rig the game!"

Dooley chuckled. "Me lad, you will be getting older, and you need to think of things other than this place. You will grow up, sooner or later. The school canna be yer home forever. What will ye do?"

There was a long, long silence. Then Fox Running spoke in a voice Dooley had never heard before. "I do not know, Mr. Dooley. I very truly do not know."

They were an ungainly pair of figures—a thin, tall Lakota boy named Tall Bear, known as Edward in the school, and a short Arapaho girl named Short Wing, whose official name was Jane.

Short Wing had made it to detention in her first week, when a female attendant crossed a line on the subject of petticoats and sought to physically instruct Short Wing on how she should wear them. Although she was far shy of Fox Running's status as a malcontent, she stood out among the other girls, who mostly resisted quietly but conformed outwardly.

Tall Bear had made his evening meal debut on his first day at the school by accidentally spilling a bowl of stew on a Comanche boy, Black Pony. The Comanche was in the process of putting the Lakota boy in his place when Fox Running stepped in and decked Black Pony, known in the school as George, with one lucky punch. Together, Tall Bear and Short Wing made up the universe of other Indians at the school who, on any given day, could be called Fox Running's friends.

Dooley, who knew that even things not allowed happened on schedule, loudly proclaimed to the darkness that he must go outside a moment.

Soon afterward, Tall Bear and Short Wing emerged from the shadows with food. Short Wing had spent a few days in the cellar and knew there was never anything fit to eat. Tall Bear simply enjoyed doing something forbidden, especially if it meant the girl's company. Although he never broke the school rules on his own, he respected and reveled in Fox Running's refusal to stop fighting against them.

"Did they search the room again?" Fox Running asked, gobbling down a piece of chicken Short Wing had wrapped in a napkin after she passed it through the barred window in the door of the detention room.

"They always do," replied Tall Bear, who was the only student brave enough to share a dormitory room with Fox Running.

"Did they find it?"

One of the students who entered that fall had brought with him a new knife, honed to a razor's edge. Fox Running, who knew where such things were kept when Petengill confiscated them before selling the best of the lot, had taken and hidden it under the floorboards of the room in case he decided to escape the school.

"No. The laundry you did not do last month, which you piled over the spot, is not disturbed. If a savage like me will not touch it, you can hardly expect civilized men to do so." Both boys grinned.

"You are both disgusting," Short Wing chimed in, smiling.

Tall Bear had been steeped in Lakota history and religion and was always amazed that the school believed Indians had neither culture nor faith. Now he smiled as he shared what he had overheard. "They do grow impatient with you, but from something they said, they are worried about what others think and do not want to expel you. I think they are also not sure if it is worse to send you away, where you can return if you want, or to keep an eye on you to be sure you cannot hurt them. One of them said Petengill has a gun in his room for fear of you."

Fox Running laughed grimly. The men who ran the school were of mixed purposes. Darby was a zealot who believed Indian culture was somehow a blot on the landscape, to be scrubbed away with harsh methods that would turn Indian children away from the paths of their ancestors and onto the path of white society. Fox Running knew the man was dangerous because he deeply believed what he taught. He hated everything Indian about his students, but he believed he cared for them and would be doing them a favor once all that "Indianness" had been bleached away, as though such a thing were possible.

Petengill was different. Petengill was like many men Fox Running had met who latched on to others for their own gain. He believed some of what Darby taught, but mostly he believed the school would be successful and those who developed it would become rich and famous. There was no level at which he felt any emotion for the students he oversaw. The Indians at the school were products made of inferior raw material to be manufactured into white men and white women, and his job was to find the most effective means of enforcing the harsh discipline both men believed was their duty to provide while also never missing an opportunity to make money on the side.

"There is talk the school might end," Short Wing said hopefully.

Fox Running doubted it, but it was a hope to dream on when his friends had gone.

Short Wing left first. Reaching the girls' dormitory involved crossing a yard, and she needed to hurry. Tall Bear walked her to the doorway, where they had a private moment, and then returned.

"I fear for you, Fox Running," said Tall Bear, believed among the Lakota to be able to interpret the spirits. "You cannot fight them all the time. It is not the fight that matters, but what it does to your spirit. The spirits do not want us to fight for the sake of fighting. What is it you fight for, my friend? Use your time here to walk free with the spirits, for they will guide you." He stopped. Dooley was whistling to warn them he was returning. "Understand your place with the spirits, my friend. I shall see you tomorrow!"

Fox Running did not say to his friend what he might have: *Crazy Horse understood his place with the spirits, but the white soldiers betrayed and murdered him.*

Then he remembered that even as Crazy Horse died, the Lakota hero had given him a message similar to that of Tall Bear.

Spirits! What good did it do to listen with his soul when his body was a prisoner?

Katherine McGillicuddy brooked no nonsense from anyone, least of all from either of the men looking back at her. Accustomed as she was to weeding out the charlatans from the compassionate, she was uncertain into which camp Petengill and Darby fell. Neither were rich; both were ambitious. Petengill seemed more drawn to the comforts of life, while Darby seemed determined to acquire fame as a reformer with a vision. There was, however, a core of genuine commitment in Darby that made her continue to meet with the men who were anxious that the estate of her father, Cornelius McGillicuddy, help them in their charitable enterprise.

Certainly, educating Indians was important, and different means could often achieve outstanding results. Yet she sensed in some of the staff at this school a willingness to discipline for the sake of brutality more than an understanding of it as a harsh tool meant to ultimately achieve a kindness for the recipient. She was also astounded at the numbers who were sick, despite the claim that children who lived far from anywhere would naturally be brought low by diseases to which those living in the city had become accustomed since birth.

Her father's wealth, and his death a few months ago, had put her in an unusual position in which an unmarried woman controlled enterprises and made decisions normally made by men. Until his death, she had pursued individual acts of charity as best she could, but now she had a vast new opportunity. She did not plan to squander it.

Others from her circle were helping Indians in various ways. Her cousin, Annie Campbell, had actually gone out West to write about the awful things that happened. She would be returning soon before going back out there, where she planned to marry a man who worked with Indians. Katherine was not sure she wished to carry her commitment that far. Her father had funded missionaries, and she was a strong believer that education was important to lift up classes of people at risk of being corrupted. Perhaps charity could do for the Indians what it did for others even farther away.

The business interests her father had left her were profitable. She knew having a woman at the top unsettled some men and was—so far—ruling her new commercial empire with a light hand. As long as the profits rolled in, she wouldn't interfere with those who were capable.

Wisps of light-brown hair framed a thin, intelligent face that sported steel-rimmed glasses through which she viewed the world. Her wide mouth was pursed in what appeared to be disapproval, and she was stroking the square jaw she inherited from her father. Her face projected the strength of her character. Gray eyes went from one man to the other as Darby and Petengill waited like children in the headmaster's office. She had come to her decision.

"Either I speak to the students, or we do not have an agreement, gentlemen," she said. "I shall select those to whom I will speak."

They agreed hurriedly and swallowed anxiously. They asked for time to allow the children to be told who she was, assuring her the children were often confused by strangers asking questions. She had no doubt they would use the time for coaching pupils on how best to respond, but she had played this game before and with better players. In truth, she was pleased to see they understood there might be room to improve. Those who were perfect had no need of her, or she of them.

"I shall join them for dinner tomorrow," she said, hearing the clock chime the hour. "Supper, rather. At six."

She rose and left the building, taking a carriage from the converted armory and warehouse that served as the school and its dormitory to her mansion on Beacon Hill, where she would have a light meal before going back out to continue the work she had begun in secret while her father was alive—to bring the vote to women. She was also active in causes that sought to change life for the better by addressing the horrible conditions of families that lived on the streets. Men talked about these women and children as if they were rejected parts for a machine! Women knew better.

That boys and girls who might otherwise be tearing flesh off the burned carcass of an animal were more or less sitting in rows trying not to spill soup was certainly notable, but Katherine McGillicuddy was more interested in what was taking place far away from the stage-managed performance she was witnessing. After very correct, very wooden, and very fearful answers, she snorted her disgust as she looked around the dining room.

"How many students are in your infirmary?" she asked. Upon hearing the answer, she noted that adding those eight to the forty-six present at the meal would leave the school one short of the number of students its operators had claimed.

After hemming and hawing, it was revealed a student was in detention.

"Take me to him," she demanded, only to be met with complaints that the boy's punishment was not yet over, and, since it would end tomorrow, he could be available then. Fox Running's actual stay in detention was to last another week, but Petengill and Darby were more concerned with her appeasement than the facts. They could lock him back up again if need be.

"I find myself concerned that you expect me to keep coming back," she said. "It is a black mark against your cause. I will send a carriage for him. I shall speak to him away from here, for I fear you may be coaching your students. I shall also have a doctor present if an examination shows bruises. Be forewarned!"

Amid cajoling and threats, Fox Running was prepared to meet Katherine McGillicuddy. They told him things he must say with no hope they would be said. They wanted him to wear new clothes, but he refused. Threats gingerly entered the conversation as well, with no indication he heard them. Darby and Petengill's only hope was that the barely concealed aggression boiling within Fox Running would radiate forth while he was with her, leading her to understand the depth of the challenge they faced and discount any negative things he might say about the school.

When he was leaving, Darby tried to ride in the carriage with him, but the driver said his orders had been firm. "I'm to bring the boy only. No one else."

The carriage clip-clopped through a part of the city Fox Running had never seen—houses instead of large, dirty brick buildings. He asked about buildings, streets, and parks. The driver answered kindly. People walked in what he knew from his classes were fine clothes, even if they looked silly. After too short a time, they arrived. He thanked the driver for his courtesy, understanding that beneath the level of those who gave orders, those who were expected to obey had much in common.

From an upstairs window, Katherine observed the Indian boy walk into the mansion after surveying the green lawns and iron fences that surrounded the fine houses of Boston's elite. He first walked to the side of the house to look at the garden that grew behind it. Once his curiosity was satisfied, he walked confidently back to the front door, looking less awkward than the owners of his school would have been! She saw him greet the butler with a smile and offer a hand, then he moved out of view.

She left the room and went downstairs. He rose from the chair where he had been seated as she came down the staircase. They had taught him manners, at least!

"Good afternoon, Andrew. I am Katherine McGillicuddy. I see you like my garden."

"My name is Fox Running. I am only called Andrew at the school," he said blandly. "My Lakota name is Blazing Fire. If we wish to have a real talk, please use one of my real names. If I am here for you to talk to me about Indians and how terrible they are, Andrew will be fine, so that Fox Running does not need to listen and Blazing Fire does not feel compelled to do something you white people would call rash."

Her eyebrows lifted.

"Are you a healer, that you grow healing herbs?" he asked.

"No, those are flowers."

"Why?"

"Why do I grow flowers?"

"You can grow herbs to heal. Why waste the space on things that are not necessary?"

She swallowed her first answer. He was impertinent. "I like them and they make me happy. Because this is my house, I can do what I want. Does that meet with your approval?"

"Savages and flowers may not be a good mix, Miss McGilli-cuddy. The flowers might be scalped."

"Then they will grow back next year," she said, "and again and again and again. Flowers are harder to kill than . . ." She was going to say "cavalrymen" but thought better of it, wondering how he had taken charge of the conversation so quickly. She could see a smirk; he knew what was coming and had goaded her into it! The scoundrel!

Fox Running was aware this woman was important to the school. She was not important to him, although in a way as they fenced with words she reminded him of the clan mothers who ensured the young learned their lessons. He recalled the one who made his sister eat a meal she had burned. It never happened again.

"Why are you smiling?" she asked as she started to mull over the importance of names to these people.

He told her.

"Yes. My father also believed our mistakes were our best teacher. Do you know why you are here?"

"The school wants money, and you have it. You asked others about lessons and beatings. You are not sure the school is a good one. You have chosen me because I was in detention. You expect me to be honest and not answer the way they want. I do not know if I can tell you what you want to know."

McGillicuddy was impressed. The boy knew the world, if not his subjects. "Why not?"

"Because I do not understand."

"Understand what?"

"Why this is here. This school. When I was a young boy, I knew I would grow to be a warrior. That is what I was taught. Then came bad things and the Custer fight and the Rosebud, and I have been in the white world and the Indian world, and there is no path for me. The books we read about what took place long ago will not help me become a man. Adding big numbers will not help. I do not need to sing stupid songs."

"They should teach you about things you did not know. The frontier is filled with violence. There is much more to life than violence. The school should teach you to live without it."

"Then why do they use it?"

Her eyes crinkled. "Because it is the language you understand?"

A thin smiled flickered on his face. "Perhaps. When they insult my people, they must be told they are wrong. It is good to know some things they teach, but I am not English. I am Cheyenne. Do they not allow the Irish the pride you have in your history? Why should my people be treated any differently? Is it because so many white people are guilty for taking our land?"

That was not a conversation she felt able to have. "Is the school a bad place?"

"It is not the place for me."

"Then why are you there?"

"There is no other place to go."

"I do not understand. Can you explain it to me?"

His eyes had been darting to the French doors that opened

to her garden. "Can we talk outside? They do not let us out often."

For the sake of form she made him promise not to run away, which she could tell was not likely because he seemed to have something he wanted to say. Instead of the garden, she offered him the treat of a real walk. They went to Boston Common, where a few walkers were in evidence on an otherwise windy day.

"You do not wear a hat," he told her.

"I hate the things," she replied. "Make a woman look ridiculous and cost money."

This time, he grinned. Then he talked for real, about life and lessons and the Plains. He explained that his friend Mr. O'Malley wanted to save his life by getting him out of Kansas, and that was the only reason he came to the school.

The carriage was waiting when they returned.

"Please tell them I shall support them, for now, as befits my limited means," she said.

"You mean you are still making up your mind," Fox Running replied. She smiled at the impudence. Perhaps it was contagious.

"No. I have made it up. Move over," she said, shoving him on the seat to make room for her to sit, unchaperoned, on the short drive to the school.

When she reached the school, she delivered a blunt verdict to the educators.

"I believe in your purpose. I am not fully assured your methods should be supported," she said. "I will fund meals for the next six months. Anything after that time will depend upon the word of this young man. During this time, he will spend his Saturdays and Sundays at my house, as my ward. I believe there is much to make of him, and I dare not trust the work to you!"

She turned on her heel and left.

"What exactly did you say to her?" asked a slightly bewildered Darby.

"I do not know, sir. I do not," replied Fox Running, happily kicking off his shoes. "Shall I report back to detention, sir?"

Petengill started to agree. Darby cut him off. "No, Andrew. But do not think this new relationship with the school's benefactor gives you the freedom to break the rules."

For a moment, Petengill was sure Andrew would laugh in their faces. Then the boy's face became expressionless again.

"Yes, sir. Perish the thought, sir." He looked back at them just a little longer than necessary, then picked up the shoes and walked away.

Chapter Eight

Boston, May 1881

Fox Running was, for once, as happy as life far from home could be, as if there was a place he really called home. Days of cold rain had ended, and a soft breeze from the sea was converging with the sunshine and warm weather. Best of all, it was a Sunday, which meant a very different kind of education.

Katherine McGillicuddy had a library piled high with newspapers, magazines, and books, not the boring kind of books the school had. She would quiz him about them and help him understand what was going on around him. He was fascinated that wires could allow people to talk to each other even if they lived miles apart, but disappointed to learn it could be years before they ever would be used on the Plains.

During the cold months, she had taken him with her to the kitchens and shelters she helped operate for those with no homes. He was revolted by the poverty and could not understand why white men did not care for everyone the way the Cheyenne and Lakota did.

"There are so many we cannot help them all, but we can do something," she said.

Now, it was spring, and he was coming to an understanding that perhaps the stumbling steps that led him to the school had also led him to some life he did not yet understand. Katherine would talk about jobs, and, although he did not really understand them, she was very clear that he could be important to his people in the future. She talked about lawyers, but he did not fully understand what they did.

He wondered if this path was what the spirits Crazy Horse had talked about wanted of him. He did not know. It seemed far from the grisly massacre at Hat Creek, a scene that kept coming back to his mind.

They were taking a stroll around Boston Common, as were many others who saw in the day an opportunity to leave their labor, or their homes, for a few hours. Katherine had been earnestly explaining about elections, and how and why the Great White Father changed every few years, when a scream rippled across the open green space.

A young, blonde woman in a pink dress was on her hands and knees. A man in a soft cap—the kind worn by laborers—was running away from her. Both men and women close to the woman in pink started pointing and yelling, although none of them moved to help her.

"He robbed her!" Katherine said angrily. "Bold!"

But she was talking to the wind.

Fox Running had walked the area with Katherine often enough to know there was always a Boston police officer at the entrance to the public space on the west side of the Common, stationed there to keep "undesirable" people away. Sure enough, the man who had run to the west must have seen the officer and moved back across the green, looking to escape now into the warren of narrow streets and alleys along the south side of the space.

He was fast. Fox Running was faster and was closing the gap between them.

"Stop, thief! Stop!" Fox Running called. "Thief!" A few heads turned, and one man in a funny derby hat took a half step to bar the way, but the man being chased effortlessly shoved him to the ground, barely breaking stride as he did so.

The street at the southern edge of the green space loomed. Fox Running ran as fast as he could. He leaped and caught the man around the ankles, knocking him down. A fat, pink object fell from the man's coat pocket.

Fox Running scrambled to his feet and loomed over the man, grabbing his coat. But the thief had a knife. He waved it wildly at Fox Running's face. The boy jumped back after one stinging sweep, then pulled hard on the man's coat. He could see desperation and fear on the man's unshaven face. He was young, not much older than Fox Running. He yelled words with no meaning to Fox Running as the boy dove upon him, hoping to hold him until the police officer arrived.

But the man kicked hard at him. The knife kept swinging and slashed deeply across Fox Running's hand. As he reflexively loosed his grip on the man's coat, the thief rose and ran, making his way into an alley as the arriving police officer called for the thief to stop and tried to give chase.

Winded and bleeding, Fox Running did not pursue the man further. Instead, he picked up the pink object, which turned out to be the woman's purse, and went to return it to its owner.

The well-dressed young woman was standing in the middle of a knot of men and women. She was fixing her hat, which had been knocked askew. Fox Running pushed his way through.

By the standards of the white men, she was pretty, with long, blonde hair that had had irons pressed into it to make it curl in ways no hair did by itself. A deep brown smear of mud marred her fine dress. She was talking to someone with her, explaining how the theft had taken place.

Fox Running touched her shoulder to get her attention. She turned to face him.

"What do you want?" she said archly. Then she realized his clothes were a mess. He had a generous helping of mud on the suit he wore, mixed with blood that dripped from his hand onto

the young woman. Horror crossed her face. "You are touching me!"

"I brought you your purse," he said, offering it to her.

"Don't touch me!" she yelled.

Katherine McGillicuddy had caught up with Fox Running and pushed her way through the spectators. The girl in pink was still yelling. "Filthy. You are filthy! You ruined my dress!"

Fox Running saw blood on the shoulder of her dress, where he had touched her. His blood had also stained the pink silk purse.

"I brought you your purse, miss," he said again, looking at Katherine as though asking her to make the young woman stop screaming and understand that he had helped her.

"Fox Running, are you all right?" Katherine asked him as she finally reached his side. "You are bleeding."

"I am fine. It is a small cut. He had this." He showed her the small-bladed knife the thief had dropped in the struggle.

"Fox what?" The girl looked at him closely, then shuddered. "An Indian! A Red Indian. Oh, I have been befouled by a Red Indian! He has a knife! My God, do not let this savage scalp me!" She glanced at Katherine, who had stepped between her and Fox Running. "And you! I know you! Your picture was in the newspaper—the one who likes Indians—and you are the socialist who agitates for suffrage. He has a knife! An Indian tried to attack me! Oh, help me! Get away! Get away! Get away! Police!"

The arrival of the police officer, who could not catch the younger, faster thief, soon led to more screaming and accusations until the young woman finally grasped that Fox Running had tried to help recover what was stolen.

"He touched me!" she kept insisting. "He touched me! I will burn this dress now. Filthy Indian! My brother has friends in the army. I know what kinds of things savage hands do. And they have touched me!"

Fox Running's pain was evident, for he understood every word.

"Perhaps someone should take this young woman home before she works herself into a state and disturbs the pigeons," Katherine McGillicuddy remarked acidly, taking the purse from Fox Running's unresisting hands and giving it to the policeman to give to the woman. "That is, if she ever stops screaming."

Then, "Let us go home, Fox Running," she said. To the rest, she snapped, "The entertainment is concluded, all of you. Now go about your business!"

The crowd melted away. The young woman was escorted in the other direction, and Katherine and Fox Running went back to her home. "I do not know what will become of these young people," she said to him. "Hysterics! Making a fool of herself!"

No matter how many times Katherine demeaned the woman, Fox Running remained silent. Although she tried to explain that young women and hysterics were an inseparable couple, the incident had deflated his spirits, and he returned to the school in a somber mood.

Two days later, he was called to Darby's vast office with its immense desk and life-sized portrait of the school's master.

"What have you done?" Darby called out before the boy had closed the door. "Do you know how much damage you have caused?"

The only thing Fox Running could recall was the gouge in the wall when he was playing a knife-throwing game in the dormitory, which was banned along with all other things Indian children might enjoy. He had done it to entertain Tall Bear, who was sick again.

He was trying to determine whether to admit the damage or wait until he was certain they knew about it when Darby shoved under his nose a copy of the *Boston Intelligencer*, one of the many newspapers that flooded the city each day with a mix of news, innuendo, and pure fabrication.

Fox Running cringed as he read the headline and then continued to read the story, feeling sicker with every word.

"Bloody Brave on the Loose" the headline read. The article beneath informed readers that an attack involving an Indian with a "dripping, bloody knife" took place in Boston Common, with Amelia Currant, a socialite of impeccable standing, being victimized and brutalized by a young Indian who tried to scalp a man until police intervened. The story said the "Injun" emitted a "war whoop" in attacking a man over the "loot." The story said the Indian was a ward of Katherine McGillicuddy, "the suffragette who demands women vote and meddles in factories and alehouses to the detriment of commerce and industry."

Fox Running fought the urge to rip the paper into small pieces. It would do no good. There were hundreds of these, he was sure. He knew the newspapers copied each other, which meant this would be widely read within days.

"Well?" demanded Darby. "What do you have to say for yourself?"

"It is all a lie," said Fox Running. "A thief took this woman's purse. I chased him. There was a fight. I was cut. I gave her back the purse. The thief got away."

"Did you touch her? Did you lay a finger upon her?"

He had. He did not deny it.

Darby slapped him across the face. Hard.

"How could you be so stupid? So ignorant? We have tried to teach you for more than a year that people like you do not touch and grab and take when you are in genteel company! If she was with a guardian or a man, you would have been proper to speak to him, but never to her. Indians do not speak to young, unescorted white women. Ever! Touch her? You could be shot for touching a white woman. And rightly so! How could you do this to us? Get to detention. Perhaps before you die I will let you out. Now I must quell the uprising on the board. You will be the reason this school closes! What have you done? Stupid, stupid, stupid!"

Fox Running felt so stunned that his temper had not risen to a reply. He mutely walked out of the office and down to the cellar, one of the school's guards following behind.

Katherine McGillicuddy had threatened the reporter by the door with having his eye poked out by an umbrella, and he ran off. She remained wrathful as she entered the office within her gleaming marble mansion where she conducted her business affairs. She had a letter to write to the filthy press!

"Hello, Katherine."

Michael McGillicuddy, her father's much younger brother, was seated at her desk. He rose as she entered. He was a tall man, well over six feet, with round features and thinning, gray hair.

She managed to stay polite. "Uncle Michael. How are you?"

"With the hash you are making of my brother's business affairs, I am very distressed. The mismanagement of his companies is bad enough, but your misadventures in politics and now this affair with the Indian boy are the last straw. I am here to set things to rights."

"Uncle, you and I do not agree on many things. I do not choose to argue in my own house."

"In my brother's house, to be precise," he said, "which you retain by virtue of the continued commercial success of those businesses he built. Men of stature and prominence have come to me, disgruntled that certain things are being conducted under this roof. You are spending vast sums on orphans and children cast out of homes."

"They deserve charity."

He kept on as if she had not spoken. "However, your focus on spending money has made you blind to the way in which it is earned. Your office sees you barely three times a week. Slack and slipshod! Further, your support for giving women the vote is objectionable to good-thinking men. Socialism is abhorrent before God. Some men do not wish to do business with a woman, and doubly so with a woman who believes they are incapable of making the right decisions!"

"Uncle, this is none—"

"And now you shame the family name by supporting some bloodthirsty Indian!" he bellowed. Then he resumed his speech at a lower volume, with deadly overtones. "I have here letters from your major customers and suppliers. Absent immediate action on your part to separate yourself from these Indian lovers and these suffragettes and turn your attention to your business, all will cease to do business with you. These letters include the bank, which will no longer advance you money, as has been its long-standing practice."

"You seek to ruin me!"

"No, dear niece. You brought ruin on yourself. I can stay its hand, but only through your action to conduct business affairs as a man would properly conduct them. As I will have them conducted; do you understand?"

He picked up the top hat he had placed on her desk and set it firmly on his head.

"You have until tomorrow to decide, my dear. You may either do what is right, or find out if the charity you provide for others will be given to you when the businesses you rely upon all fail! I shall show myself out."

Three days later, Fox Running was summoned from his detention room and marched to the office. Petengill, not Darby, was there.

"You received a letter from Miss McGillicuddy," Petengill said. "Because it is from her, you are allowed to see it. You will read it to me."

Fox Running, who was seeing daylight for the first time in several days, blinked against the brightness as he held up the letter to read aloud. As he read, he realized he was sharing a letter that had been written and rewritten multiple times, until all the emotion behind it had burned away and there was nothing left but an admission of defeat couched in the formalities of language that communicated far more than it actually said.

" 'Dear Fox Running,

'These have been very busy days, or I would have written to you sooner. The foul writings of some poorly paid scribbler have led to a vast upheaval. I am now beset with concerns from the world of commerce, which regards that fabrication published in the news rag to be as true as the Gospels and demands I separate myself from the activities I have embraced to try to make this a better society. The business world, as you may yet come to know, can be unforgiving and harsh. I will thus ask you not to visit my home again until these ill winds have passed away. I have separately written the school to advise them that a connection between it and myself is, at this time, unadvisable.

'None of this is your fault, a point I have made clear to those who operate the school in a separate letter. I look forward to resuming our conversations when a more propitious moment arises.

'Sincerely, Katherine McGillicuddy.' "

The meaning was clear. She was abandoning him. Whatever vague and indistinct future she had crafted in words was now gone, like every other dream and promise. Or perhaps it had all been a lie. All of it. He had believed her. Believed *in* her. He was a fool.

"You will return to detention, Andrew," Petengill said sternly. The fool boy had done more damage than he could possibly know. Days ago, some of Boston's citizens had agreed they might take some of the school's charges to serve over the summer as groundskeepers and cooks or maids, to help with summer entertaining. They would have paid the school for the work, which would have meant income with a cut for him off of the top. Petengill was already taking in money from some of the school's vendors who wanted to sell food to the school. That was something he had not shared with Darby. Now, thanks to this boy, the solid citizens who would have taken the Indians for labor were contacting Darby and telling him they had changed their plans.

Petengill's eyes moved to the school guard as Fox Running looked at him, and through him as if he was not there. The boy calmly moved past the guard to the desk, where a long, dagger-like letter opener lay. The boy's hand hovered over it.

"Guard . . ."

The boy's eyes flitted to Petengill in mockery as he sized up the man's rising panic. Then he picked up a heavy, brass paperweight and threw it full force through the window, smashing multiple panes and rattling shards of glass around the office.

"If I am going to be punished, I want to have a reason," Fox Running said. "Unless you would like more? I would be happy to oblige."

The dumbfounded Petengill had nothing to say. Fox Running walked past the shaken man and out of the office.

Boston, June 1881

It took time, but eventually the story of the thief in Boston

Common, the newspaper article, and the school's reaction filtered throughout the school. A kind of rebellion flared, as students—feeling the hate inflicted on their fellow Indian—insisted, when asked to perform work or do a variety of things, that they needed to speak to Andrew. In class, Andrew was said to have eaten homework and other preposterous tales. In time, the only way to end the rebellion was to bring the boy out of detention.

He almost went right back in. Tall Bear was once again sick.

"He is dying in this place," Fox Running told the infirmary attendant. "He needs to go home."

"If he is sick here, what would he be like out there living on buffalo scraps and grass, or whatever you use for food?" the man replied.

Fox Running almost hit him. Almost.

"I would have gotten better by watching," Tall Bear joked when the attendant left. Fox Running did not smile.

He made his way to the cellar that evening. Short Wing and Dark Cloud were in detention. Short Wing had refused to stop chanting in Arapaho. Dark Cloud was a Seminole new to the school whose temper was even shorter than Fox Running's.

"I need to talk to my friends, please, good Mr. Dooley," he told Dooley, who had made it clear his deafness from the war meant he would not hear students talking during their hours of supposedly enforced silence.

"Be careful," the older man said. "There is a wildness in ye, boy. What they did wasna right, but you can't fight the whole world, lad."

Fox Running spoke with Short Wing first. "When are you out?" he asked. She replied that they still had four days each to go.

"Is there anything you value in your room?"

Rooms were searched often, although not well. Any trace of

home and family was thoroughly rooted out and destroyed. Short Wing asked for a jacket she often wore that was comfortable and warm in the cold. Dark Cloud offered the thought that everything in his room could burn. They asked why Fox Running wanted to know. He did not answer. Short Wing could guess.

"Are you serious?" she said.

"Yes."

"Take Dark Cloud. He can help. We cannot leave him behind to be punished after we are gone."

Fox Running looked from one to the other. Some students took refuge from the fact that humans walked the Earth alone under the eye of the Great Spirit by building relationships between boys and girls. He knew Short Wing felt strong emotions for Dark Cloud. He had often envied them the comfort they found in the existence of one another.

Fox Running agreed to her request, then melted back into the night. Dooley could not know, for if Darby and Petengill thought he did, they might fire the poor man.

Fox Running knew where every last thing in the school was kept. That night, he tried to think as he had been taught at the school to decide the order of the things that must be done. He turned them over and over in his mind until he was certain. Then, as the clock downstairs struck the hour of three, he was finished. It was time.

Grass Waving, the Kiowa, had objected to him taking Short Wing's jacket, but his reputation as a bad and violent student led her to object meekly. He put the jacket, his own coat, and Tall Bear's things in a canvas bag used to haul laundry, throwing in the hunks of bread he had stolen as well. He had spent the day planning and thinking. Price had scolded him in mathematics class for being inattentive, and for a moment he feared a detention would ruin everything. He had controlled his talk and temper, though. He was aware Price recognized the different attitude, but the teacher appeared simply relieved to survive without an outburst.

Darkness came late. Guards checked the rooms at ten p.m., two a.m., and four a.m. It was nine p.m. now. He arranged his bed to look as though someone was in it and slipped down the stairs. Bare feet made no noise as he walked slowly around the worst creaks in the floorboards.

Petengill's office was never locked. Fox Running went first to the bookcase, where the knives confiscated from students were tossed. He found the biggest two he could for the others; he had brought the one he had stolen earlier out from its hiding place under the floor of his room. Then the desk, where the lower right-hand drawer held a brand new Colt. Petengill had bragged about it. A box of shells was there as well. He knew there was money also, but that was a line he did not want to cross. They would need protection. He knew Petengill somehow stole from the school. The gun was fine to take, but the money was not. Crazy Horse had tried to say there were limits. He hoped he understood rightly, for once.

The gun helped persuade Carl, the infirmary attendant, to help Tall Bear with his clothes. Fox Running had not yet loaded it, but the threat was enough. Tall Bear was wheezing and wobbling, but for the first time in weeks he was smiling as Fox Running helped him down the stairs.

"Wait here," Fox Running said. "The guard is not due for a while."

Dooley appeared to have been waiting for him. "There's a bag there for you, lad."

The bag held bread, some meat, a few handfuls of coins, a small roll of folding money, Dooley's gun, and some shells. Fox Running stuck the gun in his belt.

"There's a piece of rope on top. You need to tie me up," Dooley said. "It is my testimony to my vigorous effort to stop you."

"Would you please let them out?" Fox Running asked. "Which key is the rear door upstairs?"

Dooley showed him but declined to let the students out. "I will not stop you, lad, but I have a line I must not cross. You came here armed, and I had no choice."

Fox Running opened the doors. Short Wing grabbed the bag. Fox Running showed Dark Cloud which key to use and told both of them to go upstairs, get Tall Bear, and then go to where the draymen waited to deliver goods. In a moment, he and Dooley were alone.

"Thank you, Mr. Dooley. I do not know if I can ever repay you. You were always kind to me. You are the one good thing that happened in my time here. I will always honor you in my heart."

"Lad, you have a hard road. It is more than a thousand miles to your homes. There is a difference, lad, between stealing a meal and killing a man. Right and wrong, lad. It won't be easy, but do not cross the line," Dooley said.

For a moment, Fox Running wondered what Crazy Horse and John Dooley would have had to say to each other if silly men had not started wars. Probably a lot.

"Now for what matters tonight," Dooley went on. "The docks are about a half mile from here to the east. That's to the right if you stand at the front entrance facing the street. Ships might not take the lass, but you lads can sign on to anywhere. The trains are a mile or so southeast. The freight yards are huge, lad. It's easy to get away, because they go very slowly in the yard, but I dinna know how to tell you which one to pick."

Fox Running left him tied in the hallway. Dooley said he would go into a detention room when it was close to the end of his shift. "I hate the dark, laddie."

Fox Running knew he would never see the man again. He wanted to find words to say good-bye. Then a footfall sounded overhead.

"Go!" whispered Dooley. "If someone comes, I have to call for help! Go with God, laddie, and never look back!"

Fox Running nodded. There was a passage from the cellar to a back door. Not caring now about noise, he broke the window and climbed out. He could hear Dooley calling for help and someone responding.

The others were waiting where he told them. Around them, the yard stank of rotting food and dank brick as a fine mist rolled in from the sea and covered Boston. But within, the sun of the Plains was on his face, and the wind of the hills was in his hair. They were free!

CHAPTER NINE

Tall Bear was feverish. Fox Running felt queasy every time he touched his friend's face. He, Short Wing, and Tall Bear were hiding in an empty railroad car in the vast yard of engines and boxcars. On this misty night, fog was their friend as they huddled out of sight in the farthest corner of the immense network of rails.

After leaving the school and moving as fast as they could for a few blocks, they had ducked into an alley to sort out what to do next. They all wanted to go home, but they were bound for different directions. They agreed to walk to the rail yard, knowing that the fastest way out of Boston would be a train. The longer they were in the city, the greater the odds of being found.

Dark Cloud had been in luck. As he and Short Wing spoke to track workers, he learned of a train going to Virginia that night. He sent her back to their hiding place alone with the message that he would go his own way. Short Wing had returned disconsolate.

"At the school, he spoke of friendship. Of trust. Of . . . of something more. Once he no longer needed me, once he was free, he cast us aside as if we no longer mattered," she said. "That is not the way of our people!"

Fox Running wanted to tell her it was the way of the world, but for now there were worse problems than wounded feelings.

Tall Bear complained of being cold, even though the night was mild. First they hid on the freight platform of a long-

116

abandoned warehouse. For fear his coughing would be heard, they found an empty railroad car to hide in until Tall Bear's fever passed. They had been there two days now. Tall Bear only grew sicker.

Fox Running felt irrational anger. He had pictured bringing Tall Bear home, having a home with a friend near the Pine Ridge Agency. He would be able to feel proud of what he had done. He would for once be worthy of being Cheyenne. Now, he had to face the reality that he had taken his friend from the school, where he at least had a bed and water, to have him die in a squalid train car.

The night passed in humiliation and mockery. Fox Running dreamed of detention in the Pit. He was only seventeen, but he was the leader now. Dead Face did not mope and worry that the life he planned would never happen. Neither did Crazy Horse. Neither would he.

He had given Short Wing all the money they had to buy food. He did not want them hunted for stealing. Tall Bear would eat nothing and barely drank. He slumped against the wall of the car, in and out of consciousness, speaking now and then but not making sense. Once, he was lucid. "We are free," he told Fox Running.

"We are," the boy replied.

"I will be home soon," Tall Bear said, before slipping back into his fevered sleep. "The spirits are happy within me."

That had been almost a day ago. Now, his breathing was shallow. Short Wing and Fox Running had seen many elders pass. There was little doubt that Tall Bear had hours, perhaps, no more. Fox Running told Short Wing of his plan. "I will not leave him here," he concluded. "I know white people dispose of the dead like they were trash. This is my friend. He shall not be treated that way."

"You mean you will risk everything?" Short Wing replied.

He nodded.

"You have all the money we brought with us," he told Short Wing. "I can give you a gun if you wish to go home on your own, but I must do this."

"It will take two to help him walk," she replied. Although only fourteen, she tried to sound casual about the risk they would take. A certain Cheyenne must know that the Arapaho had honor and courage as well! "There is an adage among my people about no Cheyenne ever being able to do anything properly without an Arapaho to help," she said.

He accepted the gift of her sharing the risk and grinned at her attitude. "We leave after dark."

"Do you know the way?"

"Yes. I planned to escape a dozen times. Once I find the school, I can find where we need to go. Perhaps I should have left on my own. Then Tall Bear would not be dying."

"Or he would be dying there, and I would be in detention."

That was true. He said nothing. At this point, there was nothing to say.

John Dooley had been given the task of searching the waterfront for the escapees, which meant he could light his pipe and watch the ocean softly lap at the wood of the pier where he stood. As he puffed, he thought of the reactions at the school when the escape was discovered.

Darby had been the more emotional. "I failed," he wailed, crying as though someone he loved had died. "I could not reach that boy. I could not reach him. Willful and wild and disobedient, but I know that in time we could have driven out all that was Indian within him and made him a good soul with a productive life! Dooley, I have failed!"

Then Darby slammed the door to his office and shut himself within to, as he said, pray for repentance after being too soft on the students, and for guidance on how to better discipline them.

Petengill, on the other hand, made no bones about his pleasure at Fox Running's flight. "He stole from me, Dooley. I want a warrant to arrest him for theft."

When Dooley asked what was stolen, Petengill became evasive. Fox Running had told Dooley that Petengill stole from students and from the school's funds.

"Might it be, sir, that a police inquiry could stray from these things you want them to focus upon and into areas you might wish they did not?" Dooley asked blandly. "All of the things at the school are complicated, sir, for the fittest of minds only it would be, sir, and often the police—simple they are, sir, in their ways—can make things worse."

Petengill nodded and pursed his lips. "Excellent advice, Dooley. Excellent advice. Yes. We will conduct a search, because we should and because those impudent children must not think this behavior is to be tolerated, but good riddance to bad rubbish, I say. The school will be better off without them. Certainly better!"

Dooley noticed that Petengill carried a revolver with him as he went out to search the rail yard. All he could hope was that by the time the man arrived there, Fox Running and his friends would have left town.

More than once on their way, the escapees stopped to feel for Tall Bear's breath. He had been able to walk a little when they started, but, after a while, Fox Running had to carry him. Short Wing thought once how ludicrous it looked, the smaller Cheyenne carrying the tall Lakota boy, but she knew Tall Bear had been Fox Running's only close friend at the school, and that Fox Running was somehow also connected to the Lakota as well as the Northern Cheyenne.

The spirits were walking with them, she concluded, and when

the spirits walked, they should not be denied.

They were in a fine part of the city. Even in the dark, Short Wing was impressed at buildings Fox Running insisted were homes. Fearing it would squeak, Short Wing opened the iron gate at the side of one fine house that allowed entry to the garden behind it. Fox Running set down his friend. "Check him."

Short Wing held her hand over Tall Bear's mouth. There was nothing.

Fox Running, who had been certain for some time his friend had left them along the journey, pulled his knife.

"What are you doing?" Short Wing asked.

"Fulfilling a promise." He cut a lock of hair from Tall Bear. "When he became sick, I promised him that if they killed him with their medicines, I would scatter some of his hair in the place he was from, so that his spirit would find its way to his true home and not be trapped forever in this dreadful place."

Fox Running checked his friend's pockets. Tall Bear had three pennies and two extra knives he did not need. Fox Running gave them to Short Wing, keeping just one knife and Petengill's gun.

"Remain here," Fox Running said. "If I do not return soon, you will have to go on alone."

He pulled his knife, pushed at something in a set of doors that were mostly glass, and went inside as Short Wing sat on the damp grass with the dead and softly prayed for his spirit in a language she could finally speak without being told it was banned.

Katherine McGillicuddy drew breath to scream when she saw the figure that had entered her bedroom.

"Please do not, Miss McGillicuddy. No one is going to hurt you."

The voice broke through her waking haze. She knew the voice. She was sure of it. Who? The boy! The Indian boy.

"Fox Running?" For a moment, she was afraid. He had come to seek retribution. She had heard about the escape the day before in a curiously worded message sent by a man named Dooley, who was a guard at the school. He seemed to think she would be interested, but it was not a warning.

"My friend is dead," Fox Running said. "He is in your garden. I want you to bury him. I could not leave him with the garbage the white people throw away. I know you were once my friend, and I ask this because there is no other place I can leave him."

"Fox Running, I . . ."

"There is no time; what has been is what has been. I must go. They will search for me. Will you do this?"

"Yes. Yes, of course." He made to leave the room. "Wait!"

She rose and threw a robe over the gown she wore for bed. She lit a candle. The clock on her dresser read 4:30.

She went to a wooden chest, opened a drawer in it, and extracted something. She held it out. It was a small leather purse. "Here."

"What is this?"

"Long ago, before my father died, I planned to run away. I was not happy. I saved money, and I have always kept it. A few silver dollars is not much, but it may help."

Under no illusions about the challenges he and Short Wing would face, he took the purse and moved toward the door.

"I am sorry, Fox Running." He stopped. "I have tried to explain what I did to you in so many letters, but I never sent them. I am ashamed."

"When I was in that school, in that terrible place where everything I held dear to me was attacked by men who wanted to destroy it because they are so afraid of us, do you know how I would amuse myself as the hours and days went by and I was

121

alone in detention? Do you recall that in those books and plays you showed me and that they made me read there are men who die and face God and have to explain their lives?"

"Yes."

"I would amuse myself by wondering what all those self-righteous men like Custer and Petengill, and that woman with the purse, and some of the others, would say if they were to learn that God is a Cheyenne. I think God would greet you with a smile if that were so. Thank you for trying. There is never shame in trying. Good-bye."

"No! Don't go yet!"

He remained in the doorway.

"You are worried about being seen. From what I can see of the state of your disheveled attire, you look the way you often did. A barefoot Indian wearing a tattered suit will be noticed. Let me get you different clothes. Do you travel alone?"

Silence. She knew he was weighing whether to trust her.

"No. One travels with me."

"Boy or girl?"

"Girl."

Katherine was fully awake now. "Get her in here. The neighbors are far too close and far too nosy. Let me feed you and get you the right clothes. Let me get a wagon to take you to one of the small stations where the train stops. If the school called the police, they will look for you at the central station downtown. Let me . . . let me help."

He said nothing. She listened for feet on the stairs. She heard a creaking board. Then a door. Soon she heard hushed voices in her garden, and then nothing.

Missouri, July 1881

The dust of south-central Missouri blew across the hard-packed dirt of the roadway Short Wing and Fox Running walked. Summer's heat beat down upon them. They had fled Boston by train. The first one they could board went to Hartford, Connecticut. Eventually, they made it to St. Louis.

Katherine McGillicuddy's borrowed clothes helped make them look respectable. A few passengers had looked at them closely along the way. One middle-aged man had come up to Fox Running as he sat next to Short Wing on a bench in the passenger car and rudely inspected him. "You an Indian?" he demanded.

"Yes. Yes!" Short Wing had replied, in a very strange accent. "Calcutta! Make restaurant St. Louis. Food good. Boston too crowded. Come eat?"

The man made some dismissive remarks and moved away.

Short Wing later said she was inspired by May Evanson, a young woman who came to teach the girls deportment but who used word games as a way to get them to enjoy some of their time. "She would use that accent when we talked about Indians when she meant the ones from India," Short Wing explained. "I just copied her."

All that was long past now. In St. Louis they purchased clothing common to white homesteaders and farmers. They did not bother with shoes. Fox Running kept the vest for no reason he could explain. Short Wing kept some material from her dress for a band to tie her hair back, and another piece to make a covering for her hair. All other vestiges of Eastern clothing went into the Mississippi River.

His shirt flapped loose to cover the two guns and two knives in the waistband of the trousers. She wore a knife in the belt around her dress. Katherine McGillicuddy had not stinted in making sure they had the most practical things they needed to survive. Fox Running knew Short Wing still had a few coins from Katherine's money, just in case they became desperate for food and needed to buy it.

They talked little now, having used up most topics of conversation in the previous eight days traveling together. Fox Running talked little by habit, and Short Wing was much the same.

He had hoped they might find a horse, but he did not want to rouse the countryside by stealing one from one of the small farms. This was strange country, and pursuers would know it better than he would. Fox Running had a rough idea of directions and knew if they went south far enough, staying close to the Mississippi, they would come to the Arkansas River. That would take them toward Indian Territory and the reservation of the Arapaho. At least, he thought ruefully as they sweated under the hot sun, it looked that simple on a map.

Horses! They moved off the side of the track and into the shade of a pair of young sycamore trees. There had been a close call on their first day of walking when one rider with a group of cowboys voiced his opinion that they looked like Indians, but Fox Running had imitated how cowboys sounded in O'Malley's saloon to the point where that rider and his fellows, who otherwise seemed not the least interested in them, had not pressed the matter. Still, now that they had forsaken their Eastern clothes and were among people who actually knew what Indians looked like, any contact could be a risk.

Three men galloped by, riding hard. Fox Running and Short Wing waited in the shade for a few moments, but no one was following them. They could hear the horses pounding the dirt as the riders moved further and further away.

They returned to the road, but with greater vigilance. As the hours passed, they heard a faint squeaking behind them. It would creep into their hearing, then fade, then return.

"Wagon wheel," Short Wing said, her voice low. "It is on the road following us, but coming closer. It moves faster than we do, but it does not move quickly. It is not a very good wagon or a new one."

She smirked. They had been showing off to one another by identifying sounds along the way. She could tell from Fox Running's reaction that she had just scored a point in their game.

Soon they heard the hooves of the horses drawing the wagon as the squeaking grew consistently audible. Then the voice of the driver calling to the horses emerged. At last, the wagon itself appeared. It was old and broken down, as Short Wing had said, and gave the impression of being used to haul things of little worth.

The driver, a small, middle-aged man, slowed down as he passed them. They waved and smiled as they had been instructed to do in Boston when they saw carriages. It usually made the occupants go away without noticing them. Not this time.

"Whoa up," the driver called to the two large, gray horses pulling the wagon.

"You folks lost?" he asked as the springs creaked their melody. Sweat-plastered gray hair stuck out from under his straw hat. A large full beard spewed across his shirt, which was also stained with perspiration from the heat.

"Our uncle has a ranch on the Canadian River near Fort Reno," Short Wing replied. "We are walking to join him. We had to leave St. Louis after our mother died. We did not have money for a train. Is it much farther?"

Fox Running tried to look mournful as he held his hands in the position that would let him get to the guns under his shirt if necessary.

The man gave them a thorough scrutiny. "Got days of walkin' ahead. Days. Weeks. Not goin' that far, but you can hop on for a few miles if you like. Hauling . . . well, carrying supplies for the Missouri and Northwest Railroad. Got a camp down the road. Move them sacks, miss, and make yourself comfortable. Not really accommodations for a lady, but this is Missouri, not New York City! Young fella, whyn't you come up here with me?"

When the subject of the weather had been exhausted to the driver's content, as well as the question of whether anyone in Washington had half a brain, a silence fell over the wagon.

The teamster, whose name was Jack Smolley, broke it by asking Fox Running a direct question. "Want to tell me the truth this time?"

"Excuse me?"

"You ain't brother and sister. Lived out in Indian Territory long enough to know. She's Arapaho, and you're either Sioux or North-like Cheyenne, not them down on the reservation. Got nothin' 'gainst anyone. Don't like being fooled. No white man would know so little about politics."

Fox Running was chagrined. He thought he had answered the questions quite well.

"Her family really is near the Canadian River," Fox Running replied. "It was almost true. As for Short Wing and I, we were both in an Indian boarding school in Boston that was more like a prison. We escaped and got as far as St. Louis. Now we are going to her home, and then I am going to mine."

"Just like that."

"Just like that."

" 'Spose you got a gun and knives and all."

"The world can be a dangerous place, Mr. Smolley."

"Think you know all about that, son. You got the look."

"We do not want any trouble. We mean no one harm. We just want to get home. We can get down and walk," Fox Running told him. "All we ask is that you do not tell anyone about us."

Smolley gave Fox Running a critical inspection. "Indian war been over here in Missouri for a long time, son. Not a crime to be seen, but it ain't what you call something you see regular, neither."

Smolley let the horses pull the wagon a little further before he looked over his shoulder. "Missy, you come up over them sacks a mite closer?"

She did.

"One of the things I'm hauling is the payroll for the railroad men. Company knows the main road has bandits. Sent the usual payroll wagon as a decoy and hired me for the payroll. About two thousand dollars. I always haul alone, foodstuffs and such, and not the payroll, and I always take this route, so they didn't give me a guard, because they didn't want anyone thinking anything had changed. That's why I am using my worst wagon. Not sure they got this right. Maybe you two help me out if we need help, and maybe at the camp there might be a couple old horses would be just as happy to carry you to Indian Territory as not."

Fox Running could see Short Wing's face light up at the thought of not walking all the way home. They agreed.

Smolley had a rifle and a shotgun. Short Wing, who had never fired a rifle, took the shotgun. She rearranged the flour sacks in the bed of the wagon so she would be almost out of sight.

"Don't really matter if you aim," Smolley told her. "They get close, just pull a trigger, and the gun does the rest. Loud, and it jumps when you fire it, but it scares the folks on the other end even more."

Fox Running took both pistols from his pants and set them on the seat of the wagon. Smolley had looked doubtful when Fox Running told him that was the weapon he would use if they were attacked.

"Never seen many Indians good with pistols," he said. "Not much use hunting."

"Depends upon what you are hunting, Mr. Smolley."

Smolley had demanded he wear a beat-up hat that had been stuffed behind some sacks in the back of the wagon bed. "One reason I started wonderin' 'bout you," he said. "Nobody but Injuns walks around without a hat."

The wagon rolled on. Fox Running could feel its gentle rocking and the warmth of the sun. He could hear . . . nothing.

With his head lolling down as though falling asleep, he called out softly to Smolley, "It is too quiet. Someone must be near."

The wagon had reached a section of the road that Smolley said bent back and forth in a series of curves. "This is where I'd do it," Smolley muttered. "Always hate this part, even when all I got is vegetables."

Fox Running continued to rock and loll as the wagon moved slowly forward. The new .45 was by his right hand.

Even though he was expecting it, he was still startled when three men on horseback emerged from the side of the road with cloth masks over their noses and mouths, firing their guns into the air. They yelled at Smolley to stop, and he gave the command to the team. Fox Running knew the tactic: scare the wagon driver into not resisting. He had done it himself two years ago; now he saw what it looked like from the other side.

Two riders galloped over to Fox Running's side of the wagon, the third to Smolley's. "Get down," called the one near Smolley, motioning with his gun to give his words added emphasis.

Fox Running had jerked bolt upright when the wagon stopped, the hat loosely perched on his head rolling off into the dirt below.

"Hey!" he called, pointing with his left hand.

The two robbers closest to him were briefly distracted. When they looked up, Fox Running had the .45 pointed at them.

For just a moment, the tableau held. Fox Running held the edge but was too inexperienced to know what to do with it. The robbers had learned life's hard lessons well. They brought their guns to bear as the Cheyenne youth realized his mistake.

The staccato cacophony of multiple guns blazing lasted only seconds, but the echoes left the living feeling as though they had just experienced a full-scale battle.

Fox Running's shot came just ahead of the robbers' gunfire. His bullet hit one of them hard in the chest. After pulling the trigger once, the boy dove off the wagon, away from the bullets that tore into the wood. As the second robber turned to dispatch him, the shotgun exploded from the bed of the wagon. The dying robber reeled in the saddle of his bucking horse as Fox Running crawled under the wagon to escape the terrified beast's hooves.

The rider who had demanded Smolley get down fired his gun at Smolley, who tried to move but was not fast enough. Even though the robber's shot hit him in his side, he brought up the rifle and fired it. The bullet went wide and into the trees. The rider aimed at Short Wing as she reloaded, only to lurch back in the saddle as first one, then a second bullet from Fox Running's gun struck him in the chest.

"See to his wound," Fox Running told Short Wing, pointing at Smolley, as he checked the bandits. Two were dead. The first one was making noises, but from the blood leaking out of him, would be dead in moments. Fox Running kicked the gun away from his hand, then let him alone.

"Turn Smolley," Fox Running said as he leaped up to the wagon's seat. Short Wing did as he said. There was a hole in the wagon where the bullet had entered. "Good. That is good. The bullet is not in him. If it was, he would die. Is he bleeding very much?"

Violence had been rare and distant on the Arapaho reservation during Short Wing's life. She was now seeing more death than she ever had before. More blood.

129

"It looks like a lot to me . . . I don't know. How much is very much?"

Fox Running made an impatient noise, then looked for himself. He stalked to the first robber's horse. There was a spare shirt in a saddlebag. He ripped it into strips. The second robber's spare shirt served as a bandage tied in place by the strips. He did all this with quick efficiency, watching the road and trees for more gunmen. As he worked, he had Short Wing gather the guns and bullets. He was not sure what the next few miles might hold, but he did not want to be surprised without a way to return the favor.

They arranged the sacks where Short Wing had been hiding as a rough bed for Smolley, then laid his groaning form there. Fox Running left him a rifle, in case. He tied the reins of the three riderless horses to the back of the wagon. The men who had formerly ridden the horses, he rolled off the side of the road, where their bodies were unlikely to be discovered any time soon.

He jumped up on the wagon seat next to Short Wing, who was clutching the shotgun and looking very small and scared. He held the reins but did not know what came next. He had seen a wagon driven, but never done it.

"I know how," she said. She was as good as her word, and, in a moment, she had the horses moving. They kept a faster pace than before, unsure how Smolley was likely to fare or how far they had to go. The lurching wagon moved, accompanied by groans from Smolley, but Fox Running guessed it was the price that had to be paid to get him to someone who might heal him.

The day was fading as they rode through a clump of trees and into a clearing that was the railroad camp. Men with rifles came running. Short Wing drew the wagon to a stop.

"Did they teach you special manners for a social occasion such as this?" Fox Running asked as he lifted his hands and urged her to do the same.

"No, but if they give us tea, I know exactly how a proper young lady should ask for sugar," she responded, cutting her eyes at him in time to see a rare smile blossom across his face.

After being thoroughly threatened by various men, taken to a large tent, and guarded by about a dozen more men with rifles drawn, they were finally visited by a man who wore finer clothes.

"Will Moffat, foreman," he said. "Smolley's a tough old bird. There are some things Jack don't recall, but what he does remember backs up what you said, so we'll figure the rest is good. Says he made a deal with you two?"

"He did," said Fox Running.

"Gonna be your choice," Moffat said. "We got some horses here ain't good for much, but you can have your pick. Horses the boys there had that they don't need no more are like to be better, but take what you want. We'll send you on your way in the morning."

"So you can count the payroll and be certain?" Fox Running asked. "We are not that stupid, to steal from you and then come here."

Moffat looked from Fox Running to Short Wing to the men guarding them. He jerked his head. The men began to move away. "Yes, we are going to count it. That's my job. Not my business if you're white or red; just making sure nobody steals from me. Don't try to run off." He moved away. "Bread by the fire. Beans. Help yourselves."

Fox Running found the bread, and also blankets. The railroad men were less abrasive than Moffat and wanted to hear the details of what happened. If they noticed that two Indians had saved a white man, they did not mention it.

In time, the camp fires died down. Short Wing settled under her blanket next to Fox Running. "Were you afraid?"

"What?"

"When those men attacked the wagon. Were you afraid? You looked as though you had done all of this before."

He thought of the Black Canyon Gang, of back roads, dark nights, and dark times.

"Robbers are usually so excited, they miss," he said. "It is not whether I was afraid, Short Wing. It was whether I could do that which must be done so we could go home. Nothing more."

CHAPTER TEN

August 1881, Arkansas

The black-painted wagon was parked on the edge of Browning Creek, at the edge of Browning's Crossing—testament to the influence of a family by that name that sent nine men to fight for the Confederacy and had two return.

"Yes, sir, it is so!" proclaimed a man wearing a jacket that had once been fancy over a pair of trousers that had once been clean. "This remedy can cure all ills. It will make you young again."

As testimony, Dr. Matthew Miracle called Chief Medicine Brew, who emerged from behind the wagon wearing moccasins with built-up soles that compensated for the inexplicable fact that, although the elixir was a wonder without peer, the man who was showing off its effects was short.

But he was young.

"From darkest Brazil, where the secrets of the Moomee tribe are still passed down by word of mouth, Chief Medicine Brew is here to show us the power of this elixir," Dr. Miracle told the crowd.

Fox Running walked through the crowd. For the first few shows, he expected to find someone who knew him and had held onto a shred of dignity. He had conquered such scruples somewhere in northeast Arkansas, and now he did flips and cartwheels for the audience, losing the robe that covered his torso in the process.

"And see that body!" Dr. Miracle called, inviting guesses as to the chief's age. When the numbers between fifteen and twenty were all used, he revealed that Chief Medicine Brew was actually fifty-eight years old, and his wife, Princess Manzapinia, was fifty-five.

"You were older the last time," Fox Running jibed as Short Wing emerged in a dress that was nowhere near modest enough for Arapaho standards.

She smiled her expected false smile and allowed Fox Running to lead her around.

"Smile, princess, so they can see those young-looking teeth!"

"Those teeth will yet bite you!" she hissed back through a broad grin.

The two Indians had joined the medicine show in southern Missouri and stayed with it for safety at a time when Indians traveling alone were more likely to be considered runaways from a reservation than anything else.

They had become part of the act immediately, and in many roles. Fox Running had shot feathers off of Short Wing's headdress. She had used a throwing knife to chop off a cigar he clenched in his teeth. They each had a dozen names to suit the temper of Dr. Miracle and whatever he thought would get their small traveling group the most money. Cures sold best, but cures also required good weather to be able to travel quickly to the next town.

Dr. Miracle explained that Chief Medicine Brew had been stranded in Missouri and was on his way to New Orleans, but as a favor had shared the formula for his medicine. He then closed by offering to sell no more than one bottle each to the customers.

The limit was only partly a gimmick. Tommy, the man's son, had problems with the latest batch he'd brewed the day before, and the aroma was so bad they could barely bottle the stuff, let alone expect anyone would drink it.

But this crowd had some toughs. One wanted a sign that required more than smiles.

"You said this stuff would make me able to do anything. Have that Chief Whatever shoot this here dollar after I throw it in the air!" The man was the kind the crowd listened to, because he was tougher than the rest, but also the kind both men and women looked at askance for the constant stream of tobacco juice he spat upon the ground. Soon, others were daring the chief to do what the man said.

Short Wing looked at Fox Running nervously. He was good with guns, but no one was that good.

"Get me my gun, Princess," Fox Running said placidly. Short Wing returned and handed it to him. Dr. Miracle nodded to Tommy, who moved the horse near in case they needed to ride and leave the wagon behind.

The tough held the coin out to Short Wing. "Princess? Would you do the honor?"

Short Wing was scared. Fox Running was far too calm. She knew they were not much more than a week from the reservation. All this could not be for nothing now!

He nodded. The one thing Short Wing had learned in the weeks with the medicine show was that, when they were performing, the show had to keep moving no matter what. She smiled broadly and flipped the coin in the air.

Fox Running never moved a muscle but along with everyone else watched the coin sail into the hazy sunshine.

As the dollar landed with a thunk and a puff of dust, Fox Running drew Petengill's revolver and shot the offending coin where it lay.

"You threw it, kind sir, and, after you did, I shot it," Fox Running said, bowing and smiling. "Are there any more requests?"

The crowd loved it, laughing at the man who had lost a silver dollar—laughing even more when Dr. Miracle handed the man who laid down the dare one bottle of elixir for nothing. "You already paid, friend."

With all the onlookers chiding him, the man drifted off. The show had again succeeded in keeping them alive until the next time, while providing a crowd of hard-working people some laughter, which they enjoyed even more than the medicine's claims. But there was one difference—for Short Wing and Fox Running, this was the last show. The medicine wagon would head south; they were going west.

"Thought they had you this time," Dr. Miracle told Fox Running, who he had found was a natural in the business of separating customers from their money.

"I did, too, until I realized what he actually said!"

"Gonna miss you two," said Dr. Miracle, born Harry Jacobs. "Offer to stay is good if you want to keep traveling."

"No!" Short Wing said. "I am going home!"

September 1881, Arapaho Reservation
Short Wing had been riding harder as they moved deeper into Indian Territory. They rested in the day and rode in the evenings to ensure they would not be apprehended. Home was filling her senses as she began to recognize the landscape.

It was all he could do to get her to make camp when they reached the Canadian River, even though they were about a day's ride east of her people. He was slightly envious that the pull of a place should be so strong, and that, even though much of her family had died, there would still be grandparents and friends who would welcome her home.

Finally, they were there, with lodges spread about, some meat drying outside some of the lodges, smoke curling from others, and a knot of elders sitting by a fire. The smells were familiar—the outdoors and smoke and grease and food. He thought back to the years of his boyhood, and even those with the Lakota. He had not fully appreciated what he had then. Now that he could never go back, he knew that what others took for granted would never be part of his life. He wondered once again what he would do when his journey to honor Tall Bear was over. Perhaps the spirits would tell him, if he was still of interest to them.

He stayed on his horse as Short Wing went down to speak to the elders. Not his family. Not his place. Yet the knot within him that was ever present on their journey was finally easing. No one was suddenly going to start pointing at him as an Indian. For once, he would not need to be told he did not belong.

"Get down off of that horse and meet my grandfather," Short Wing called. "They are going to find him."

Short Wing had been impassive at the school when not rebelling. Now she could barely contain her joy. She was talking about her childhood; about cooking something that came out a blackened husk but her family ate it anyway; about when her brothers let her on a hunt but had sabotaged her bow so the string snapped. He knew most of her family had been killed by disease. Most of the children sent to Boston had few family members left, if any. That was usually how Petengill talked his way into getting them in the first place.

A white-haired man, whose anxiety was clear on his face, swiftly approached Short Wing. When he drew close enough to see her face, his expression radiated joy. Fox Running felt a pang of hurt as he watched, knowing there could never be any such reception for him. Short Wing disengaged herself and ran to Fox Running.

"Come. Meet my grandfather. He said they never got my letters. I wonder if the school never sent them but used them to spy on us! Grandfather's name is Spotted Buffalo. There will be a feast. You have to stay! Oh, it is good to be home!"

Fox Running could see that Spotted Buffalo was pleased to see his granddaughter but did not fully understand why she was not at the far-off school. The fact that Short Wing was talking faster than a bird sings did not help, but, for now, it did not matter. His granddaughter was alive and in front of him. Spotted Buffalo was happy.

For the next few days, Fox Running wandered the village and the lands around it, resting and being feasted. He was aware that some of the younger boys watched him from a distance as though he were some sort of medicine man—a Cheyenne who somehow made Short Wing appear when she was far away. He met more people than he could keep track of, for Short Wing had introduced him to everyone.

On the morning of the eighth day after their arrival, Spotted Buffalo joined him near the riverbank. The spot reminded Fox Running of a camp his family had once made near the Powder River, and he spent time there every morning.

"My granddaughter is alive to me again. For this I cannot thank you enough," the old man said after a round of pleasantries.

"The school was a very bad place for us," Fox Running said. "Perhaps what they do will be good for some, and it is possible someone there meant well, but I think it is bad to try to make us ashamed of who we are."

"They did not say that when they spoke of a better future for children who would come back to us as teachers," Spotted Buffalo said. "They lied. It matters not whether they meant to do good or not. They lied to us and stole our grandchild through trickery."

"They are so sure they are better than we are, Spotted Buffalo, that they do not question what they do."

"Short Wing talks of you as a hero," he said.

"No," replied Fox Running. "We were friends in a place where there were no friends. My other friend from there is dead." He told the story of Tall Bear.

"I am filled with shame that I agreed to let her go," Spotted Buffalo said, shifting his seat on the ground. "The world I knew as a boy, and even as a younger man, is gone. I wanted her to have a place in a better world."

Fox Running waited. More was coming.

"When I was young, seeing a white man was the talk of the village. We counted them as friends and turned against our neighbors for war to show our pride and strength. We were wrong. Perhaps if we had made war on the white man then, there would still be buffalo. Perhaps this is not so. Short Wing tells of vast buildings and machines. Perhaps the white man would have spread no matter what we did. Short Wing also tells us you have a duty to perform."

"I promised Tall Bear to spread a lock of his hair at the Pine Ridge Agency in Dakota. I must honor my word."

"Short Wing speaks as though you may return; as though your lives may intertwine. I ask that you do not."

Fox Running took the news impassively. He watched the river in silence.

"We are in your debt, Fox Running, but you are a young man filled with many things. You are a warrior without a people; you know the ways of the white men as well as those of the Cheyenne and the Lakota. In you I see a spirit that is yet troubled, that wars with all you find around you, that still has miles to go before it finds the place where it belongs."

Spotted Buffalo sighed deeply. "Young men, some much like you, ride out from this place from time to time. They sometimes call us old and cowardly. They believe they can fight a war that will send the white man back. They end up as outlaws. That is not all. The women who go with them end up living from cave

139

to cave; having their babies alone and dying alone; wasting away until their warriors admit defeat and return broken. That I sent my grandchild to a bad place is a mistake I regret; I will not allow her to live a life that would destroy her. She will be unhappy if you go, but she is young, and she will find another warrior. You have done much to give her a life where she may have children and live here in peace amid the love of her people. I ask you to do this as well."

"Is this her will?"

"I have told her it is my duty to her to talk this way to you. I say this from love, not hate or anger. I believe she thinks I do not understand being young. She is angry. In time, she will be obedient."

Fox Running stared into the water of the Canadian River. Spotted Buffalo's words were not a surprise. They could even be true. In Boston, he was an Indian. In the Arapaho camp, he was a Northern Cheyenne, part of the people who brought chaos to their country when they escaped the reservation to go back home.

He wanted to tell Spotted Buffalo that the old man was wrong, but the voice in his head he always thought was Crazy Horse told him Spotted Buffalo was telling a truth Fox Running already knew. He was reminded once again that Dead Face did what was right even unto death, not asking whether it was the easiest road.

"If I must go, I should go now. Tell her my life is the richer for her friendship, for she was brave on the road that led us here. Tell her I will value her friendship and courage forever. Tell her good-bye." There was anger in his voice and wetness in his eyes at the thought of leaving behind the only person he knew from the last two years of his life. He started to walk away.

"Fox Running!"

He turned back at the old man's call.

"On a raid long ago, one of the warriors took a belt that holds two pistols. It was a useless thing, but it was of fine leather, and it was something to take from a raid. I have left it by the place where you sleep along with your other things. Take it with our blessing that it protect you. Know that as long as we live, we will hold your name in our hearts for all you have done. Go with the spirits," said Spotted Buffalo.

"And may the spirits rest with you," replied Fox Running. As much as he disliked hearing what Spotted Buffalo said, he could not tell the man that he was wrong after all. Eighteen now, Fox Running was a man. He would make his way. Perhaps, as Tall Bear once claimed, the spirits would tell him his mission in life. For now, he would honor his promise.

His guns were there, as was the belt with its holsters and some food for the journey. He buckled on the belt. It was heavy with two guns, but he would get used to it. He put the extra shells and the food in a leather bag, checked the precious handkerchief with Tall Bear's hair inside it and put it, too, in the bag, threw a blanket over the back of the horse he had ridden, and turned to the north. He did not look back.

October 1881, Fort Riley, Kansas

O'Malley's saloon was run by a man named Forrest, who had bought it from the town after the old man died in the spring. Van Diver, so Forrest said, had been given a new assignment in far-off California. He left a few months after Fox Running went to Boston.

Fox Running wondered if any of the letters he'd labored over to the two men were ever sent. He'd never heard from them. Forrest said some old things might be in the back. He offered to buy Fox Running a meal if Fox Running would hoe out the things that needed to be discarded and put some order to the collection of boxes.

Meals he did not cook were few and far between. He accepted. There were papers almost as old as Fox Running, a tintype of a younger version of O'Malley with a woman and child, some clothes that might fit Fox Running if he doubled in size, and books that were turning moldy. Some sacks of flour that had been stored far too long in a damp place were crawling with worms. A box of some kind of liquor in fancy glass bottles was underneath the mess. He saved the tintype, gave Forrest the fancy liquor, dumped out the flour, and burned the rest.

The saloon was busy when he finished. Forrest told him to walk down to the Star, which he said was the best restaurant in all of Fort Riley, and tell Jack Jenkins, the owner, that Forrest was paying the bill and to give Fox Running whatever he wanted.

"Old man O'Malley was a good man, from everything I heard," he said. "If the stories are true, I guess you were like a son to him. Wish I had better news to give you, but the world don't make life easy, boy."

Jenkins, a bluff man in his forties, made it clear from his expression that Fox Running was not his usual brand of customer, but, when the youth invoked Forrest's name, all became well even if he did make Fox Running sit in the dimmest, farthest corner of the restaurant.

After consuming a rare steak, and asking for extra bread for the trail instead of the loads of pie white men ate, Fox Running rose to leave. As he was trying to thread his way among closely-set tables, the butt of the gun he wore on his left hip jostled the right arm of a man eating dinner. The man exclaimed as a bit of his food fell to the floor.

"Watch where you're going!" he called out loudly as Fox Running passed. There was, as O'Malley had often told him, always one loudmouth.

142

The man was about ten years older than Fox Running and made far more noise than was necessary for a simple accident. Fox Running knew when white men drank liquor, they became angry with everyone.

"I apologize," Fox Running said, turning back. "Please excuse me."

"You cost me my dinner; knocked it all on the floor."

Fox Running knew this was not so; he had seen the man pick up what had dropped to the gritty, dusty floor, and it was barely a mouthful—especially for one with such a large mouth. He decided not to antagonize the man. An Indian in a soldier town needed to be careful. All he wanted was to leave.

"My apologies," he said again, recalling how the school taught them to apologize over and over. He turned away.

"Not so fast!" the man called out. "You owe me a meal. Jack! I want another meal. This fella ruined my dinner! You think I'm going to tolerate this? Jack, you know I'm a man to be reckoned with!"

For a moment, Fox Running stood still instead of leaving as quickly as possible to avoid any incident. The man used that moment to look at him more closely. "You an Injun? Jack, you let Injuns eat in here? This brave hit me. I think he may have one of them tomahawks. Jack!"

Fox Running wondered if the man was a bully when he was not drunk as well as when he was. Either way, it was best to let him rave.

But the man rose, stepped closer, and grabbed Fox Running's arm. Fox Running could see the man had a gun at his hip, and that the holster looked worn. He wondered if the man was some kind of cowboy or gunfighter. That would only make getting out of this harder.

"Who you think you are, coming in here to eat with white men? Jack? What kind of place you runnin'?"

143

Fox Running shrugged off the man's grip. The man stumbled, knocking into another nearby table before regaining his balance. Fox Running was certain the man was drunk. *White men must hate life if they have to go through it drunk,* he thought. He shook his head in disgust and started moving toward the door, only to find onlookers who had stood up from their meals blocking his path.

Jenkins came running from the back with his hands out as if to ward off catastrophe. "Clay, Clay, this boy done work for Hank Forrest, and Hank, bein' a good man, said he could have a meal on him. Not my wishes, but Hank's a good man tryin' to do a good deed, so I let it go. Just let it rest, Clay. I'll get you another dinner. No need for you to get all bothered. I'll get it right now. Let it rest. Meal's on me, Clay. Don't you get yourself worried. Get you another bottle. Meal's on me!"

"Let it rest? He and the ones like him come through here back in '78 and killed a hunnert or more men. We all know that. Army says we got to all let bygones be bygones. Not me! I'd have my Martha if not for them. Them filthy Cheyenne! Remember what it was like, everybody, when they were murderin' people in our beds last year? Slinkin' in the woods in the dark. Afraid to meet a man face to face. You a coward like that, Injun? Want to meet a real man fair and square, or haven't you got the nerve?"

The owner's imploring gaze rested on Fox Running.

"When I meet what you call a real man, I will know," Fox Running replied. "For now, I will leave you to eat your food and wallow in your liquor and look ridiculous in front of people so that they may amuse themselves."

Clay roared and then lunged at Fox Running, knocking the bread the Indian wanted for the trail onto the filthy floor. Jenkins held the man back.

"Got no guts, Injun! Let's see what them two guns of yours

can do. Men in these parts know what Clay Atcheson can do, and you're gonna learn about it!" Atcheson said as he struggled against the restraining arms of the restaurant owner. Chairs scraped and feet stomped as customers moved to get out of the way and find a spot to watch the gunfight that by now was certain to come.

"I will wait for you outside," Fox Running replied, as he saw the pained face of the owner. "There is no reason to ruin this man's establishment. Try not to injure yourself getting to the street. It is that way." Fox Running pointed, then walked through the crowd that parted to let him pass.

He walked out into the sunshine, looking up and down the street as he wondered how what began as a free meal could end up in a gunfight.

Fox Running had seen cowboy gunfights before. Sometimes the cowboys were too drunk to do more than fire wildly. Sometimes they were deadly. Sometimes comical. For a moment, he wondered if he could keep walking and no one would notice.

Too late. The wildfire of gossip had spread word of the fight. He could guess the man named Clay had done this before, from the way the crowd was acting.

He walked into the center of the dusty street, checking his guns to be sure both were loaded in all chambers. He set Dooley's old pistol into the left hand holster and Petengill's newer weapon in the one on the right. He thought of Spotted Buffalo's admonition that violence would follow him. The old man was right.

Atcheson emerged from the dining room. He wore just the one gun on his right hip.

As he stopped on the steps that led from the wooden sidewalk to the street and looked at Fox Running, the Cheyenne was certain that if this was not the first time Clay had challenged a man, it was the first time he'd been surrounded by this many spectators who were openly guessing how many shots it would take Atcheson to kill Fox Running. Or perhaps the man was one who killed in secret and was unhappy to have an audience. Or, the thought came, Atcheson was so drunk that the sunlight made him stagger.

Fox Running held up a hand as Atcheson moved to a spot about forty feet away. "I am Fox Running of the Northern Cheyenne. I do not seek to fight any man, and I have no quarrel with drunks and fools, but I will fight any man who desires it."

"Shut yer trap, Injun," Atcheson called out. "Just say yer prayers if you got any."

"I do not wish to kill you."

"Well, I am looking forward to killing you."

They had to walk closer for anyone to be able to hit anything. Fox Running had often fired the pistols he carried. His nerves should not be jangling; his heart should not be pounding. But he had never stood this alone in a crowd that, he was certain, would shed no tears if the man who had bullied him into a gunfight were to kill him. In fact, from all he could overhear, it would make Atcheson a hero among many.

Fox Running felt one drop of sweat running down the ridge on his face where the scar remained from his fight at the Rosebud. His mouth was suddenly very dry. If the townspeople were still talking, he could not hear the words anymore, only a faint buzz that reminded him of a bee.

Atcheson's right hand hovered over his gun. Did the man mean to pull his weapon now? At this range, a good gun could be accurate, but few guns could pass that test, and few arms were steady enough to guide a bullet accurately even if the weapon was good.

Fox Running extended both arms toward his guns. Atcheson took a slow step forward. Another. Fox Running felt rooted;

146

that and pride were all that kept him from running. Another step from Atcheson. Another. Fox Running flexed his fingers. Another step. Atcheson was licking his dry lips. Another step. Atcheson's face showed a sneer as he moved closer to Fox Running, as if he could read the emotions within that refused to still themselves. Then the spell inside broke as if a flood of ice water had calmed the heated nerves that were screaming incoherent messages only a moment ago.

Fox Running saw not just a bully with a gun, but a man carrying death—his death. His right hand moved.

Surprise showed on Atcheson's face as Fox Running reached for his gun while the two were still more than twenty-five feet apart. He missed with his first shot. Atcheson fired back and missed as well, although Fox Running felt something sail past his head.

Then Fox Running did as he always had and not as the cowboys did. He braced his right hand with his left and fired, cocking the hammer and pulling the trigger three times in succession as the gun's explosion echoed off the false fronts of the town's stores. As he fired, his legs stung from the rocks and dirt kicked up by one bullet that plowed into the ground inches from his left foot. One rock hit his face, and he closed his eyes reflexively.

He opened them as Atcheson fired again. This shot went even wider than the first two. The white man was weaving now, but not from drink. The sweat-stained shirt he wore looked darkened with more than his perspiration. His lower teeth showed on his pain-streaked face as he tried to cock his gun one more time. His wobbly hands could not manipulate it.

Fox Running walked forward. Atcheson tried to line up his weapon with the moving target until Fox Running was close enough to take the gun out of his hand, close enough to see a wet, red stain that had spread across the right side of Atcheson's midsection, and close enough to see the man's eyes trying to focus but with little success.

"If you want to keep this man alive, someone needs to come help him," Fox Running called as he holstered his own weapon. "Or you can let him die."

Fox Running took the gun out of the weak and wobbly right hand of the man who wanted this showdown. With disgust, he threw Atcheson's gun far into the street and turned away from the gut-shot drunkard.

"I am finished with him," he told the crowd as he walked away without a backward glance. He was certain Clay Atcheson had friends who might shoot him, but he also feared that if he ran, the watching crowd would become a lynch mob. He walked straight down the street, looking at none of them as his heart pounded and his ears listened for sounds of pursuit.

In a matter of moments, he had reached O'Malley's old saloon. Forrest had come outside. He looked at Fox Running as though he was seeing a ghost but wordlessly watched as Fox Running slowly mounted his horse. With one hand, Fox Running held the reins. With the other, he drew a pistol. In case.

He guided the horse down the street at a walk. He sat tall in the saddle, proud in the saddle, defiant in the saddle.

When he was no longer in sight of the saloon, and well out of sight of the crowd, he kicked his heels into the animal and urged it forward. In time, the townspeople would follow. He must get as far away as fast as he could, for there was no question in his mind that when an Indian killed a white man who bullied him, the Indian would be to blame.

Chapter Eleven

Fox Running made camp for the night on a bluff a few miles west of Fort Riley. The high ground overlooked the road from the town. He needed to know if they were pursuing. He had to get to the Lakota reservation. That was a sacred mission. It was getting late into the season when the Moon Turns Its Hard Face to the Earth, and soon the ground would freeze before the killing snows of winter. If the people from the town did not follow, he could move north freely. If they were on his trail, he would need to find a place to hide until they gave up looking for him.

Through the early hours of the morning, the road was clear except for a couple of lumbering wagons. He wondered if Atcheson did not die, or if something else distracted the cowboy's friends from pursuit. He was convinced of one thing: in saving his life, he had lost it. Spotted Buffalo need not have worried. There was no way now he could ever return south, for fear there would be a price on his head. This would not be like Montana in 1878. That was a gang of wild youths breaking the rules in a time of great turmoil. Now, he had killed a man and everyone there knew his name. He had told them!

He decided to head west and then turn north. As a boy, they had told him of a trail from the lands of the Northern Cheyenne to the south. The trail wound through hills where the soldiers would never pursue. If he could reach that trail, he would be safe.

Several days of battering rain forced him to slow his pace, taking shelter where he could. The wreck of a homesteader's part-sod, part-wood cabin was a refuge for two days of downpours. Not much was standing, but enough for him and the horse to have some shelter.

The sun that shone upon Kansas as he rode was warm and brilliant, highlighting drops of rain on waving stalks of grass and grain. He would need to eat soon. The horse had been able to graze on the grasslands. He had no such luxury. Even water was denied him until the mud receded in the creeks.

In the distance he could see a thin blue line of smoke, like strands of faded blue string dangling from the sky. He rode for it. His hair was still short by Indian standards, although it was long by white ones. He had a hat as something of a disguise, even though he despised wearing it. He could hope that the farmer would not see an Indian and consent to offer a meal in exchange for a few chores. After all, he could certainly sound civilized!

The cabin where the smoke was coming from was crude and rough. There was no one nearby. He dismounted. There was a field of grain, some still beaten down by the hard weather. At the far end, he heard the angry voice of a man. Smaller, higher voices were cringing out a reply.

He recalled gathering corn when he was small—children racing around with little idea of what they were doing, with mothers and grandmothers enjoying the spectacle until at last it was time for the order to harvest food they would need for the winter. Every kernel would be saved, and a child who ate food meant for the winter would soon learn how it felt to be humiliated in front of the village. Even so, it was a time of rare enjoyment.

What he witnessed as he moved through the waist-high grain was nothing like his memories. A man with black hair sticking out from under his brown, battered hat was brutally beating something hitched to an ugly, cumbersome machine that had once been red but was now mostly rust. He could see the man's suspenders crisscrossing his back, holding up a homespun pair of pants.

Fox Running pitied the poor animal. Men who beat animals deserved to come back in the next life and be beaten.

As he moved closer, he realized something was not right. He could see two small, dark-haired boys holding reins as the man continued to beat his victim, who had fallen to the ground. The man was screaming rage and cursing. The horse must have collapsed from the blows.

Then it struck him: The boys were not holding reins. They had been harnessed to one side of the reaper, a massive piece of metal designed to cut grain. That meant there was probably another boy being pummeled.

"Stop!" he shouted. The man kept swinging a stick at his victim. The boys were pointing at Fox Running, saying something the man ignored.

"Do that will you?" the man screamed. "I will not tolerate it!"

The gun was in Fox Running's hand before he knew it was there. The shot echoed as the bullet whined far above their heads.

Everything stopped.

"Stop this!" Fox Running called out.

"Who are you?" the man screamed. "Someone she was sneaking around with? I should have known. I should . . ."

The next shot went into the soft dirt a few feet from the man, spraying him with clumps of rich, brown soil. He was quiet.

"You two," Fox Running said, gesturing with the gun at the

151

boys. "Get whoever that is out from there, if he is not already dead."

After fussing with harness straps, they eventually disengaged themselves from the battered, rusted reaper and knelt out of sight as they argued about how to untangle the one left harnessed to the machine. Fox Running slowly walked closer, keeping the gun focused on the man. The man was unarmed, but Fox Running could smell liquor. He remained wary.

The boys continued to fuss and argue. "What is going on over there?" Fox Running called.

"We can't get her out."

Her?

Fox Running instructed the man to lie down in the dirt. The man wanted to fight, but the gun cowed him. As Fox Running neared the reaper, he was startled. The victim of the beating, face bloody and more blood oozing down the back of her coat from an opening where it had torn, was indeed a girl, whose long, red hair spilled down and grew matted as her blood flowed into it.

"Stand clear," he ordered the boys. He holstered the gun, pulled out a knife, gripped the harness straps, and cut through every piece of leather he could see, watching in case the man thought this was an opportunity to attack. The man did not. *Coward,* thought Fox Running.

"Get her now," he said, returning the knife and gun to where they belonged. Soon the boys were leading the girl out of the tangle of leather. Cuts scarred her ruddy, swollen cheeks. One eye was almost swollen shut. The thin coat she wore had been ripped through to her bloody skin in more than one place. Even with the boys doing their best, she staggered as they held her.

Teachers at the school in Boston had beaten Fox Running and others for breaking the rules, for talking in their own languages, for the purpose of breaking their spirits. Fox Running had suffered his share. This beating was worse.

"Get up," he told the man on the ground. "Why? Why did you hit her?"

"She wouldn't do no work," the man spat. "Said the reaper was too heavy. Didn't get her to let her stand around idle."

"So you tried to kill her?"

"Not feedin' her if she don't work!"

Fox Running turned to the boys. "Where is your mother?"

They looked at him, terrified.

"Got none, they do, is the way of it," the girl slurred, spitting out blood as it flowed from her mouth. "None of us do, if ye want to know the truth. Jacob, tell him. Hurts, it does, too much for me to talk."

Irish. Yet again.

One of the boys explained they had been sent from the East because they had no homes and families.

"The orphan trains," Fox Running muttered. Katherine McGillicuddy had kept something about them in one of her piles of material on the causes she supported. Children who were abandoned, or were more than parents could or would care for, or who ran loose in the streets and were arrested over and over, were packed up and sent West to families that might want them. The brochures made it sound as though children needing homes were loved. It said nothing about them being beaten half to death.

"Samuel and I came from Baltimore," the boy said. "Maggie is from Boston. We came here in the spring."

Fox Running thought idly of spring in Boston. Was it only a few months ago he saw one future for himself that now seemed so ridiculously impossible? He was not sure if he should feel sorry for himself for considering it or laugh at his naïve stupidity. He wondered if the girl was cast out when he was.

"Mr. Bowen's wife died of some fever. I don't know anything

about it, but he did not pay his bills and the bank took his horses. We pulled the plow this summer. The reaper is too heavy. We just couldn't do it!" Jacob said. "We told him we would cut the grain with the scythe, but he said it would take too long and that he bought the reaper to harvest the grain, and we had to haul it!"

"Is that the truth?" Fox Running asked Bowen.

"They were fed every day, which is more than they had where they came from," he said. "I had a small section cleared. Estelle and I, we worked. I bought more land and bought the reaper. We needed hands, and they came around telling us these children would work for a good home. Estey caught the fever, and she passed. My first crop failed. Then I planted late. And now these good-for-nothing children will not help!"

"We were only fed when I cooked, ye sot!" Maggie snapped. "Ye spent more time with your liquor than your fields. I told you I could na' pull it! Huge old rusted thing. Not a mule. Knew I was a girl when ye were drunk, ye did, but not when it was time to haul that thing you could not even pull!"

Fox Running had read that farmers used machines now, but this one was very old. It must have been sold from farmer to farmer to farmer.

Maggie stopped and pressed a hand to her side. The boys holding her were waging a losing fight as they tried to keep her upright.

"Enough!" snapped Fox Running. "Take her to the cabin. I will be along in a few minutes."

He had no idea what to do next. If he resumed his journey north and left them behind, the girl would get another beating, probably a worse one. The man, Bowen, was as pitiful as he was disgusting. Fox Running could not shoot him and leave him there. That was murder. Yet it was a risk to allow him to walk freely while Fox Running decided. Farmers kept guns handy.

"Stand by your machine," he said and grabbed pieces of leather. Soon, he had tied the man's hands to the reaper. The leather would not hold long, but it would give Fox Running time to think.

"Do not think I will not kill you if you force me," he told Bowen. "Depending upon what they tell me you have done, I may do it anyhow."

The boys had guided the girl to a bed made of a few boards nailed crosswise that held a mattress of straw.

"Did this happen often?" Fox Running asked when he arrived inside. He took a piece of a spare shirt and dipped it in a bucket of water, then wiped off the blood on her face so he could see the damage.

"Enh," she grunted as he hit a tender spot. "Nae a' first. True, he brought us here to work because we were cheaper than buying animals. Always a hard man, he has been. The streets of Boston were no better or worse. The lady sometimes tried to be kind, but she was sick and then died, and then all was gone of humanity in him. The liquor owned him. I thought about leavin' him to rot in his own fields, but I couldna."

"Why did you stay?"

"The twins could not be left alone. They canna travel. Nine, they are." Fox Running was surprised. They were as big at nine as he had been at fourteen. "He would ha' killed them."

"He almost killed you."

"He used to know when to stop." She coughed. Blood came up.

Fox Running knew little of healing the wounds that took place within. Coughing blood meant bones were broken by the places where men breathed, or there were very bad wounds that went deep inside.

"I must see about the wounds on your back," he said. "Can you sit?"

155

She sat up and carefully took off the coat. He touched the wet cloth to the bloody tears in her shirt. Only one caused her much pain. The coat had absorbed more damage than he expected. She had no wounds on the front of her that had bled into her shirt.

Fox Running looked at the three outcasts. Every minute he delayed made it harder for him to reach the Lakota before winter, but he could not leave them behind to be beaten.

"I am going to Dakota Territory," he said. "You can stay here with him, or go with me. I am sure there are farms along the way with better families, where you can be fed and not be beaten, but I will not force you to leave if you wish to stay."

"He told us once if we ran away, he will follow us and kill us," said Jacob. His brother nodded.

"If you ride with me, he will not dare," replied Fox Running.

The girl had been studying Fox Running. He knew the question was coming. "Some kind of Injun you are?"

"I am of the Northern Cheyenne," he said. "My name is Fox Running. I am going north to the reservation of the Lakota, that many of you call the Sioux, because I promised a friend who died that I would go there. I am not here to capture you. I will take you to any town you want that is on the way north. I travel alone. I spent time at the Indian boarding school in Boston. It was a bad place with men who gave beatings like yours. I am going to do something I promised my friend, and then I will go home. I promise you can go wherever you want, but I do not think you are safe here."

"We got to talk this out," she said. "I canna speak for the children."

"I will wait outside, but you must hurry. I tied Mr. Bowen to the reaper, and he will be free very soon. Also, if you do not come with me, I must go now. Every day of travel before the snow hits must be used."

They did not take long.

"We will go," said Jacob as he came outside.

"Take whatever clothing you have, for it will be cold," said Fox Running. "If there is food, take it. We will not stop again this day."

The roll of clothes for the three was pitifully small. They took some bread and dried meat. Fox Running lifted Maggie, who winced and grunted when he touched her, and the two boys onto the horse. He took the reins and led the animal.

"I shall walk. We must go."

As he looked for Bowen, he saw that all three of the riders kept their eyes forward. They passed a spot where Bowen, trying to get free, could see them leave. Fox Running heard the man's shouted threats. Soon, they were nothing but an indistinct noise. Then they were gone entirely.

Fox Running kept up the pace until well after dark. None of the orphan train children had ever ridden a horse. They were all sore by the end of the day. Maggie had made bread before they went to the field, so for this day there was plenty to eat. Fox Running made a fire for warmth.

"I will stay awake and keep watch in case we are followed," he said, instructing them to spread their spare clothes over them as a blanket and to huddle near each other for warmth.

The boys, who both said they had never slept in the open before and voiced fears of wild animals, were asleep within minutes. Maggie sat with them on the opposite side of the fire from Fox Running. He had noticed when they dismounted that when she was not bent from pain, she was his height. He had seen some people in Boston with hair the color of orange fire, but never this close. He wondered idly if hair so red felt different to the touch. He wanted to ask, but recalled the blonde girl in the park in Boston. Talking might be one thing, but touching was something else.

"Never seen an Injun up close," Maggie said.

"After three or four days we can look for a place for you and the boys," he said. "If you stop running too close to where you left, that Bowen man might find you. Do you know the name of the closest town where he would go?"

"Do you scalp people?"

Fox Running laughed inwardly. It was the one thing white people always talked about. He did not want to laugh in her face, because her thin face looked so serious when she spoke. He guessed she was around fourteen.

"It is far too much work," he said. "I do not have any interest in trophies. Your hair is safe, if that was what worried you."

"You don't wear feathers. You don't really look like an Injun. Why?"

"I have lived in the world of the Cheyenne, the Lakota, and the white," he said. "I take what I can find and nothing more than that. We wear feathers for ceremonies. I have been traveling for many months. I wear what I can find." He fell silent, studying her. "How old are you?"

"Sixteen," she said. "Born I was in Donegal. We came here when I was very young. My father was a blacksmith, but when the business failed he caught work with the railroad. One day, he left. I do not know where he went. My mother had six children. I was the oldest. We had no money, so I would steal what we needed from the shops in the street and the rich people with fancy clothes. When I was caught, we could not pay the fine, so they put me in jail. When I was let out, I went back to stealing, because my mother's sewing work could not support everyone. They caught me again and told Mother this time I would either have to go to prison or they would send me away. They paid my mother something. She needed the money. They put me on a train. When we got out here, men would come to decide which they wanted to take. One man poked me as though I was a cow. I hit him. I had cared for the boys on the train. Mr. Bowen wanted them, and he took me as well. At first, I thought it was good. It did not stay very good for very long."

Fox Running idly wondered how many people like her, or like him, there were—people who drifted from place to place because they had no home, no family. It was not something to talk about with a stranger.

"It is time you slept," he told her. "We must start early. I do not trust that man not to follow us, or get others to ride with him to hunt us. I know he is a coward, but cowards can be dangerous when they are humiliated."

He could see she was wary.

"I do not ever trust strangers, either," he said after a time when he was certain she was still awake. "But how many strangers can hum you this?" He softly hummed "The Rising of the Moon," the old Irish rebel song O'Malley taught him and that he sang with Dooley.

"On wi' ye now," she mumbled softly, drowsily after humming with him as she smiled the first smile he saw upon her face. "An Irish Injun."

She did not sleep at first, but, in time, her breathing eased. And Fox Running kept watch over the family that had now become his.

CHAPTER TWELVE

October 1881, Fort Riley, Kansas

Wallace's *Frontier News* had made a specialty out of telling Eastern readers the dramatic doings of life out West. Deadly gunmen, bold horses, marauding Indians, vast, powerful storms, and courageous soldiers were its stock in trade, as were dewy-eyed maidens who managed to continually find themselves in predicaments well beyond their ability to resolve on their own.

In between the advertisements for patent medicines, there was sure to be at least one sudden, violent death at the hands of a colorfully named outlaw. Although the death of Billy the Kid that summer had ended one of the best-selling stories ever to grace its pages, authentic accounts of the dramatic death and life of New Mexico's most famous outlaw had kept its columns filled for weeks.

Carson McAllister, who from his weeks in New Mexico had generated dozens of stories that thrilled readers regardless of any connection they might have to the truth, was now passing through Kansas.

He was bored. He had spent so long out West as a correspondent for the magazine that in his annual sojourns East, he found himself feeling trapped among the bricks and horse-drawn streetcars of the city. Even Kansas now seemed placid. The Indian raids were over. Most of the news he could manufacture came from the trail towns like Dodge City, where gunfights were common and life was cheap. However, the editors were complaining that every breathless description of a Texas cowboy shooting another drunk cowboy sounded pretty much the same.

He was humoring them now with a trip to Fort Riley. Perhaps the cavalry had found raiding Indians, or something that could be made into good copy. Once winter set in, he would be back in the East, but he did not want to go yet.

While having a drink at Callahan's saloon in the town, he heard talk of a gunfight a couple of weeks back that was different from the rest. An Indian? A real Cheyenne Indian? Indians never went off the reservation any more, never had been gunfighters, and never bested whites at any contests involving guns. It had to be whiskey talking. but anything would be better than the same old stories, so he decided to investigate.

He hunted down Jack Jenkins, who confirmed that Clay Atcheson, who some thought was a pretty good man with a gun in his own right, was shot down in the street by a young Cheyenne. Jenkins did not remember much beyond the fact that the Cheyenne wore two pistols.

Atcheson had lingered for a while and just the other day died of his wounds, with no one in Fort Riley feeling much sorrow at the loss of a man whose foul temper and facility with a gun made him someone most cowboys tried to avoid. McAllister was told the Cheyenne youth had simply shot Atcheson down after some scrape and then left town as though he had done nothing remarkable. A cold-blooded killer!

He found Forrest, who said the young man was heading north, but that he knew little more beyond the young man's name—Fox Running.

Within hours, the telegraph at Fort Riley was clacking a dispatch that Wallace's *Frontier News* would soon trumpet as the latest dastardly killing from what the magazine would term the "gunfighting desperado known far and wide as the Cheyenne Kid."

November 1881, Northern Kansas
Five days had passed since Fox Running met Maggie and the boys. They had pushed north and west every day as best the trails and tracks allowed. They were sore and hungry. Rain pummeled them again this morning, but they did not complain.

Fox Running wished he was better at hunting. Maggie had asked why, since he was an Indian, he could not hunt their supper. He admitted he was a poor shot with a rifle, which was why he did not carry one. Pistols did not shoot very far, he told her.

He was not living up to whatever image she had of an Indian, but he was unconcerned. Soon the Irish children would be gone, and he could fulfill his pledge to Tall Bear. Meanwhile, he enjoyed their company. Maggie had recovered from her beating faster than he would have expected. She sometimes walked or rode as though her back still hurt but was too proud to complain. She seemed pleased to have him guiding them, but he did not think they would want to stay much past the first large town they reached. The thought of the girl's impending departure left him with mixed feelings, but he had no words to express them. They never taught that at the Indian school.

It was important to get to Nebraska. Laws in one state ended at the next. That would make it hard for Bowen to lay claim that the children were his. The lines on the maps did not exist in the world of plains and hills, but they loomed large in the minds of men. Soon it would be safe to find the children a home. He hoped it would be a good one. He liked Maggie, for all her odd ways of white children. She was kind, and they laughed often. She sang to him. Even if his head said they would be leaving him soon, his heart had other notions.

★ ★ ★ ★ ★

They were approaching a small town. From a distance, they could see what looked like two strings of buildings on opposite sides of a street, with other buildings clustered nearby. They did not have any money to buy food, but at least they would know for sure where they were. Perhaps they could work for a few meals before starting north again. They could also learn if Bowen was on their trail.

"And we can sleep in a stable inside!" Jacob said. "No more rocks for pillows!"

Fox Running had misgivings, but with no food, they also had very few choices. Riding around the town would take them into rough country and consume more time. They would take the risk. He debated whether to tell them about Fort Riley and decided against it. If he was wanted, he would find out soon enough. The gunfight there had been about three weeks ago. More than enough time if there was going to be a manhunt, and he had seen no sign of any hunt for him—so far.

"Folks look like you come far," was the blacksmith's greeting as they approached the stable. He told them the name of the town was Rock Springs, and that they were barely a mile from the Nebraska border.

"Wondering if we could swap some work for some oats for the horse and a few meals for ourselves," Fox Running said, trying to imitate the way he heard cowboys talk. "Heading for my cousin's place near the Sand Hills. Been a longer walk than we thought."

"I can finish those shoes," said Maggie, pointing to where a set of recently pounded-out horseshoes sat on a table. "Get me a file, and I'll do it."

"Over there," the blacksmith said, after telling them they were welcome to stay. "Boys, get yourselves shovels and rakes over there. Do what your ma tells you."

Fox Running started to correct him, but Maggie shook her head. He said nothing.

The smith then looked at Fox Running. He took in Fox Running's two guns. He was asking a question without saying a word.

"Met up on the road," Fox Running said. "Family left stranded. Couldn't say no."

"Nice of you," said the smith, who identified himself as Jack Evans. He kept examining Fox Running far longer than seemed necessary. "Travelling can be dangerous. Lot of outlaws. Injuns, sometime."

The man's tone made Fox Running uneasy. Evans locked eyes with Fox Running. "You hear a lot about wild men and guns on the trail," he added.

"We did not have any trouble," Fox Running remarked, feeling the urge to mount the horse that was now in a stall and run.

"Good for you," Evans said. "Tell you what. You keep them boys workin'. I'll go get some food. Young 'uns pack away food, don't they?"

Fox Running made noises of agreement.

Evans then moved away far too quickly.

Fox Running knew something was wrong. A man didn't just leave a stranger with his business unless he had an urgent mission.

Maggie was the happiest Fox Running had ever seen her. With a file, she was scraping down the shoe so it would better fit the horse. It was clear as he watched that she had done this many times before. Fox Running abandoned his plan to warn her they might need to leave quickly. After all, they were not trouble. He was.

The longer Evans was gone, the more nervous Fox Running became as he waited by the door. Then he saw the smith heading back toward the stable. Two men were trailing him. One wore a star and had a gun at his hip. The other man carried a rifle. There was not enough time to mount and ride to get out of range.

When they reached the stable's entrance, the man with the star on his worn, brown, leather vest spoke. "Hello, son. Sheriff Dan Porter. Mind tellin' me what brings you and those kids to Rock Springs?"

Fox Running repeated the story about heading to the Sand Hills. "The trail goes through the town, Sheriff," he said. "The girl and the boys, they needed some food, so we stopped."

"This is a peaceful town, son." Fox Running waited for what might come next. "Don't need no gunplay here."

Voices grew audible from beyond the doorway.

"Zat him?"

"Sheriff, that him?"

"Sheriff's got the Cheyenne Kid!"

Fox Running was not certain what the voices meant, but the word Cheyenne could only mean trouble. His hands had unconsciously drifted to his gun belt. The sheriff noticed before he did.

"Now, now, we don't want no trouble. Get what you come for and leave. We don't want every half-witted fool to come here looking for the Cheyenne Kid. Don't like gunfights and gunfighters. Not having that in this town."

"Sheriff, I . . ."

"You call yourself Fox Runnin', right?"

"Yes." How could the man know that?

"And you shot Clay Atcheson in Fort Riley?"

"Yes, but . . ."

"And the newspaper said you shot ten men in Missouri and a whole bushel more in Kansas? Said there might be some kind of old scores settled in Montana and Dakota and Wyoming?" The sheriff had a copy of the newspaper. "Right here. See? If you can read, that is. Read it to you if you can't."

Fox Running grabbed the battered copy of Wallace's *Frontier News,* which had already seen many hands, and read. He crumpled it and threw it to the ground as the sheriff yelped that his copy of the paper was ruined.

"Sheriff, I do not understand what this is all about. I do not know who this Cheyenne Kid is, but it is not me. Yes, I had a gunfight in Fort Riley because a man who was a bully would not let me go, but I do not have any such absurd nickname, and I did not kill all the people this article claims I did. There has been a mistake."

"Newspaper said it all. You escaped from some place in Boston."

"No!" Maggie yelled.

By now, Maggie and the boys had stopped their work. They crowded to hear what was being said. She looked at him in horror.

"You said . . ." she began. "You said you were just trying to go to Dakota! You are a gunslinger and a killer and who knows what else, and we've been with you! You joked about scalping us. You were looking at my hair. I know you were. You were! What were you really thinking?"

"Maggie, I am not whatever it is . . ."

The boom of a shotgun discharging both barrels drowned out any conversation.

"Sheriff, don't you protect that murderin' Injun." The voice came from a young man who stood in the middle of Rock Springs's main street. The shotgun was pointed up at the sky. Its owner was dressed all in black. He, like Fox Running, wore two guns at his hips.

"C'mon, Red Man Cheyenne," the young man taunted in a singsong voice. "Newspaper said you was fast. Show me how fast. Whole town wants to see. Whole town wants to see if you got the guts to face a man, there, Cheyenne Kid! Bet you back shot that man in Fort Riley, all them other men, too."

"Sheriff, this is a mistake," Fox Running said. "This is your town. Tell that man to go away."

The taller sheriff looked down at him. "Not me that made the mistake, son. You live by the gun, I always say, you die by the gun."

Shaking his head, as if in frustration at the failure of his effort to forestall a gunfight, the sheriff turned away. Then he turned back. "Son, Garret Hightower spends about every day practicing with his gun. Seen how fast he can draw. You go out there, the only thing I want to know is if you want the body buried or burned. Not sure they'll put an Injun next to white men, but I can ask."

"You should ask him, Sheriff," Fox Running retorted. "White men have tried to kill me since the day Custer attacked my village. I am the one who is still here. Go tell the fool I will meet him."

He took off his hat, tossed it into the dim recesses of the stable, and shook out his hair. There was no sense trying to disguise who or what he was. Anger flowed through him. He had tried to live by everyone else's rules. Look where it had gotten him!

The sheriff moved away with a contingent of townspeople and hangers-on to find good places to watch the entertainment.

Fox Running turned to Maggie and the boys.

"I have been in one gunfight, Maggie, and it was forced upon me. I do not know why that newspaper said what it did, but I am not a gunfighter. All I want to do is go to the lands of the Lakota, pay my debt to my friend, and find a place to live without someone fighting me. I do not care if you believe that or not, but it is the truth."

Her silence and rigid face said it all as she pulled the boys closer to her and farther from him. He turned and stalked away.

Hightower had tossed the shotgun into the dirt of the town's only street. He waited with his hands clasped over the silver buckle of his black-leather gun belt. His face registered surprise as Fox Running approached, walking fast. The Indian didn't know how this was done!

"Slow down!"

Fox Running did not. He was soon fifty feet away.

"Gonna shoot you down, you don't do this right!"

On walked the Cheyenne, boring in on Hightower, who could feel the Indian's hate like a fire. Twenty-five feet. Less. The Indian was scratching the back of his neck. Or something. Had to be some Indian magic trick!

Hightower scrambled to draw his gun. As it cleared the holster he saw something glint in the sun; then the knife struck his right arm. The impact froze his draw as his arm shook and shivered from the damage done by the thick blade. His hand was on the butt of the gun, but the gun would not clear the holster. He tried to thumb back the hammer, but his thumb did not have the strength.

Fox Running was inches away now. The spectators were silent. Fox Running looked into the eyes of the man who wanted to kill for sport. "This is too good a knife to leave in a man such as you."

He grabbed Hightower and pulled out the blade, pushing hard against Hightower as he did so. The pain spiked, and Hightower crumpled to the ground. Fox Running bent down.

"He's going to scalp him!" someone called.

Rifles were cocked, and guns emerged from holsters.

Fox Running wiped the knife on Hightower's black coat and put it in its sheath at the back of his neck, kept in place by the loop of rawhide he wore around his throat.

He looked through the crowd until he saw the sheriff. Anger

and contempt radiated from his lone figure as Fox Running looked at the men ready to fire, as if daring them to act. He stared into every pair of eyes that met his. Few did.

Then he silently turned and stalked back to the blacksmith's stable.

He threw the blanket over the horse and was leading him out when Maggie approached, with the boys lagging behind. She had the wrinkled newspaper in her hands. "I'm sorry I . . ."

"These people will find homes for you. If the newspaper people who have written about things they know nothing of come to find you, please do not lie."

"Fox Running, I am sorry . . ."

"That words some fool put in a newspaper would mean more to you than the fact that I took you from that place where you were being beaten worse than any living thing deserves and tried to care for you reminds me that white people always believe the worst of an Indian." He jumped on the horse's back. "I must go before they decide they need to be brave and kill me to save themselves from whatever it is I might do to them. Good-bye, Maggie. Oh, I have been a fool to ever be kind to anyone who is white!"

She was trying to speak as he galloped away. She saw him go through eyes that were misted with tears.

Fox Running rode the horse as fast as he could, as long as he could. He kept to the west. Sooner or later he could turn north, but not now. For now, he needed to get as far away from anywhere as possible, before he did what he wanted. Before he killed every last one of them just to ease the screaming rage within.

Carson McAllister felt as though he needed a bath after talking with Hiram Bowen. He was certain Bowen lied, but he had enough details to prove that something at least had happened.

Bowen was overjoyed that his story was worth a whole five dollars. Fool! Now, as he left the Silver Dollar saloon, McAllister needed to find a room. The town, Kean, had nothing to offer but the stable. Perhaps there would be a back room in the general store. The saloon was too primitive for his taste.

He stopped on the street. He was certain someone was calling his name. It was the Western Union man! The man ran until he caught up with McAllister, who by now was becoming the West's leading authority on the Cheyenne Kid. There was a telegram for him. The Cheyenne Kid had been sighted, and the townspeople of Rock Springs, Kansas, were asking for McAllister.

McAllister swelled with a just pride. This collection of stories would soon put him ahead of even Mark Twain in fame. Perhaps there would be lectures about how he led the pursuit of this outlaw. True, the Indian had broken no laws, but he was certain this was a detail his readers would be happy to overlook!

November 1881, Boston

Katherine McGillicuddy moved closer to the fire as the late autumn rains rattled the windows. She had risen to her uncle's challenge by taking firm and total control of her business enterprises, from the factory that made shoes to the mills that turned cotton into clothing. She had stepped back from public involvement in the causes in which she believed, knowing that beating a strategic retreat was necessary for her long-term survival. She became careful to ensure as few as possible knew about those causes she still supported financially.

She had proven time and again that a woman could be every bit as shrewd as a man in the world of commerce, but there were days when she needed to escape it all. These were the days when she sorted through the clippings her office staff compiled from the newspapers and magazines that were not the least concerned with facts as long as someone bought the paper to be entertained by its tales. Some of the fabrications were so ludicrous as to be amusing. It was as though the frontier were invented to be a place where the most unlikely occurrences were commonplace events. Then she came to a series of clippings from Wallace's *Frontier News.*

Her eyes widened. These she read with intensity. It could not be. Yet amid the vast helpings of purple prose from a writer who was clearly skilled at making one sentence worth of facts into reams of type was an undeniable truth: the "desperado" the newspaper called "the Cheyenne Kid" was the same young man she thought, not so long ago, would have a future. As she waded through the clippings, she could see multiple newspapers picked up the same story, adding and rearranging details as they chose.

Her heels tap-tapping her emotion, she strode from the warm study to her office, where a map was marked to indicate the railroad holdings in which she owned some or all of the company. Yes. There was one in Laramie, Wyoming. She would have a wire sent first thing. There had to be some mistake! She had no real idea how far it was from Laramie to where her friend, Annie Campbell, was living with the Cheyenne, but someone could make the trip. Letters took weeks. She did not want to wait that long!

She looked at the clipping, wondering if it might be worth her while to buy a newspaper; if their tentacles to the West were as strong as their writers made one believe. It was a project she would pursue if it could be profitable. It might also be necessary.

That settled, she re-read one clipping about children from an orphan train marooned in some place in Kansas. The story said they had been brutalized. She composed a stern note to Grandison Edwards, who oversaw the arrangements between children and adults, to determine how this charity that could not remain operating without her contributions could have made such a dreadful mistake. She had the note delivered immediately. Then she ordered chamomile tea and sat by the fire in her study, wondering what could possibly be taking place most of a continent away out West.

The clippings that so alarmed Katherine McGillicuddy were read no less avidly by others in the city. At the Boston Indian School, room searches had turned up more than five copies of the various articles. Darby and Petengill were alarmed, for they expected daily that some enterprising newspaper man would knock on their door.

Among the school's students, the reaction was equally emotional. Among the older boys, many of whom came from the Plains states where the Cheyenne Kid now roamed free, the clippings were proof that an escape from the school could lead to freedom, and more and more who had reached their limit of brow beatings and actual beatings slipped away even in the harsh weather of a New England autumn.

And in the basement, where a guard named John Dooley still hummed "The Rising of the Moon" and waged his own revolt against authority to the point where the school's leaders were close to firing the man for undermining their rules, the clippings were read with a fear that whatever Fox Running had done would end in his death, and a certain respect that the boy had managed to escape. Now all he needed to do was survive.

CHAPTER THIRTEEN

November 1881, Nebraska

The Cheyenne trail was marked with rocks piled in ways Fox Running learned to read as a child. He took his time. He had been lucky enough to shoot some game early on his travels. He mostly burned it when he cooked it, but it was meat, and it kept him alive. As the days grew shorter and colder, he began to look more for some form of shelter. A thin coat, thin shirt, and thin pants—and no shoes—would not keep him warm.

He also knew he needed to leave the trail at some point and head further west. The trail used by the People wound near the Sand Hills, and he was certain that because he had mentioned the place, it would be crawling with gunfighters who wanted to test the Cheyenne Kid and writers who wanted to tell lies about him. He was uncertain which he hated more, and which he feared more. The dark clouds to the north were a reminder that snow was coming.

As he cut across fields, he could see the changes homesteaders had made. Where once there had been nothing but grasslands, vast brown swaths of earth showed where farmers had waged their battles to grow crops. He could understand people who lived in a place like Boston wanted to get away. But taking Cheyenne and Lakota land to give to others was still wrong, no matter how much those who took insisted they were right.

He had been daydreaming and was closer to the next cabin than he thought. He could see a woman, man, and child by the open doorway. The man had a rifle in one hand. They must get few visitors, he mused, if one rider was an event.

He thought about riding past, but he was low on food. They had already seen him. What could he lose? This was too far for news to travel.

"Howdy," called the man as Fox Running rode slowly to their cabin. "Get down and come in."

"Hi!" called the little girl, waving with the exuberance of youth for anything that was different.

"Jim . . ." The woman placed her hand on the man's arm. She leaned towards him, pointing at Fox Running.

"All right, Injun, you stop right there!" the man shouted, all friendliness gone. "Lucy, get back here."

Fox Running stopped where he was, hot anger burning that he'd changed from welcome to hated once they realized he was an Indian. He waited. A man with a gun was a man not to be trifled with.

The little girl did not understand a word being said. "Hi!" she said, coming to within a few feet of Fox Running.

"Hi, little one," he said back.

"Don't you even talk to her," the man yelled. He turned to his wife. "Allie, get her."

The wife started toward the little girl, who ran away, thinking it was a game.

"Lucy!"

The girl darted past her mother, not looking where she was going.

Echoes of Fox Running's first shot and Allie's scream mingled. The second bullet went into the wall of the cabin, sending Jim sprawling as he was shouldering the rifle, which fell into the hard-packed mud.

"Stay there!" Fox Running commanded. He dismounted. Lucy was crying and screaming in fright. Fox Running ran to her, gun drawn, but Allie ran faster and scooped up the girl.

"You want to take her, you have to deal with me!" she declared defiantly.

With a look of disgust, Fox Running kicked toward Allie the dead timber rattler he had shot after the little girl had disturbed it. He kept a wary eye on her husband, who was trying to inch closer to the rifle.

"No thanks necessary," he said bitterly.

He holstered the weapon and mounted. "And when some scribbler with ink where his brain should be comes by, tell him you witnessed another killing by the Cheyenne Kid," he said.

He kicked the horse to a gallop.

He did not know it, but the hunt for the Cheyenne Kid was taking place in Missouri after a teamster named Jack Smolley recalled hauling an Indian named Fox Running and decided he wanted to speak his piece to the newspaper.

McAllister found him a disappointing interview.

"Threatened me? Saved me! Fella just put holes in those robbers as cool as a fall breeze. Heading somewhere in Arapaho country," Smolley said in the St. Louis office of his hauling company as he outlined everything that happened when Fox Running and Short Wing rode with him.

Smolley would later indulge in an angry stream of letters to Wallace's *Frontier News* when he found that his rescue was portrayed as robbers falling out when the story was printed. A long letter he laboriously drafted in rebuttal—one the newspaper promised to print—miscarried, the newspaper said. The legend of the Cheyenne Kid grew. But of the desperado himself, there was no word.

The season of death was upon the Plains. The grass that had been green weeks ago was fading to brown as the morning frost turned from the light covering that made the prairie an endless expanse of white for a few sparkling moments into a killing blanket that left bushes barren and grasslands limp and lifeless.

Fox Running rode without hope. He would never reach the Lakota before the snow.

Since leaving Rock Springs behind, he had seen several cavalry patrols. He did not know if they sought him or if some group of Lakota or Cheyenne had decided to break away from the lands where their people were confined. He could not believe soldiers would scout for one man, but if what was being said in the Kansas town was any example, he was being accused of—or given credit for—all manner of shootings.

At first, the solitude of traveling alone had seemed strange. From the time he had surrendered at Hat Creek, he had usually been near others, or alone at most for a few days between towns. Now, he was alone for as long as the days stretched before him.

No, he told himself, there were simply no people. The lands he was slowly riding through had been the home of the Cheyenne and Lakota for countless generations before him. After him? Who could tell? These were the lands where the Rock Warrior lived, who could turn to stone when his enemies were near. He could recall Doe Leaping having him look at the steep rock sides of the canyons to see if he could find the Rock Warrior. Over these Plains rode the Spirit Horses, the legendary animals who decided the People were worthy of riding instead of walking in the days when the Northern Cheyenne were chased by enemies and first settled on the vast open lands that had become theirs. Above him, every night, were the stars, the children of the Star Maiden, who left them for the small ones who would stray, so they could always find their way home.

And there was the land itself. The brutal, uncompromising blasts of cold that collided with eternal rock. The rugged buttes and hills that rose above the prairie and defied the worst of the winds. The cracks and crevices that could be streams in the spring, raging floods in the days of the storms, and dry, cracked dirt in the August heat. It was the land the spirits gave to the People, a land that would test them, for it was only given to those who were worthy.

Was he worthy? Or was he nothing more than a very lost boy looking for a home he would never find?

Corporal Caleb Gant once again looked at the lieutenant, wondering how anyone so stupid could have been made an officer. Correction. Remained one for more than a day! Just because they had been ordered to sweep the High Plains to find the Cheyenne Kid's gang did not mean they actually had to do it! Had not the fool learned? Two or three days, then back to the fort, where there were good fires and food that did not turn cold before a man ever got to eat it.

He looked around at the collection of twelve miserable men with him. Every one of them knew a big snow would be coming soon, but here they all were—sitting as close to the fire as possible without burning their feet and waiting in silence for the fool to come to his senses and turn back. If the Cheyenne Kid was as bad as they said, twelve half-frozen cavalry troopers were not going to stop a gang that some of the ranchers said numbered into the dozens. Not that any of them had seen a thing. Everyone knew someone who knew someone who had seen something, but no one ever had any details. He privately wondered if this Cheyenne Kid was made up by some of the newspapers, but since the army was now officially worried about him, nothing would do except to send perfectly good men out to freeze to death looking for someone they were not sure existed!

He looked around. For a moment he was afraid he'd muttered his private summation of the army aloud. No one was paying attention. Everyone had eyes fixed on the fire as if looking at the flames would somehow make them warmer.

"Well." Lt. Gillespie Wendover cleared his throat. "Tomorrow we will circle through Laramie County. If we do not find anything, we shall begin to turn back. I have been told that the early snows out here can be profligate, and I can only assume that this gang of Indians we are tracking has already gone into some hiding hole for the winter. I believe that even with the weather tonight it would be acceptable for the guard on duty to remain by this fire."

Wendover had heard tales of men freezing to death on the Plains. He had been torn by wanting the glory of capturing the Cheyenne Kid and fearing the humiliation of losing his men to the weather. He had decided to give his quest one final day. A rancher two days ago had spoken of one rider moving this way. It might well be a scout for the gang, or even someone hiding from the law, but he wanted to be sure before he turned back and gave up his chance to be hailed as a hero for capturing the vicious, massive gang that was a threat to the territory.

"Good evening, gentlemen." They all heard one hammer click, followed by another. There were rifles nearby, but none had them in their hands. Holding cold metal in numb fingers was no man's idea of how to spend time.

The voice came from the edge of the fire's glow. They could see the outline of a small man. Just one.

"I hate to trouble you, but I have run into a very difficult situation," Fox Running continued. "I am out of food. I believe you have a surplus. I propose that we trade."

"Trade for what?" piped up the lieutenant. "I am Lt. Gillespie Wendover of the United States Army. I will not be confronted in this fashion. I demand your name and your purpose and that you immediately put down the guns you have and surrender yourself."

"My name, Lieutenant, is Fox Running. My purpose is to survive long enough to do something far more important than your mission to find this fabled Cheyenne Kid of yours. As for giving up my guns, well, no."

A soldier reached for something. "No!" Fox Running snapped at him. "I do not want to shoot any of you, sir, but I will shoot all of you if necessary."

One of the men was muttering. Wendover blanched as the words sank in. This was in fact the man they were hunting—the Cheyenne Kid. He tried to pierce the darkness beyond the fire's light. How many had surrounded them? How strong was this gang?

Fox Running could read the officer's thoughts as the man's eyes darted, looking for others in the night. For the moment, he could use fear of the phantom gang, of which he had heard tales, if it immobilized the soldiers.

"I need bacon and flour," Fox Running said.

"I will give you nothing!" Wendover declared.

"Then I shall take it," Fox Running replied. The soldiers could hear him humming "The Rising of the Moon" as he moved to the supply horses. They could hear hooves moving softly against the hard ground. Then Fox Running stood at the edge of the light again, the fire highlighting features the soldiers would later describe as "terrifying." In one hand he held a pistol. The other held the reins of several horses.

"Do not move!" he warned. His eyes swept the circle of men. Again. He backed away.

The soldiers cringed as two shots rang out, then righted themselves to look at others as all denied being afraid. They could hear hooves pounding away to the north. The Cheyenne Kid had spooked their horses.

"This way!" called Wendover, drawing his sidearm and pointing where Fox Running had been standing. But no one was there. The Indian was gone as if he had never appeared.

The soldiers threw every stick they had on the fire, to give them light and heat. In the morning, they rounded up all but two of their mounts and all three supply horses, which had been robbed of bacon and flour.

They all agreed that the signs on the ground made it clear the gang surrounding them outnumbered them, perhaps as much as three to one. And upon their return to Fort Laramie, they added another page to the legend of the Cheyenne Kid, who was foiled in his plan to wipe out a cavalry patrol after a fierce battle—or at least, so it would be said.

December 1881, Wyoming

The snow was piling around the hooves of the horse as he and Fox Running slogged through a storm that brought a curtain of cold, wet white onto everything around them. Fox Running looked for someplace—any place—to get out of the weather. He had never been this cold in his life. There were hills on his right, or there had been before the blizzard started, but the snow robbed the flatlands of every feature. There was no place to stop. He would just keep riding. He wondered if they would end up frozen—a dead rider no one knew who was discovered when the snow melted in the spring.

He recalled when old ones left the camp in bad weather, when they had reached the time they wanted to die, that the men said they would just go to sleep and never wake up. If that were true, there could be worse things.

For a moment he wondered if he had been talking to himself again. The Lakota boys always made fun of the white trappers who lived alone for months at a time and who talked to themselves endlessly. He did not want to be one of them!

No. The voice was not his. It came from somewhere off to his left. There it was again! Then came two shots together from the same direction. A signal. It could be a trap, but if someone was out in this weather, it could be someone in even worse condition than he.

He turned the horse toward the sound. He called. No answer. He pulled his left-hand gun and fired it twice into the air.

Two answering shots came quickly. They were close enough that he could see the flame from the gun as it fired. He almost rode into the man, who was hobbling in the snow, limping badly as he waved his hands to attract attention. Fox Running leaped down from the horse to grab him. "Are you hurt? Where is your horse?"

The cowboy had ice hanging from the large mustache that drooped over his upper lip. "Run off. We hit ice. Went down. He took off. Think I busted my leg. Can't walk much."

"Is there shelter nearby?"

"Line shack." The man looked around in the swirling snow. "Can't say which way is what in this weather. Find the tracks we made getting here if you can, and they'll guide us back. No idea where they are."

Getting the man on Fox Running's horse was not easy, but the boy pushed until the injured man was safely on its back. Fox Running walked and held the reins, looking for anything that could be tracks in the featureless gray-white world. This way? Snow drifting over rocks and bushes gave the irregular appearance of tracks. There! A line of disturbed snow. The tracks lasted a few feet and then faded out, blown over by the drifting snow. There was no horizon. He could not be sure of any direction, but he knew he could not remain in the snow long without becoming too numb to find their way out.

He was so focused on looking for tracks that he all but missed the square shape off to his right. He moved faster now. The shack was small. There was an open-sided shelter for animals.

One horse was in it. He could smell wood smoke. He reached the door and pounded. The door opened, and a blast of heat hit Fox Running. The man who opened it stared dumbfounded at the boy, then saw the man beyond.

"Stringer!" He ran past Fox Running. "Get in, you fool," the man yelled as he carried his partner inside.

Fox Running turned from the doorway and led his horse under the shelter. Snow was still gathering there, but the roof shielded the place from the wind. Fox Running touched the horse for a moment longer, to say whatever thanks it might understand, then staggered inside.

A blanket was drawn tight around his neck as Fox Running sat on the shack's hard dirt floor, as close to the fire as he dared. He and Teddy, the cowboy who greeted them, had hauled one of the rough bed frames near the fire and set Stringer upon it. The wind howled outside. Fox Running shivered as feeling returned to his hands in the form of pain. He realized as he sat how close they had come to death.

The hot coffee Teddy gave him was bitter, and he could not understand why white men drank it, but it was warm. Teddy talked as he looked at Stringer's leg, deciding the leg might not be badly broken. He had tied two sticks around the lower end of the leg, from knee to ankle. The leg was swollen and red. The two cowboys talked about the missing horse and the cattle Stringer had ridden out to find. Then they turned their attention to Fox Running.

"Long way from home, fella," was Teddy's comment. "Where you bound?"

"I was going north," Fox Running said. He could not think of a good lie.

"Sonny, 'bout now there ain't much that matters 'cept bein' alive," said Teddy. "Indians don't ride through here all alone like you, specially boys your age, so we're a mite curious if you got more people with you. You Cheyenne or Sioux? I used to live up in Montana. You got the right accent for one of 'em."

"I am alone," said Fox Running. "I am Cheyenne, but I have lived with the Lakota. My name is Fox Running."

"For now, son, it don't matter if you're Billy the Kid come back from the dead. Saved Stringer there. Not that he's a prize, but he can cook tolerable." The rescued man responded to the gibe with a smile.

"This sounds like a three-day norther, so we'll hole up and see what happens," Teddy continued. "We got food. Laid in firewood. When this blows itself out, we'll take a look-see at what happens next. For now, we're alive, and that's about as good as it gets. Might just be you want to learn how to be a cowboy for the winter!"

March 1882, Wyoming

Fox Running rode slowly through the watery snow as he squinted against the blinding glare of the sun on the field of white interspersed with brown where mud showed through. The icebound creeks had returned to life. They gurgled with water from the melting snow.

In the distance, he could see dark shapes of cattle poking their noses through the slush to find grass below. It was hard to believe now the drama that had marked his winter as a cowboy, chipping ice out of water holes so animals could drink, helping rescue some from deep ponds that froze over and then cracked when a steer walked upon them, spreading bales of hay so in the worst of the blasts there would be something for the cattle to eat, so the cowboys would not find their dead, frozen carcasses.

Teddy and Stringer had been good companions. He had come

to trust them. Under different circumstances, they might have been enemies, but in a time when the entire world was three men on their own against nature, it was hard not to be honest. They had clucked and shaken their heads when he told them how the newspaper had so distorted things to make him appear almost an outlaw. They had never been East and were interested to hear what a big city was like.

They taught him what it was like to be a cowboy, laughed uproariously at his mistakes, and made sure that when he left they shared everything they had to spare, including a rifle so he could hunt something other than men.

Best of all, they had given him directions to Pine Ridge that would take him through little-used mountain passes. He had started while many travelers might still be winter-bound, just in case the army wanted to resume its patrols.

They had told him the Cheyenne were largely gathered in the Tongue River Valley south of Fort Keogh, so he need not ride to the fort if he wanted to see his own people. He did not know if he would be welcome, but he had decided he would head there after he did his duty by Tall Bear. The boy's hair remained wrapped in a cloth handkerchief that Fox Running had carried for close to a year. Soon, it would be spread where the boy wanted his spirit to roam. Soon.

A week of slow riding brought him to the White River, which he would follow to Pine Ridge. Going through Nebraska near Fort Robinson might have been faster than taking the Wyoming route through Dakota and the foothills of the Black Hills, but he was more interested in avoiding anyone. He also did not want to ride past Hat Creek. He could not but feel that the spirits of those who died there would reproach him for having done so little in the days since they had been slaughtered at the Pit.

"I do not forget," he said to their spirits one day when he

passed what he thought he remembered as the trail that would have taken him there. "When I am worthy, I will return for your blessing."

From time to time he saw a smudge of smoke that bespoke a settlement. Each time, he rode well around where the smoke was coming from. Although for the past few months he had been able to live without the nonsense of the newspapers making him into someone he was not, he had to assume that, sooner or later, someone would be waiting to either write about him or shoot at him. An Indian in a white world stuck out; an Indian in an Indian world would not. He needed to reach the lands set aside for the Lakota. After two days without sighting a single plume of smoke, he decided he must have finally arrived.

"You are almost home, my friend," he said as he reached into the pouch where Tall Bear's hair remained. He needed to be sure, and he put the handkerchief and its contents in a pocket of his pants.

A few miles later, from a rise overlooking a shallow valley and a plain that stretched for miles, he could see lodges. The emotion the sight stirred took him by surprise. He was glad he was alone. Warriors did not see with blurry vision from wet eyes. He had made it! He had left Boston almost a year ago. It seemed a lifetime. All he wanted to do was sit on the horse and look, as though moving would break the spell of feeling that, even though this was not his land, he was home.

When his eyes were through looking and his mind was done showing him memories of the days he belonged to a camp like this, he started moving slowly toward the lodges, assured that his emotions were under control, as befits a warrior coming home.

Tall Bear did not have any close relatives, or none he had mentioned to Fox Running. The Cheyenne looked around, trying to imagine a place that would have meaning to his friend.

Perhaps there would be family members Tall Bear never named. He hoped so.

Two men galloped to intercept him. Fox Running could understand. He was dressed in cowboy clothes, so to the Lakota, he appeared to be a white man riding onto their lands.

"Greetings," he said in Lakota as they came close. He reined in the horse and was careful not to put his hands anywhere near his guns. They did not greet him in return.

"I am Fox Running of the Cheyenne. I was known as Blazing Fire to Crazy Horse and lived among the Lakota when you were at Fort Robinson many winters ago, and I fought with you at the Greasy Grass. I am here on a mission to fulfill the final wish of a young warrior named Tall Bear, who died at the Indian school in Boston in the East."

The men inspected him. They took their time. It was a reminder that he had left the frenetic culture of the white man behind.

"What is this mission?" said the older man, a stalwart warrior of middle age who identified himself as Lame Bull. He sent the second man to see if Fox Running traveled alone or had brought others.

"My friend asked me to bring a lock of hair here and scatter it to the winds so his spirit could rest here instead of where he died."

"How is it you were once with the Lakota and vanished? I recall there was a boy who followed Crazy Horse, but your face is not familiar to me. Where have you been?"

Fox Running tried to explain.

"It is a journey like no other I have ever heard," said Lame Bull. "Your Cheyenne relatives are in the Tongue River Valley now."

"I am glad the People are safe," Fox Running replied. "I have no family there, for they all died on the Rosebud in the year of the Custer fight."

"Why do you wear guns?"

"To kill those who get in my way," he said, more bluntly than he meant.

Lame Bull smiled faintly at the direct speech. He agreed to take Fox Running to a sacred circle set aside for worship of the spirits. He sent the second warrior with a message to be spread to others at Pine Ridge.

"We will have others join you in the morning as you remember your friend," said Lame Bull. "His name is not familiar, but Tall Owl has gone to learn if any related to this young man are with us, so they can join us and thank you for bringing him here. For this night, please be the guest of my family, for you have come far."

Fox Running walked his horse through the village. Many stared, for newcomers were rare, especially newcomers who looked like cowboys.

"They find you a strange thing to see," said Lame Bull. "I recall the day Crazy Horse received his horse. I was among those given the honor of going with him to the camp of the Cheyenne. Much has happened since then. The boy on that day was small. How many years have you now?"

"I am eighteen years," replied Fox Running. "I will be nineteen this summer. I did not grow tall, Lame Bull, but I know how to survive. I have gone from Boston to the lands of the Arapaho to here to fulfill the wishes of my friend. I recall the days of Crazy Horse and mourn his murder."

Lame Bull looked far in the distance as they walked to the horse pen. Fox Running felt a slight twinge as he left the horse behind. The animal had become a silent piece of him.

"It is like yesterday," Lame Bull said, "when Crazy Horse tried to set his feet on the road of peace, and yet so much was lost so fast. So many friends are gone." Then he brightened.

"Yet there is life, Fox Running. Where there is life, there can be hope. See my children!"

Four children of varying ages burst from the lodge and ran to their father, calling greetings. A young woman Fox Running's age remained at the entrance to the lodge. She looked sullen at the interruption. She was tall for a girl, perhaps taller than Fox Running. She had been cooking on a large iron pot over an outdoor fire. A thin leather band circled the hair she wore in long braids, framing a thin face with extremely prominent cheekbones and a small nose. Her eyes barely bothered looking at Fox Running.

"Who is this, Father?" she asked. "If this is another one who spends his days telling everyone how brave he will be someday when cows leap the moon and jackals swim the lakes, tell him to leave now or I will poison the stew."

Lame Bull appeared to take this remarkable speech and lack of time-honored hospitality in stride.

"Fox Running, this is my eldest daughter, Morning Shadow, who as you can see is the subject of the attention of many young warriors. Fox Running has come to pay honor to a dead friend, Daughter. Until the moment of your rude greeting, he was not aware you existed, for I wished to show hospitality and did not wish to frighten him away by warning him."

This was delivered with near-amusement on the largely impassive face, which split wide in a grin when his daughter muttered something and moved to stir the stew.

"Morning Shadow is of age to be married," Lame Bull explained, "but she has made it very clear that the tradition of having her parents arrange her marriage is one she chooses not to follow. Because I, as an older man becoming less keen in wisdom, agreed so that my dinner would be properly cooked, she has become insufferable."

"And correct in my judgment of young men who can preen

but not provide," Morning Shadow replied, gesturing toward her father with a dripping, long, wooden spoon. A thin dog pounced to lick the drippings, almost knocking her over. Lame Bull laughed.

"What manner of bravery is it to talk and talk and talk and demand food for more talking? Let them feed themselves, listen to themselves, and perhaps, one fine day, drown themselves, and we shall have less work and more quiet!" Morning Shadow waved the dripping spoon as the dog pounced to slurp each drop.

Father and daughter locked glances, each looking vaguely amused as though this contest of insults was part of their daily conversation. Morning Shadow then turned her attention to Fox Running, as if trying to understand him in a look. The glance turned into an inspection that began with his scar and ended with his clearly well-worn guns.

"Welcome on your journey, traveler," she added, falling back on a traditional Lakota greeting as she looked at Fox Running directly. "What we have is poor, but we are richer if you share it with us."

"I am delighted to accept your hospitality," Fox Running said. "As long as I am not to be drowned for saying so!"

Lame Bull roared.

"White Deer!" the girl called to a young girl near the pot, who ran off when the words were spoken. "Out of that!"

"Their mother passed from a disease," said Lame Bull. "Morning Shadow, as my eldest, became their sister and their mother. In truth if she were to marry, I do not know how we would survive, for although I have three daughters and one son, my children all wish to be brave warriors and practice their craft constantly by attacking one another." He laughed loudly as a child no more than three or four came running to be lifted up

189

in her father's arms, babbling loudly. "I shall leave you to her mercy!"

"Why do you dress like a cowboy?" Morning Shadow asked. "Who made those moccasins? The dogs could sew straighter."

"I made them," Fox Running replied. "I spent the winter with some cowboys in Wyoming. Had we met at another time they might have been my enemies, but we met in winter when there was only life or death, and there was no time for that. I could not wear their big heavy boots, so I made these."

"You shall have a proper pair. Why do you wear guns? No one here wears them like that."

He did not want to tell her about the newspaper people and their lies. "I have come a long distance, and it was safer to travel this way."

"Did you know the trader at Fort Robinson? Or do you come from Fort Keogh?"

"I do not know anyone at the first," he said, not wanting to mention Fort Keogh. "I was last there as a child. I came from much farther away. I began my journey here in Boston."

"I do not know that place," she said. "Is it near the Yellowstone River or beyond the Black Hills?"

"It is far beyond them, in a land very different from this one."

She caught an inflection in his tone.

"Father will let you stay as long as you want. No one will care. The soldiers count us, to be sure the young braggarts are not becoming young warriors—as if they have the energy. The last time they counted us, the children ran off with some of the papers." She laughed. "To see white men running to gather pieces of paper as though they were the gold that drives them mad was amusing. When they realized we were laughing at them, they stopped."

He explained why he was there.

"Crow Rising!" she called. A boy of about ten peeked around the edge of the lodge.

"Take Fox Running to the Medicine Place." She turned back to him. "This is where we have our ceremonies. It is where they will want your friend's hair scattered. It is . . . it is a very holy place that is deep with spirits. You may wish to walk with them before your friend's ceremony."

Crow Rising led him to a clearing that was separated by trees from the main camp. "This is the place," said the boy. "Crazy Horse once had a vision here."

"Crazy Horse was a great man," Fox Running replied.

"You knew him? He has been dead for many years," the boy said.

"I was not much older than you are," Fox Running said, recalling his introduction to the famous warrior. "He was always very kind to boys, even as he was very hard on the enemies of the Lakota." Fox Running fell silent then as he took a measure of the circle, which had posts with ceremonial carvings around it.

"I will go back," Crow Rising said, clearly feeling uncomfortable.

Fox Running let him go, understanding the boy's reluctance. He had never been a child who spent much time with the spirit world. That the dead could reach into the world of the living and touch them was something that, when he was young, scared him more than comforted him.

He sat on a log at the edge of the circle of dirt. The boy's words had struck a nerve. Five years ago, he had met Crazy Horse. Five years. A matter of inches in the life of a tree; forever in the life of a boy. Crazy Horse had told him once that he believed many of the white people would never forgive the Lakota and Cheyenne for defeating Custer. However, from what Fox Running had learned in Boston, the white people reacted the same throughout history: if Indians resisted, they were attacked until they were dead. If they did not, their lands were simply taken away as if the Indians never existed. There were no ultimate victories, only perhaps spirits who would live in circles like these, until one day even these would be no more.

For the past five years, he had walked between two worlds, belonging to neither. Tall Bear's spirit would come home tomorrow. Would the same ever be said of his?

The ceremony to spread Tall Bear's hair was a mix of solemnity and celebration. The Lakota mourned the loss of a young man whose family had crossed the bridge to the spirit world before he did; yet they welcomed that a spirit who might have been trapped in some far-off white man's city would now be free to roam among the lands where he belonged. Lame Bull had told Fox Running that Tall Bear's family had been dead for years; that he was alone in the world when he went to the school.

As the leaders of the family that was sponsoring the ceremony, Lame Bull and Morning Shadow walked with Fox Running as they approached the fire in the center of the circle. In the next life, they said, Tall Bear would have two families—his and theirs.

Fox Running held tightly to the handkerchief that wrapped the hair he had carried with him for a year. The medicine man chanted about walking beyond the stars. Fox Running thought of the boy who was so sick for so long in Boston. Those final moments trying to find him a place where he would not be tossed with garbage. He almost jumped when Morning Shadow gripped his arm.

"They await you," she said. The scorning, scoffing girl was replaced by one wearing a wide-eyed, solemn mask.

Fox Running's hands trembled as he fumbled with the handkerchief. For a moment, he was afraid he would lose Tall Bear's hair in the wind. He threw the handkerchief and hair into the fire.

The flames flared a brilliant yellow. The Lakota gasped and murmured.

Then the medicine man sounded one long note that slowly rose as the voice of the elders, rose and rose until it was as high as that of a young girl. Silence hung upon its ending; then the drums began to beat.

Lame Bull and Morning Shadow were smiling now; no, grinning, as though something marvelous had taken place.

"Your friend has gone home," Morning Shadow told him. "The spirits sent him with yellow fire. Few spirits burn that brightly. It is a special sign from the spirits. They are happy; he is happy. You have done what your friend needed; he is now here forever with the trees and the rivers and the sky."

Both old and young started to dance around the fire. "What . . ." Fox Running began.

"Before, we mourned for the death of a young man so far from his people," she said. "Now we rejoice that he is home and will never be alone again. Come! Celebrate your friend's journey. Dance with us!"

For once, Fox Running had not worn the guns that had become a part of him. Now, he was glad, as the drums beat, a wooden flute emerged, and the Lakota celebrated that a spirit once caged by the white man had gone home. At first, he felt awkward, for as a boy his clumsiness at dancing had been a subject of constant mockery, and in the years since he had no reason to join any dances.

"Are you made of wood?" Morning Shadow mocked once as he tried not to make a fool of himself while she and her sisters and brother flowed with the sounds of the flute and drum.

"Like this!" Crow Rising shouted as he launched into an exuberant circuit of the circle while his family and the other dancers cheered. And Fox Running danced. He did not know if he danced well or poorly, but he could feel that, in the celebrating of the Lakota, he was, for the first time in years, beginning to feel whole.

Fox Running's plan had been to honor Tall Bear, then ride to the Tongue River Valley, where the Northern Cheyenne dwelt. He still had to find Rides a Crow and give her the message from Dead Face. He knew this was wrapped up in his destiny. Yet as the moon rose and fell, he remained with the Lakota.

"You are torn, young one." It was Blue Sparrow, one of the elders, who would stop from time to time when he sat by the river. She was revered for her wisdom and had watched Fox Running closely from the day of his arrival.

"There is given to me work that is not done," he said, "but I know not what it is, Grandmother. I can feel it calling, but I do not know what it wants of me."

"And you do not want this work?"

"For six years, Blue Sparrow, I have been without a place that was my home. Longer, if you count the time my family lived with the Lakota instead of the Cheyenne. I am tired of being without that which even the smallest child takes for granted. I do not want to take up any challenge, or fight more fights. Others can walk a road that does not demand this. Cannot I?"

"You speak of Morning Shadow."

For a moment, the young man smiled.

"She is a gift. Is she a gift for me? Was I sent to the Lakota to be with the Lakota from now until the day the sun turns dark?" He related his conversation with Dead Face shortly before the warrior went to his death. "Those few words remain even after all these years. But what do they mean? Must I leave to do what I must, or will that which I am meant to do find me? Life is hard and cold, Blue Sparrow. Must I turn aside one of the few good things I have ever found?"

The old woman was quiet. Then she spoke again.

"There will come a time when the spirits tell you what you must do. You know this and you fight against it in your heart and mind. Yet I can tell you that the ease you seek—and even the happiness you seek—will be nothing more than the rotted core of an apple that has been eaten by a worm until you have understood who you are and that which you are given to do. The spirits have preserved you on this journey for a reason. I do not know this reason, and you may not know it either, but you must learn it, or there will be no happiness for you or Morning Shadow."

Lame Bull closely observed the way his eldest daughter, who had once threatened a young warrior of broad chest and deep courage with having a pot of water dumped on his head for committing the affront of speaking to her, grew close to Fox Running.

The stew told him when she had one of her sisters tend the meal so she could walk with the Cheyenne. Crow Rising added to this store of information by spying on his sister when she walked away from the lodges with Fox Running, who remained a quiet presence with Lame Bull's family. The young man said little, but if there was a chore to be done, a word to be said to one of the children, or something for which a family needed help, he was there.

Morning Shadow had hidden Fox Running's moccasins and presented him with ones she made herself, telling him the ones he made were too ugly to be seen. She had also asked him to teach her how to shoot a rifle, which he did.

"She tells him stories about the Star Warriors, and they watch the river," Crow Rising told his father. "He touches her when they shoot the gun, and their hands hold each other's by the river." Yet Crow Rising made it very certain that nothing wrong took place between them.

Still, Lame Bull knew the young man would need to be spoken to. It was clear he needed schooling in proper Lakota customs if he were to become a Lakota and marry into their family, for the family could never be parted from its people. If he were serious about Morning Shadow, there were ways this must be expressed.

Lame Bull was also troubled that soldiers from Dahlgren Post, the army camp outside the Great Sioux Reservation's borders, seemed interested in Fox Running. Questions had been asked about him specifically not long after he arrived, which was unusual. Lame Bull knew the army had spies within the reservation. Army interest in anyone could be a sign of trouble. Lame Bull would watch and wait.

Warm days merged as spring greened the land. Young Lakota warriors who were the age of Fox Running began to appear at the lodge. Some were trouble and wanted to make war to be famous. Others were simply young in the ways of the young, who knew their fathers and their fathers' fathers earned respect by their deeds against the enemies of the Lakota. Fox Running turned aside their various schemes for raids. Sometimes, the young men replied to his rejection with scorn. At times, he could see Morning Shadow trying to understand a warrior who would not fight. But to him, war and fighting were not play. They were nothing more than death, and he had not come to the Lakota to wallow further in what he hoped to avoid.

CHAPTER FOURTEEN

May 1882, Great Sioux Reservation, Dakota Territory
Far Trees staggered in from the northern part of the Great Sioux Reservation. He had been following a deer when he came upon prospectors who were well within Lakota lands. Hunting for gold was prohibited there, as all the Lakota knew. The men had shot Far Trees in his arm.

The young warriors began to clamor for permission to avenge the slight to the law and the Lakotas' dignity. Messengers were sent to Dahlgren Post and the army to complain about the incursion and the attack. Lakota young men said this was useless. They feared these prospectors might be the first wave of new ones the army allowed on the land as a pretext to further reduce the size of the reservation.

Although still too young to be a warrior, Crow Rising had been asked by the young men to serve as a scout, for he was a restless boy who knew all the trails that could allow them to surprise the prospectors.

Fox Running had gone down to the river alone once again. He was unsure of his feelings for Morning Shadow. He knew they were both of an age when men took wives, for life was often short. Yet he had lived most of his recent life alone. He was uncertain of her feelings, for he had never spoken to girls and knew none of their ways and was leery of saying words that would change the pleasant nature of the weeks he had spent here.

"Fox Running!" Morning Shadow was running through the trees.

"What is wrong?"

"They are going to attack the prospectors! Crow Rising is going with them. You need to go to protect him. He is the only boy in our family, and he wants to prove himself. He is only a warrior in his own mind, Fox Running. They want him only to scout, but he will not hang back."

"What do you want me to do?"

"Go with them, of course! They are boys, Fox Running. They think this is some kind of game. I know I am a girl and women are not supposed to know anything, but even I know that white men do not play at war. They fight to kill. The young men will think they can be heroes like Crazy Horse and ride men down, but they will be killed. I know you are like them in age, but you know more about war than they can imagine. Please?"

Part of him wanted to reply that he was younger than Crow Rising when he fired a gun at the Greasy Grass, and that warriors needed to learn on their own. Yet she was intent and came to him for help.

"I will go," he said. "If he wishes to be foolhardy, I cannot stop him, but I will go."

She nodded. "I am glad to see you are learning to do what I say," she added. "It is something that is good in a Lakota husband!"

Laughing at the way his mouth hung open, she grabbed his arm and pulled. "We will talk later. Following Hare told me I needed to say something or you never would. She knows much of this. Now we must hurry! I hope they have not left."

With a mix of emotions, Fox Running followed her through the trees and back to the camp.

The young men were mounted. A cheer emerged as Fox Running announced he would ride with them. He buckled the belt around his hips, the first time in days he had worn it. The horse was almost fat from rest. Fox Running visited the horse daily to check on him but had ridden him sparingly since they had come to Pine Ridge. Now, he would ride hard.

Fox Running could tell from the sun they were taking a wide circle east before turning north. Although the prospectors were in a heavily wooded area of the reservation, all of the Lakota young men stayed mounted as they picked their way through the trees. None would consent to be left behind with the horses.

Fox Running rode at the rear, telling himself he would be content to let them make mistakes so long as nothing hurt Crow Rising. In time, the line of horses moved slower and slower until it stopped.

The prospectors had set up a considerable camp. They had been there some time. The cabin looked stout. Fox Running counted eight men. There could be more inside. There were fourteen Lakota young men. Now he was concerned. The Lakota would be at a disadvantage fighting hardened prospectors, who must have known that sooner or later they would run into trouble and would be prepared for it. He could see rifles propped against some wooden structures through which water passed. There were men at them, probably looking for gold. Others had flat metal dishes and were in the creek itself. None seemed aware they had been spotted.

Right Owl, the oldest youth, told the Lakota to split up and charge the men, one group coming from each direction. To Fox Running, it was a sensible way to attack if the men had been animals being hunted. They were not. These animals would fight, not run.

A creek separated the Lakota from the prospectors. Fox Running was unsure how deep it was, but it would be hard for the Lakota to attack across it while they were under fire from the gold miners. If the prospectors retreated into the cabin, there was little the Lakota could do about it.

"I am sure this plan is very good, but if we take more time to circle around them and attack from those trees on that side of the creek, they will not expect it," Fox Running said. "They will have the creek at their backs, and they cannot run. They will have to surrender."

"I do not want them to surrender," said Right Owl. Others murmured their assent. "They have come upon our land. They need to learn what it means to show disrespect to the Lakota. They should pay the price!"

"You cannot kill them all," said Fox Running. "And if you do, the army will ride in to avenge them. Take them alive."

"That is not how the Lakota fight," replied Right Owl, who Fox Running knew was one of the warriors Morning Shadow had rudely told to leave her alone when he told her he wanted her to move into his lodge. "If our Cheyenne guest who spends his days walking with women wishes to watch, we will show our brother how it is done."

Fox Running lifted the guns from their holsters and set them down again lightly. They would be needed soon. He looked for Crow Rising.

"It is the way of my people to think and talk before we attack," he replied. "I have said what I felt should be said. Where do you wish me to be?"

Fortunately, Right Owl put him near Crow Rising on the far right end of the group. At least he could help keep an eye on the boy.

The time the Lakota had spent talking was more than enough for birds and small animals to know there was danger and leave. One quick-witted prospector either saw motion or noticed how the wild things were reacting.

"Zeb! Think we got comp'ny!" The miners were large men, rough-hewn in a rough world, but they moved fast to grab rifles.

As their hands closed around their Winchesters, a howl emerged from the center of the Lakota line. One dumbfounded prospector, knee deep in the creek, held his mining pan in both hands as he saw the yelling face of Right Owl emerge from the trees. Right Owl jumped into the water, but his moccasin-clad foot slid on a stone.

Clang! A bullet glanced off the pan. The man's arms shot into the air. He dropped it as though scalded and surrendered to Right Owl. A wild volley of rifle fire came from the Lakota, who stopped to fire as they reached the creek water.

Fox Running, whose first shot had hit the mining pan to be sure Right Owl did not die from his rashness, sent his next bullets into the wood of the cabin to keep anyone with a rifle from having an easy shot at picking off the Lakota.

One man took cover behind a trough to aim at Crow Rising. Fox Running's bullet hit him in either the leg or foot, sending the man to the ground. Fox Running fired twice more, exhausting the gun, then drew his other pistol. Although he could not fire a gun accurately with his left hand, he always liked to have one ready. He holstered the empty one and snapped off six quick shots at where the miners were clustered together. He ducked behind a tree, broke open the cylinder to reload, did the same with the other pistol, and then realized why the gunfire had slackened and died.

Four of the men grouped together now had their hands up. The man who had fired first was on the ground, dead from the looks of him. Two others were wounded, both men at whom Fox Running had aimed. The man who had surrendered in the creek was already in the hands of the Lakota, who had only to grab hold of him to make him plead with them not to scalp him.

Right Owl looked at Fox Running with a different face than before as the Cheyenne came to where the Lakota young men kept their rifles pointed at those who surrendered.

"You have won," Fox Running called.

"I have never seen anyone but a cowboy shoot like that," said Right Owl.

"I lived in their world; I had to learn their tricks," Fox Running replied. "You have won a great victory. You will have to show the village what you have done!"

The miners, it was agreed, would be marched to the village. Right Owl was savoring his moment of glory. Then they would be turned over to the army. Fox Running breathed a sigh of relief that no one else would be killed. Killing started a wave of retribution that would never end. Miners who lived to tell the tale of being caught would be a warning to others to leave the Lakota lands alone. For now.

In the meantime, the Lakota young men energetically set about the task of wrecking the array of wooden boxes and structures the miners had built. The wood was piled next to the cabin to be set on fire.

"That's ours, and we bought it!" said one of the miners, who became bolder as they realized they would not be killed. "They said when we hit gold we'd be rich. This is all legal, they told us!" The prospectors were adamant that they had a perfect right to be mining gold on Lakota land.

"Who told you that you could seek gold on Lakota land?" Fox Running asked.

The miner who did the talking for them was silent. Fox Running's fear was not that occasional miners would evade the rules and seek gold on reservation lands. That was to be expected. These were neither the first nor the last. His greater fear was that someone in the army was telling miners to come pan for gold on the Lakota reservation, knowing that in time an incident like this would happen. If that was the case, the young men might have unwittingly helped their enemies, and he with them.

Right Owl lit the flame after all the wood was piled. They had doused it in kerosene from a jug in the cabin. Fox Running doubted it would all burn, or that it would take the cabin with it, but the Lakota had won a victory, and all were coming home alive. Days so good were rare.

Fox Running lagged behind the rest of the warriors. He told Crow Rising to tell them his horse appeared lame, but he would catch up. It was a lie. He did not wish to be part of a parade of young men and miners. He had already been far more famous than he ever wanted. He rode the horse to the pony herd and then drifted through the village to the lodge of Lame Bull. There was a conversation to be resumed with Morning Shadow.

Time to speak privately was measured in the beating of birds' wings after his return to the lodge. First, she had been hauling water. Then Crow Rising returned and had to tell a story that was often the same as truth multiple times. Lame Bull arrived and needed to hear both the boy's story and that of Fox Running. There was a feast in the evening, and the families of all who participated were being honored.

He was certain the words they spoke were on her mind, for their eyes met often during the feast, and also in the long hours after, when the fire burned high, and the Lakota celebrated that, despite their losses, the warriors of the future were proud and strong.

Thumping feet heralded the morning. Lame Bull rose when his name was called.

"You must come," said the panting, urgent-faced boy to Lame Bull. Then he saw Fox Running emerge from the lodge. "And you as well."

A small cavalry contingent had arrived at the ceremonial gate that marked the entrance of the reservation. Some others were with them, in Eastern clothes.

Fox Running hung back as they reached the contingent of soldiers. He recognized Malvers, who so many years ago had spoken of his desire to rid the Plains of Indians. He was the leader of the soldiers who had come from Dahlgren Post. Without a glance at Fox Running, Malvers rushed to intercept Lame Bull.

"What have you done? Yesterday one of your runners told us there were prospectors on your lands, and now before I can decide what to do about it, I hear that you have killed them!"

"Men broke the law," said Lame Bull gravely, as befit a leader of the Lakota designated to keep the peace and deal with the soldiers when the peace was broken. "Men who break the law are criminals under my law or your law. We summoned you, but there were only words that came and nothing more. The young men did not wait. They do not believe in your justice, because it does not protect our people. There were eight. One was killed and two are wounded. The rest are . . . there they are!"

A collection of fearful, bedraggled miners walked toward the soldiers. Two were carrying a man with a bandage around his lower right leg and foot. Two others carried an improvised stretcher that bore a miner shot glancingly in the chest. The man was in pain but would live. A miner and a soldier carried a stretcher with the blanket-covered body of the miner who was killed.

"They shot at the young men. The young men shot back. If your people break the law, they must suffer what happens to those who break laws. That is what you tell us when our young men break your laws," Lame Bull said defiantly.

"They have broken the law by shooting these men," said Malvers. "I will take them with me."

Enough Lakota knew enough English that the impact of his words caused anger to ripple through the growing crowd.

"That would not be wise, Captain Malvers, unless you want to start an Indian war and be the first to die." Fox Running stepped forward. He was afraid the Lakota might fight back if their young men were arrested. Unless Malvers wanted to provoke a fight, he needed to know that would be a mistake. Malvers needed to be told in a way that made it look like it was in his best interest, because he would be happy to kill Indians if given the chance.

"Who are you, that you know me?" Malvers said with asperity. He turned to Lame Bull. "Who is this?"

"My name is Fox Running, and I am the Cheyenne boy you knew many years ago when Shoulder Bar Van Diver was your friend. The one you told how much you hated Indians. Remember?"

The officer's mouth hung open. He stared at Fox Running.

"In the time since I saw you, I was sent to school in Boston. They tried to beat the Indian out of me. They failed. But they taught me much. They taught me about the laws of your treaties. Under the treaty between the Lakota and the United States government that was passed by Congress, it is trespassing for white men to be on Lakota Indian land for purposes of taking from the soil any gold or other deposits. The army is required to arrest those guilty of trespass and assist tribal authorities in preventing such trespass. I can recite some of the treaty if you wish, but it means that just as you would beat about the head a thief who came to dig for gold in your cellar, the Lakota have the right to defend what is left of the land that has been granted to them and to defend themselves as necessary. If you arrest them, you are breaking the law, and your superiors will hear of it, and you will be broken to a lieutenant, if not drummed out of the army, and you will be the one left with nothing, Captain Malvers."

Fox Running was quite proud of the speech once it was finished. It might even be true, since treaties were always filled with generous promises the white men who wrote them never intended to honor.

Malvers was still staring. He grew red in the face and chewed at the ends of his mustache as Fox Running continued.

"The only ones you have authority under the law to arrest are those who have broken the law. The Lakota held them for you. You may even look under the blanket to be sure that the dead man was not scalped; I know there is a fascination with that among your people."

"You! I told Van Diver you were trouble. All of you are trouble. He should have taken my advice."

"You have taken much from the Lakota, Captain, but you have not taken the right to defend themselves against those who steal, unless you wish to tell Lame Bull and all of the Lakota here that the treaty was nothing more than a sham?"

Behind Malvers, a lively discussion had broken out between a civilian and some of the soldiers who accompanied Malvers.

"What is it, Greenwood?" Malvers snapped at a sergeant trying to whisper something in his ear. The sergeant finished what he wanted to say, speaking softly and looking repeatedly at Fox Running.

"Is he sure?" Malvers asked. The sergeant nodded.

"Well, then," Malvers told the man, a sly, sick smile forming. "Very good." Something had been said to make him swagger and sneer. "On my signal."

Fox Running had lived wild long enough to know when men were trying to hide what was really taking place. Something bad was happening. His heart raced. Instinct said to fight or run, but he could do neither.

Malvers spoke earnestly with Lame Bull as if stepping back from his threats in words designed to ease the tension. But the men behind him were not relaxing. They were taking very deliberate, casual steps apart from one another. Not one of the soldiers was looking at him, even as they looked at the others. That meant he was the one they were focused upon. He had left his guns at Lame Bull's lodge. Malvers's horse was too far away to be reached quickly enough that he could mount and outrun eighteen rifles.

"Now!"

Every soldier pointed his gun at Fox Running.

Malvers did not make the mistake of blocking their shots. "Sergeant Greenwood!"

"Sir!"

"Please ask Mr. McAllister to step forward. We shall do this properly."

Carson McAllister, the veteran Wild West correspondent for Wallace's *Frontier News,* strolled into view. "This is the Cheyenne Kid!" he said with self-conscious theatrics as he pointed dramatically at Fox Running. A man with a pencil, sketching furiously, was trying to draw the scene.

"Him? He's the one that killed Harry," said the miner Fox Running had shot in the leg. "Shot him from behind, he did."

"Ought to hang him!" called out another miner, courage appearing in proportion to the number of guns protecting him.

"What is this?" protested Lame Bull. "This is Blazing Fire of the Lakota. He was adopted by Crazy Horse into the Lakota."

"No!" retorted Malvers. "This is a Cheyenne named Fox Running who is off the reservation without permission because every mother's son of those heathens escaped, and that makes him subject to army law!"

Fox Running looked at McAllister. If he could have reached out his hands he would have grabbed the man by the neck and shaken him. Or worse. Instead, he tried to speak mildly as if this was all just a mistake.

"I do not know this 'Cheyenne Kid' person you speak of. I have never seen you in my life. How can you lie that you know me?"

"That scar!" retorted the writer. "The folks in Fort Riley said it was burning red when you shot Clay Atcheson. Heard the same at Rock Springs when you attacked that man with a knife. That Kansas farmer told me about it; that Irish girl with the red hair said you was just the height you are. Even that man in Missouri who lied for you described you the same way with that scar. I got you!"

Fox Running was no stranger to hate. The night he left Boston, he wanted so much he could taste it to take the gun into Petengill's bedroom at the school and shoot the man to repay him for all the beatings. Yet nothing he felt was close to the hate he felt for this man who had lied about him and stalked him and now made the army arrest him. He knew he had done wrong in his past, but that was years before, and since then he had tried to live down that shame.

"I am Blazing Fire as named by Crazy Horse, who declared me his ward," Fox Running declared. "As a Lakota, even if I was also born in the lands of the Cheyenne and am known to the Cheyenne as Fox Running, you have no grounds to arrest me on Lakota land."

"You can't let him talk his way out of this!" McAllister expostulated. "I tell you, he's the Cheyenne Kid!"

Time. He needed time. He was vaguely aware of Lame Bull and others with him, but he felt alone.

"You say I have broken laws," he told McAllister. "Yet from the things I read when someone once showed me your scribblings, there was nothing that was not common to life in one of your towns. You can hardly pretend that your newspaper carries the truth. Just because you wrote it does not mean it happened."

Fox Running looked at Malvers. "Did this man who claims I am some name he has made up to sell newspapers ever have proof I have broken a law? Does the army now arrest men just because someone wrote a tale that was published?"

"Keep your guns on him," Malvers ordered his soldiers. "McAllister, I must talk with you."

Lame Bull studied the sky intently. "The miners' cabin," he said randomly, speaking Lakota. The man's head seemed to have developed a twitch.

"No talking to the prisoner. Move away from the prisoner!" Lieutenant Greenwood demanded. He moved in closer to push Lame Bull away.

Malvers wagged his finger in the correspondent's face. "Was there a wanted notice? Did any of those places actually want this man arrested? You said he was wanted. Is that the truth? If I arrest an innocent man, my colonel will bust me to a private."

McAllister would not let Malvers deny him his greatest triumph. He could see there was bad blood between Malvers and the Indian and tried to exploit it. "Of course he was wanted by the law. I don't carry the posters with me, but, once you arrest him, I'm sure there will be even more crimes that will come to light! That is, if he does not get killed trying to escape."

Malvers's lips twisted into a vicious smile.

"Yes. Yes. That could easily happen."

The two men each took a step back toward Fox Running.

As Lame Bull argued with the soldier, Fox Running could see Crow Rising holding the dog that often lived with Lame Bull. The dog was bucking to be released. Fox Running's eyes met the boy's.

One soldier, nerves stretched to the breaking point, screamed as the dog lurched against his leg. He sent a bullet whistling over the group. Greenwood ducked. Lame Bull lurched into him, and they both went down.

Lame Bull pointed at the dog and began to yell at the boy to catch him. The boy darted into the line of soldiers chasing the dog, which ran into their legs and bounded off. Malvers turned away from McAllister at the sound of the shot.

Fox Running knew this was his only chance. He ran into the line of soldiers—who could not fire for fear of hitting one another—then, as they were trying to regain order, ran twenty feet beyond them to where their horses were left.

"Escape! Escape! Prisoner escaping!" he heard one voice call out.

"Kill him!" That from Malvers.

One gun fired. Another.

Pushing aside the horse-holder grabbing the reins of five horses, Fox Running put a foot in the stirrup of one and used the horse as a shield as the other horses, now loose, galloped into the pack of soldiers seeking a clear shot. He heard the rifles fire wildly. He was on the horse's back. The other horses had run past. The soldiers were in line.

He dug his heels into the horse's flanks. One ragged volley. He guided the horse to the right side of the path, and then to the left, in hopes they would miss.

The next volley found him. One bullet skinned his left leg. Another caught him under his right arm. A third stung him in the neck.

There were two more volleys he heard, but he was out of range, having rounded a curve in the trail. Pursuit would come soon. He dismounted. Wounded, he would be no match for fresh horsemen. If he was hit, the horse might have been wounded, too.

He pulled the rifle from its scabbard and stuffed as many shells as he could in his pockets. There were two spare shirts in the horse's saddlebags, a dented metal flask that contained foul-smelling liquor, and the kind of thick stockings soldiers wore under their boots. He took those and swatted at the horse, which was soon gone.

Fox Running tried to orient himself by the sun. North. He would go north. He started to move into the trees and out of the puddle in which he was standing. Then he noticed it was not water, but blood from his leg wound. He took one of the stockings and wrapped it around the place the bullet had ripped his leg. It would bleed as long as he moved, but there was no choice. What mattered most was that the soldiers have no trail by which they could find him.

After reaching the trees, he heard the mounted soldiers ride by. The sound made him walk faster. It would not be long before they caught the riderless horse. If any were smart enough to backtrack to where he had bled, they could find where he went into the woods.

The sun, as best he could see it through the trees, was high in the sky. He stopped. He looked down on his right side; blood from the wound in his neck had saturated his shirt. He could feel weakness, as though if he were to lie down, he might not ever rise. The pain under his right arm was throbbing and hot. He must keep moving.

He was lost. He could feel panic rising but sought to control it. He had not come from Boston to die here. Or had he? Would his spirit walk with Tall Bear if he died on this spot? There could be worse fates.

He braced his left hand against a pine as he gulped air. There had been no trail to follow through the trees. He was guessing directions. He was very thirsty now. He breathed deeply. Smoke. It was faint. It could be a fire from someone camping alone. It could be something else. He followed the smell. His eyes soon told him he was getting close as they watered. There it was—the cabin of the prospectors! Charred up two walls, but it was still standing.

The creek was running clear. Water. That was what he needed. He reeled to its edge and dropped to both knees. He drank as deeply as he could. He splashed his face to revive himself. Then he rose to his feet and watched as the cabin moved left and then right, but no matter which way he walked it did not get closer. He closed his eyes to make them work properly and then reopened them. The cabin slid on its side. Then the sun dazzled against the leaves. And then there was nothing.

CHAPTER FIFTEEN

"Mother?" Long, soft fingers were pushing the hair off his temples and touching his head with something wet.

"Shhh," came the woman's voice.

Doe Leaping was alive! She was there. It had been so long. He wanted to tell her where he had been. She would be proud. But rough bark lips would not part to speak, and the effort of moving them was immense. He would tell later. Soon.

The world was black. There were legends of a world like this, where unworthy warriors went to spend forever in darkness and cold, where their eyes would never see the sun.

"No!"

A hand touched his arm; his forehead.

"What is this place?"

"Shh!" The hand softly covered his mouth. It smelled of earth and something bitter—a medicine from roots.

"Where am I?"

"Speak softly," the woman cautioned. "Do you remember the soldiers? They shot you. We are hiding. You must be quiet. They may be near."

"I tried to shoot them, Mother. I am not a coward, no matter what they say."

"Shh," the woman said. "We will talk later. Sleep now."

He felt his head being moved to lie upon her shoulder. Her arm held him close. She was warm. He could smell a scent of pine smoke in her hair. Her breathing was slow and even. In time, he followed it to a place of peace.

There was light filtering in. He could see something. He did not know where he was. He tried to move. His side was fire and pain. The place where he lay moved sideways as he pushed himself up. Tree bark was at his back. A square of light was ahead of him, beckoning.

He lurched. Pain rose. He fought it down. He lurched again. Sudden bright light made him cover his eyes. Something made noise, and then it was dark again. Feet ran.

"Sister, he is walking," he heard a child-like voice say. It was familiar, but everything was strange.

"Stir this," came an order. That voice was also familiar.

The blinding light was back. So was the woman.

"It seems you did not wish to die," she said. She took his arm. She held on hard. "Let us hope for both our sakes this is a good thing. Walk toward the light."

He was blinking and all but blinded. Then he understood as he felt the warmth of the sun on his face.

"Where am I?"

"You are at the miners' cabin, Blazing Fire, or Fox Running, or Cheyenne Kid, or whatever other name you have that I do not yet know."

"Oooh." It was coming back. The soldiers. Morning Shadow was here. For a moment, he felt sadness, recalling his delusion that his mother was alive.

"They spent days looking for you, but they gave up."

"Morning Shadow."

"We have been caring for you," she said.

"I thought . . ."

"You called me your mother for the first days."

"I . . . she has been dead since the fight on the Rosebud," he said. "She and my sister went off with the others, and I never saw them again. I thought . . ."

"I know. When warriors would come back from a raid, many of those dying or badly wounded thought they were being cared for by their mothers. Perhaps it is because all warriors are only overgrown boys!"

The smile behind the words was kind.

"Blue Sparrow pulled the bullet from you. She has pulled bullets from many men. She said you will heal, but you will be sore for many days. The other wounds stopped bleeding the first night after we put a mixture on them from the roots that grow here. Father came the first night. We dragged you inside the cabin. The prospectors believed the cabin was burned, and no one thought to look for you here. The army still hunts for you, but Father has managed to keep them from looking everywhere that is reservation land."

"How long has it been?"

"Nine days," she replied. "Did you really know Crazy Horse?"

"I was not much older than Crow Rising," he replied.

"Why did that mean white man call you the Cheyenne Kid?"

She knew little about newspapers. He explained that in the East, people liked to read about the West, and that newspapers often told stories that were wildly exaggerated.

"This man makes it sound as though I have done wrong, and I have not," he said. "I can explain."

"If you wish to, you should do it on a day when you are healthier," she said. "I do not care. I do not really understand. You are like no one else I know. You do many things that white people do, but you are an Indian, and the soldiers want to arrest you. You have been good to me and to my family. I know what I see, and I care not for what people say who I do not know. The soldier you spoke to was very angry when he left, but he seemed as angry at the man in the checkered vest as he was at you."

Fox Running went to pull his right hand through his hair. The wounds in his side and neck reminded him abruptly that it was a bad idea.

"You are alive, Fox Running," said Morning Shadow. "You are not healed. You must stay here for now. I shall return, but not often."

She had something else to say that she clearly did not wish to express.

"Father warned me there could be young warriors who saw us in the days before you were hurt and were jealous, and they might tell the soldiers where you are as a way to be rid of you. He warned me to stay away as much as possible so that no one suspects. He believes there are Lakota who have been turned into spies by the army. I will be gone perhaps a day, but I will return. You must not try to leave, for we do not know who may be in the woods seeking you."

He reached out his left hand. She touched his fingers with hers.

"We did not talk of the things I wish to speak about," he told her.

"I will bring more stew," she replied, with a glint in her eye. "Of what else could you possibly be speaking, unless the fever from your wounds is making you say more things that are mine to recall and yours to wonder about?"

"What did I say?"

"I shall consider telling you another time." Now she was openly smiling. "I will be back!"

She was, and they talked of many things. She was the only one to whom Fox Running confided the story of all he had ever done. She told him the spirits understood that people made mistakes. She talked much of the spirit world to him, of how whether he knew them or not, his ancestors were trying to guide him. As time healed his body, his soul began to heal as well.

Carson McAllister was livid. He was certain there would be a showdown that would be a fitting end to the story of the Cheyenne Kid. Now, only two weeks after the daring escape he'd chronicled in his columns, he had received a telegram from the newspaper's office in Boston that he was to come back by train as soon as possible. Meddlers! When he asked to remain, the order was repeated in increasingly stern words and with the harsh tones of an ultimatum.

Bronson Malvers was equally enraged.

"This is ridiculous, sir!" he told Colonel Harold Meyers, who had summoned Malvers to his office and told him that his request for a full-scale hunt for Fox Running had been rejected. Malvers remembered that Fox Running had been possibly linked to the Black Canyon Gang, which operated in Montana in 1878. He wanted that used as a pretext to arrest Fox Running for being the Cheyenne Kid. Another report had confirmed that Fox Running took five pounds of bacon and ten pounds of flour from an army patrol last fall.

"That boy is a hostile who deserves to be hung now before he begins another war. I was this close to arresting him. My request to return with a full battalion, sir, will ensure that we find whatever hole he went into and pull him out of it! In the weeks since we failed to arrest him, he has had time to create a new war that will kill civilians."

Meyers looked at Malvers intently. Intense soldiers were like loaded weapons. Only sometimes useful. "What is our job here, Captain?"

"To kill the Indians, sir, until they are no longer a threat!"

"NO!" Meyers slammed his palm on the desk and rose. "Our

217

job is to protect the peace, Malvers. I have reviewed the incidents that the newspapers have used to describe this so-called Cheyenne Kid, including the gunfight in Fort Riley. I can see little that warrants an arrest. Did he ride with a gang four years ago? What if he did? He was fourteen or fifteen! He killed one of them! Will a jury support you?"

"We do not need to try him, sir. We can just arrest him, and let nature take its course."

"And kill him? No, Malvers, that is not how the U.S. Army operates. As for the escapade last fall, do you think the army wants to tell the story of how one man faced down a dozen soldiers and walked off with rations without firing a shot?"

"I want him out of the way, sir!" Malvers insisted. "He is a malcontent and a hostile. He should be put down."

Meyers tried to hold in his anger and explain to Malvers why he was wrong. "Some of you soldiers operate as though exterminating the Indians is the way to peace. It is a path to war. If he were white, we would laugh at anyone who said we should arrest him. The army does not arrest gunslingers, much as we might wish to. Captain Van Diver sent me a long letter from San Francisco. Apparently the frontier rags sell very well there. He said he does not believe the young man is a threat to the peace unless we make him so, and by doing so make him a hero for every Sioux or Cheyenne warrior-child who wants to follow him. Then there will be a Cheyenne Kid gang roaming the territory!"

"But sir . . ."

"I am speaking!" Malvers was silenced. "From what I hear through those who we pay on the reservation to warn us, he is not a hothead, not a war chief, and not a leader of any group. What is even more disturbing are the comments from the prospectors, who said they were told by a soldier that panning for gold on Lakota lands would entitle them to the protection of the U.S. Army."

"Sir, my words . . ."

"Are hanging you, Captain. Did you fight in the War Between the States?"

"No, sir."

"I did. I killed Southern boys, some of whom I now command; some of whom sent their children to fight in this army. Some of them killed Northern boys. What is my point, Captain? The war is over! We are not killing each other today because we have accepted the war is over. The war against the Indians out here is also over. Most of them, like Red Cloud, know that. Sitting Bull understands it. Even Little Wolf—that Cheyenne who led his people back from Indian Territory—only wants a place where they can live by themselves. For my money, Captain, Custer was a glory hound who got what was coming to him by trying to kill every Indian he found to make a name for himself."

"Sir, I . . ."

"We may yet have another war up here, Captain, but it will not be because you manufactured it! Dismissed! If you tell one more miner to pan for gold because you will protect him, you can do so on your own and not as part of this army. If you continue to consort with shady characters who believe the army will protect them, I will get to the bottom of the rumors I hear about your conduct and those with whom you associate when you are off this post. You will not like that one bit! Go!"

The train from St. Louis would be idealized in the brochures as luxurious. After two days, it was dirty and cramped, at least according to McAllister's back and legs. Every time he wanted to get up and walk, the engineer sped up, and they rocked from side to side, spilling part of the mediocre whiskey that was the best the railroad served.

He reached the offices of Wallace's *Frontier News* expecting a royal welcome only to find there were hardly any familiar faces. He would speak with Trent the editor about the lack of deference shown him by the clerks. No one asked him if he wanted coffee or tea while he waited.

When he was finally allowed into Trent's office, by a young woman who looked at him with little respect and less interest, his vulgar summation of the state of the newspaper offices was quickly silenced by the presence of an imposing-looking woman who stood behind Trent.

"I am Katherine McGillicuddy," she said. "I now own this newspaper. You will recount for me all of the facts behind your stories about the Cheyenne Kid. I understand your craft, as you see it, requires a certain fluidity in your handling of the truth, but in this case I wish to know the facts as they are. Do you understand, or are you too drunk? Only those things that are certifiable, verifiable, and honest facts."

An hour later, after extensive stammering, vast probing and continued thunderous tapping of a very expensive black leather woman's boot on the floor, McAllister finished wiping the perspiration from his forehead.

"You may leave now," the McGillicuddy woman instructed him. "Remain in the anteroom."

Several moments later, she swept out of the place without even appearing to notice his presence.

A shaken Trent summoned an equally shaken McAllister into his office. He poured them both generous measures of liquid from a cut-glass decanter. "The Cheyenne Kid is history," he said. "Over. No more. If you want to write about him, you can do so for another publication."

"I made that story!" McAllister fulminated. "No one else could have taken that material and created a tale that would sell! I know there's more to the story. That brave is going to go on a scalping spree yet!"

"If you want to write for us, you can go to Missouri. I convinced her no one could write the story of Bob Ford shooting Jesse James like you could. There will be James stories for weeks and weeks. If not, it was nice knowing you."

"Just like that?"

"Just like that. She owns the *Frontier News*. She bought it over the winter. She made it clear she is going to run it. She has some source out in Wyoming or Montana that is feeding her information, and she's killed any further Cheyenne Kid stories. I have no idea why. This is final. A train leaves for Missouri in the morning. We will buy your ticket, unless you wish to make other arrangements and go back to Dakota."

"The same rates? I'm not being cut?"

"Same rates, Carson. I'll send a boy to buy your ticket and another to get you a hotel. The Grand, as I recall? I think under the circumstances we can afford to cover that and your meal."

McAllister agreed to the terms that offered him little room for argument and left the office building. He needed the money, so he would let the Cheyenne Kid get away for now. He would keep the soldier, Malvers, informed, though, that if there was anything new about the Cheyenne Kid there would be money for Malvers if the tip panned out. There would be other magazines to write for, and he would start looking once he left Boston and was back in the world where women knew their place. No Indian lover would get in his way. He had lost this round, but sooner or later, he would track down that Cheyenne Kid and get revenge. Sooner or later.

John Dooley counted again. Twenty-one dollars and eighty-eight cents. With the monthly rent due next week to Mrs. Callahan for his rooms, he would be down to less than fifteen dollars. He could hardly not pay her, for the notice of a few days would be wrong for a woman who had been kind to him in the four years he had boarded with her.

But money was now going to be scarce. Not surprisingly, the Indian School refused to pay him his final wages after he announced his intention to quit. Darby, in fact, told him to leave immediately. Petengill, who had wanted Dooley fired for months, was gone recruiting.

The final blow had come when a boy named Porcupine Song was injured when "resisting discipline," when the truth of the matter was that math teacher Price had slammed his head into a wall to prove a point. Dooley had given Price a taste of his own medicine, then announced his plan to quit.

That was two weeks ago. Since then, the warehouses Dooley knew needed guards had no openings for him. To him it was clear: Darby was telling others not to hire him. Dooley was contemplating leaving Boston, but there was no place to go. His body was perhaps healthy and strong enough for a job on the docks, but he knew he was getting older. Perhaps a season there while he hoped for some other position.

A horse clip-clopped past the neat rooming house. He heard the rattle of a carriage bouncing on the rough paving stones of the street. He had idly noted the sounds because they were unusual in a working-class neighborhood. Some new driver. Or a drunk. The sounds stopped abruptly.

A short while later, Mavis Callahan swung open the door. It was, Dooley noted, the first time ever that she had not knocked. She was so flustered he knew some excitement caused this breach of manners. "You . . . you have a guest, Mr. Dooley. I showed her to the parlor."

Her?

"Mrs. Callahan," said Dooley, who knew the woman was as good a soul as could be numbered in Boston, "you must be confused."

"No, sir. I do not get confused. She asked for John Dooley,

late of the Indian School of Boston and once of the Fifty-seventh Massachusetts Infantry," the landlady said, precisely mimicking the tone of the guest.

Dooley had been lounging in a shirt and vest. He threw an old jacket over them and followed Mavis Callahan to see who could have any business with a man no one wanted.

He recognized her immediately.

"Miss McGillicuddy," he said, inclining his head as he tried to recall how single women who were powerful and important were supposed to be addressed. "It has been some time since I saw you. Are you well?"

Katherine McGillicuddy enjoyed pleasantries almost as much as coddling fools. She gave Dooley a quick, thorough inspection. He passed.

"You were Fox Running's friend," she said directly. "Are you still so?"

"Ahh. The lad. Aye," said Dooley. "Such stories they make up about him in those rags of theirs."

"That's what I want you to find out."

Dooley did not understand.

"The school fired you."

"I quit."

She waved away the difference. "You have no ties here," she continued. "I want you to go to the Great Sioux Reservation in Dakota Territory and find him. Or wherever else you need to go. I want to know about these Cheyenne Kid stories. Who is he now? What is he doing? Once I hoped he could be a lawyer for his people, fighting in the courts for the rights they surely have on paper, but that no court ever hears about. I do not think that can ever happen now. Is he an outlaw, or is this all the newspapers making things up? I bought the worst of the lot, but Annie says they all do that out there, and in some cases the people enjoy reading tall tales as though they were true."

223

"Annie?"

"Annie Campbell, the writer. My cousin. She was the woman who wrote about the massacre of the Northern Cheyenne a couple of years ago and drew those sketches that the museum refused to allow, and so I found a place that would display them instead. She will be writing for me soon. But not about him. I need to know. You may be the only person he trusts, and you have to find him. Fifty dollars a month until we know what we need to know. This should cover expenses." She laid a fat stack of greenbacks on an end table. "I shall hold these rooms for you for the next four months until we see what there is to see. I do not know. There might be something permanent out there, because I am certain he will never come East again. It is hard to know what is true out there. It is wild and distant, and I can trust no one. He trusted you. Are you interested?"

"Miss?"

"A train leaves the day after tomorrow that, if the connections as advertised are true, can get you in Dakota Territory in five days. I will arrange for the ticket. You need clothes. You need a gun if you do not have one, because they all have them out there. You were his friend, and I think you can help him."

"Lovely it is to see you, madame, but all of this is a little fast for an old Irish head. Like him you sound there, with all the pieces of the story coming together at once. Can you start near the beginning?"

She did, explaining everything from the pressure put upon her by her uncle to Tall Bear lying in her garden to her concern that Fox Running was now an outlaw on the Great Sioux Reservation.

"I need to know what to do," she said. "I have resources. The business reverses I was facing have been addressed, and I felt the need to make up for what I . . . for having him think he was as expendable as most of our society believes people are. I did not realize the world could be so full of hate for those who try to make it a better place, but I have learned my lesson. I understand now that men who have business interests here mix them with politics, and anyone who disturbs their little world is a threat. Me, the Indians, anyone! I backed down once. I will never do so again! I have learned how to hide the things I do so that no one will ever again back me into a corner like that. In fact, if everything comes to fruition, I may be the one putting *him* in a corner one fine day not too far away. But you do not wish to hear about my uncle.

"If Fox Running is not irretrievably lost, I must help him help his people. I do not know how. I have bought the terrible newspaper that spread lies about him so it cannot do any more damage, but I do not know what the truth is, Mr. Dooley! You can help me. He trusts you. He spoke of you before he left. I cannot move to the wilds of Wyoming or Dakota or Montana or wherever, but I am hoping you will at least go there. I know it will mean a fight, somehow, some way, in some place, because everything in that young man's life is a fight. That does not scare me, not any more, and I hope it will not scare you away."

Dooley weighed his options. Find a warehouse to guard through the dank Boston nights, or take the chance that a young man who wanted to fight the world had not yet taken his battle beyond all limits.

"Ahh, I so often forget to be scared, lass . . . I mean, Miss McGillicuddy. And how is it we shall communicate and manage this business with all this distance between us?" he asked, matching Katherine McGillicuddy's smile with one of his own.

"You must leave today," Lame Bull told Fox Running as they sat in the younger man's accustomed place by the river.

"Father!" Morning Shadow was outraged.

She understood that Fox Running needed time to better

understand himself, for he understood nothing of the spirit world, only the world of guns and war. She knew that a spirit quest of the kind talked about by Blue Sparrow meant he would need to be alone for some time, but she was not prepared to have her father announce it so abruptly.

Fox Running waited quietly, knowing the man had a reason. Lame Bull was a practical man, who put the welfare of the Lakota before everything else.

"There are soldiers who watch on the edge of the reservation, who look and who spy. They are watching for you. They know you are here, even if the army does not dare enter for fear of sparking a fight. You need to prove to them that you have left."

He held up his hand to silence his daughter. "You may speak with Crow Rising to plan your return, for he knows all the ways in and out that the soldiers do not. He can help you find a way they will not know, but they must see that you have gone. Until they do, they will continue to wait and watch, and one day, one of the young men and one of the soldiers will shoot each other. This will bring more soldiers, and *this* will bring what the Lakota seek to avoid. We saw what happened to the Northern Cheyenne. They were almost wiped out. We endure. There must not be war."

He turned to his daughter. "You are my daughter, Morning Shadow, and it is not a step I take lightly, but for now it is what must be. I am called to what is right for the Lakota. I cannot turn from that path, even for you." He turned his eyes to Fox Running to hear what the youth's response would be.

"I have not seen the lands of the Northern Cheyenne in many years," Fox Running said. "I shall go there. I have another duty to perform. Your daughter and I had talked of this, and we agreed it must take place." He looked intently at Morning Shadow.

"I know that what you say is true, and I would not risk a fight. They will watch after I leave for several days to see if it is a trick, if I gather warriors in some hidden place. I shall remain away for at least two moons, but I shall return before the frost, for longer I will not wait." He looked back at Lame Bull. "I shall bring with me that which a man presents to another man to marry his daughter. For all shall be done as is fitting and proper."

Lame Bull nodded.

"Will it be a spotted cow or a brown one?" Morning Shadow said as she tried not to shed a tear of weakness. She knew in her heart Fox Running needed to know who he was, and being alone would help him find that truth. She wondered, also, how that truth would change everything. "Perhaps one of each? For certain I am worth more than an old one!"

"It is a day I will be glad to see," Lame Bull said formally. "Let us agree the price will be as my daughter has said, for it seems that in this I am behind the pace of the young. You are wise, children, for bending to the will of what is necessary."

He extended a hand to Fox Running. The two gripped forearms. "I will walk with you as you leave. Meet me at our lodge."

Morning Shadow and Fox Running watched as he walked away.

"If this were the time of our fathers, we would not marry until after the hunt," he told her. "We must wait. Your father is right. I would not have a war that could take lives, including those of your father and brothers."

"I shall come to this place every day. I shall drop a rock in the water, Fox Running. If you do not want the rocks to build until there is a flood, you will return." Her eyes probed his face for reassurance.

"That is not the reason I shall return," he replied. He opened his arms, and she stepped into them, holding tight until he loosened his grip. "In the Moon When the Streams Grow Hard I shall see you here in this place."

"This is a Lakota camp, Cheyenne Who Makes Bad Moccasins. You will return in the Moon when the Last Leaves Are Shed. And should you begin to forget Lakota ways, I shall come find you and drag you back by your ear as befits a wayward child, which is simply another way to describe a warrior."

They embraced a moment longer. She stayed by the water as he walked away, tall and proud and almost glad as he reached the distance that would prevent him seeing how wet her eyes had become.

A crowd watched Lame Bull walk with Fox Running to select his horse and lead the young man's reins as the horse and rider walked to the ceremonial entrance to the reservation.

"Keep her safe," Fox Running said softly.

"Return," Lame Bull replied, before they exchanged loud and formal farewells.

CHAPTER SIXTEEN

June 1882, Tongue River Valley, Montana
"When you have seen all you need to see, you may come out of the woods."

The dry greeting to the young man in the trees was spoken by Rides a Crow, a Cheyenne Spirit Walker who was revered as a Wise Woman for her role in helping to lead the Northern Cheyenne from the southern reservation back to their beloved home. They had been urged by the army to move south from Fort Keogh and occupy lands along the Tongue River as a precursor to the creation of a reservation.

"Perhaps it is best if you stay hidden," she said after a minute when no one appeared. "The army tells me that I must tell them when I see the notorious Fox Running, who they insist is someone called the Cheyenne Kid, and who has done something very, very wrong that they cannot explain in any sensible way. If I never see him, I must never worry about telling the army a lie."

Silence.

"I will admit that I am curious. The army paints you as a threat to the West. I know there was a blood feud your father, Red Eagle, took to the grave and which falls upon you, although, with all that has happened since then, I do not know who cares enough to pursue it. My friend Annie Campbell, a white woman who writes about the People as though she were one of us, told me that according to a woman she is friends with in Boston,

Fox Running was a young man who went to an Indian boarding school and suffered greatly and might make mistakes but would never seek to do wrong," she said. "Lame Bull of the Lakota sent word weeks ago about you, wondering much because he could not believe the Cheyenne would have cast out a warrior such as you."

She stopped. Waited. Watched the lazy smoke from the fire.

"And so, Blazing Fire of the Lakota or whatever other names you use, who are you?"

"I do not know," he replied, emerging.

Rides a Crow beheld a young man dressed in a mixture of cowboy and Indian clothes, wearing the guns of a white man, carrying the knife of an Indian, and wearing his hair long like an Indian.

"Let us talk," she said. "For I know much about you and little of you. Tales can tell us much of what is done, but little of the reasons."

"I know you," he said. "The day the soldiers attacked at the Rosebud. I saw you. I did not know who you were, but I remember you. You were gathering berries by the river. I thought you must have been killed in the charge."

"There was a time when I wished I had been," she replied. "My family, like yours, was killed that day." She shivered, as if to shake off the past. "We are not here to talk of that time. You are here to ask questions."

"There is something that must be said first," Fox Running said. "I bring a message, and I feel great shame at not bringing it sooner, but the winds of the spirits have blown me like a leaf. I am now here to deliver it."

Rides a Crow at first thought he was joking, then realized his mood was deathly serious.

"Let us sit by the fire," she said. They did. "Now tell me."

Her face dissolved at the mention of Dead Face's name. Fox

Running told her every detail he could remember, from Dead Face's words about their place in the world beyond to his calm acceptance that death with honor was preferable to more captivity.

"I must be alone," she said. "The spirits have found a very strange messenger to give me this gift, Fox Running. I must think. I must pray."

Hours later, she returned, holding tiny Wrapped in a Blanket, who was orphaned when some of the Northern Cheyenne captured on their trek north sought to escape from Fort Robinson but were hunted and killed.

"Tell me your story," she said. "Leave nothing out."

After hours of talking, Rides a Crow asked Fox Running to follow her to a spot far from the homesteading taking place as the Cheyenne sought to take possession of the lands that were once theirs. It was rough and rocky. One section was known as the Buffalo Spine, where the rocks rose high with steep sides to a narrow top.

She had a little bread and some meat for him to eat.

"You may be here for a day, or a week," she said, "but you must stay here until you understand what it is to be Cheyenne, or Lakota, if that is who you truly are. We are not who we are because we are not the white man. To be a Cheyenne, or a Lakota, is to understand that we come from the earth, and we come from the spirits, and we live in harmony with what exists around us. You have lived your life as a warrior, but I do not know that you understand what you are fighting for. To spit in the eye of those who hate you is easy, Fox Running. To know your place, and live to hold that place, is hard. But without it, you will be a dead leaf blown across the Plains that will crumble."

Morning Shadow had told him the spirits were waiting for him to find them. As Rides a Crow left him alone, he wondered

231

what they would think, what they would say, and what he would do about it.

Morning Shadow was comforted by the messenger sent from the Cheyenne wise woman. She knew that Rides a Crow was a famed Spirit Walker. Morning Shadow also knew that for all she was aware of the spirits and sought to live among them and according to their will, she was but a novice compared to the legendary Cheyenne woman. The message said Fox Running was with Rides a Crow, that he was safe, and the spirits were watching over him. It was very little, but it was enough. She would wait.

As she continued with the tasks of her life, for the work of a family never ended, she learned that a white man had come to speak to the Lakota. The white man, she was told, was from a far-off place called Boston. She knew this was the place where Fox Running had been. She left her chores and went to the place where various white men came to speak when they wanted something, out of curiosity about this city that had been part of Fox Running's life.

Even if she had known him from earlier years, she might not have recognized Peter Petengill, who was growing fleshy from too many good meals and fine wines. Churches had begun to support the school, and there was talk the government was thinking that a chain of these schools might solve the problem of what to do with Indian children who had been born into a tradition of wild feats to show bravery but now lived in a world where wild exploits were criminal behavior.

The school was proud of its results. True, few graduated, many escaped, and in this past humid summer a few had died, but time would show their efforts to be notable. Even better, they were already becoming profitable—the more students, the more money. That was not a part Petengill shared with those he wanted to send their children to the school.

"I am here to help the Lakota people have a good tomorrow," he began. "To make the Lakota strong in these times that are not those of the past, your children need an education. The Indian School of Boston can provide an education that will help your children come back to you ready to make the Lakota proud and prosperous."

He was aware of a young woman glaring at him as he spoke. There were often hostile listeners. This one, however, was advancing on him. She held a knife as though she understood well how to use it.

"This man lies," Morning Shadow called to the assembled Lakota.

When Petengill named the school, Morning Shadow understood he had to be one of the ones who had hurt Fox Running. At first, she vowed not to interfere. Then she realized she could not allow Lakota children to endure what Fox Running had.

"He promises to send children back to you with a white man's education. Do you recall the ceremony we had for Tall Bear, when Blazing Fire brought here all that was left of him? That boy was killed by this man, in the school where he wants to teach your children to be ashamed they are Indians. There was nothing left of Tall Bear to bring home except a piece of hair. Is that what you want for your children?"

"The Indian School of Boston helps Indian children look to the future, not the past," Petengill replied, wondering who Tall Bear could be. He could never remember their heathen names, only their Christian ones.

"You beat students. You beat boys and girls. You make them work and take their wages. You give them names that are not their own, cut off their hair, beat them for speaking the language of their families, and lock them in a dungeon when they break rules you created that are nothing but torture so they will stop being Indian and start being white. Your school makes war on all that is our heritage. You want to kill all that is honorable about our people and make our children yours. Leave here and do not come back!"

"The Indian School of Boston has a proud history," Petengill began, aware that his audience was listening more to the ill-educated Indian girl than it was to him. "The Great White Father believes in the school. The missionaries support our school."

"Then let them send their children there," Morning Shadow called out, advancing further on Petengill, who looked in vain for one of the Lakota escorts that served as the tribal police. They were enjoying the entertainment and, from their posture and the smirks on their faces, clearly had no intention of helping a white man deal with a Lakota girl.

"You will leave now, and you will never come back," she added as she came close. "Or I shall tell Fox Running, and he will come with his guns and shoot you until there are so many holes, all the lies flow out of you!"

"Fox Running?" That was a name Petengill would never forget. "Him? He's here? He's here in this village?"

"He is my pledged husband," Morning Shadow replied, glorying in the tremor that passed through Petengill as she said so, while ignoring the buzz of gossip she had instigated. "And he will be glad to take the vengeance that must be taken, if I do not take it first."

She lifted the knife. Petengill stepped away in obvious fear. She snatched the hat off his head and sliced it to pieces, throwing them with contempt to the ground. Morning Shadow put the knife back in the belt at her waist and spoke in Lakota. "This is the brave white man who wants to teach your children courage!" she said. "Shall we cut off his pants to see if he has wet himself?"

The women and men who had gathered began to laugh as they turned away from Petengill. Not one Lakota offered to sign his or her child up for the school. Morning Shadow smirked at Petengill as she walked away, leaving him alone and humiliated. Fox Running would be proud of how she squashed his enemy! She could hardly wait for his return to tell him!

Fox Running had been alone for a week. He was frustrated and angry. If the spirits spoke, or had anything to say to him, they had so far not shared a thing. He had promised, and he would keep his promise, but this was a waste of time.

The saloon was called Boots and Saddles. Avoided by anyone whose army career was moving up, it was the off-post home for the malcontents such as Malvers, who had come to realize that the best the army might ever offer was a series of postings in forts where there was little to do now that the government had decided to coddle the Indians instead of following up the army's advantage after most of them were confined to reservations.

The saloon was small and spared as little expense on light as possible, which meant the dirt and filth on the floor remained largely unnoticed. Petengill had retreated to the saloon after his humiliation at the hands of Morning Shadow. Its customers were receptive and sympathetic as he described the Lakota witch who'd stalked him and flayed him with her words.

After he was done sharing his story, Malvers approached the Easterner with a question. "He's there, on the reservation?"

"Who?" asked Petengill. He'd lost no time drowning his sorrows in whiskey that was raw, if not rancid, but had a kick like a mule.

"Fox Running. The Cheyenne Kid. The renegade. The girl said he was on the reservation now?"

"She said she would sic him on me in a vicious and unprovoked attack because we are trying to save their miserable souls and lives," Petengill responded. "I would think the army would rid the place of a gunfighter who threatens innocent people. She proclaimed him as her husband. As if she was proud of being the wife of a criminal and a violent thug who should be brought to justice!"

"You were threatened?"

"Of course I was threatened," Petengill exploded. "Have you not been listening? That Lakota harridan vowed to have her gunfighter man come and shoot me full of holes if I stayed there any longer. She said he was there, and she would summon him to kill me, and I was forced to leave in fear of my life!"

Malvers ordered another drink for the man and moved to the table occupied by Seth Tallridge. Tallridge was known throughout the region of the Pine Ridge Agency as a man who did things others would not, for a price. He led a gang of riders, all as rough as he was. This table was his, whether he was seated at it or not, from the time he shot a man who took his chair and then sat down for his whiskey with his feet on the dead man.

Tallridge and Malvers had long ago come to an understanding that there were things the army need not know about or investigate, and that a financial partnership between the two men was the best way to help the army keep its nose out of Tallridge's affairs. This time, it was Malvers who did the talking.

"I cannot go there to arrest him, but I can hold him if you bring him to me," Malvers said. He had come to fixate on Fox Running's escape as a blot on his record that he would set right as his last hope of promotion.

Two hundred dollars tempted Tallridge. That would amount to what he had paid Malvers over the past year or so. He could hire a couple of men who usually worked alone and did not work for others cheaply. However, there was risk. Going in would be simple. Getting out could be difficult. Malvers promised to be ready with information from spies about how to leave the camp without being stopped. Tallridge would need a few days. Malvers agreed, then went back to the bar and approached Petengill.

"The army might be able to investigate a sworn complaint," he said smoothly. "Why don't you write down everything that happened?"

"And face that killer?"

"No, no, no," Malvers reassured him. "You can be long gone once we have the complaint in writing. We just need a reason to go on the reservation to arrest him. You know how much they coddle these Indians. Just write down what happened—describing every outrage you have suffered—and sign it. Leave the rest to me."

There was food and water left, but Fox Running had not touched either in three days. He had gone out on the rocky walls of the canyon, beyond the place where Rides a Crow had left him. He could not have explained it, but it was suddenly important to reach the very peak of the narrow ridge she called the Buffalo Spine. His fingers were raw and bleeding as they gripped the rocks. His arms were sore from pulling himself up, and his legs felt rubbery as he reached each new ledge. Up. Up.

The top of the ridge ran for about fifteen feet. It was perhaps ten feet wide at its widest, and barely a foot at its narrowest. He sat there. The wind roared in his ears and seemed to flow through his head. His heart pounded.

The sun-baked rock was hot as he sat with one leg over each side of the ridge. His movements were slow and sluggish from exhaustion. The sun began to sink to the west. From the perch he had reached, he could look down upon it as it turned the sky yellow, then orange, then the color of blood for a moment before it faded to the gray-blackness of night. A shiver of fear, or cold, shook through him as the night wind stilled itself with the sinking of the sun.

Around him, the dome of the night sparkled on each side until, at last, the fading streaks of light in the west were gone, and there was nothing around him but the stars hung for the People by the Spirit Warrior. And so he sat, and he breathed in the air of the land that was old when the People were young and became filled.

The army was shrewd in its dealings with the Lakota. Each village within the reservation had a few Indians picked by the soldiers as above the rest. This created jealousy and rivalry. Those who were by nature jackals became the best spies the soldiers could hope to have. Thus, it was easy for Malvers to give Tallridge the precise way to find the lodge of Lame Bull in the middle of a vast plain of Lakota dwellings.

Tallridge and three other men moved quietly through the lodges and avoided any still-burning fires that could have shown them for who they were. They wrapped themselves in blankets and wore no hats, so their profiles in the dark would resemble those of Lakota men.

But the sound of boots is not the sound of moccasins. And if the Lakota village was never still, its noises were those of animals scouting for food or men and women being respectful of the sleep of others, not the furtive stops and starts of men whose chief interest is to avoid detection.

Lame Bull was wide awake as he lay still. On the warmest nights, like this one, he often slept outside, wrapped in a blanket at the entrance to his family's lodge. His knife was with him, though the rifle he used for hunting was inside the lodge with his children. He drew the blade silently and waited.

"We grab the Injun and git. Fast," whispered Tallridge. "Ready . . ."

He howled as the blade of Lame Bull's knife sunk itself in his thigh. One of Tallridge's accomplices had a .45 ready and fired. The shot tore through the lodge. Lame Bull pulled at the knife to free it. The second shot struck him. He flew backward into the skin wall of the lodge and then to the ground.

Crow Rising had been taught to reach for the rifle the moment there was an alarm. Before he could grasp it, a man with a pistol entered the lodge and slammed the boy across the side of his head with the gun, sending him toppling to the ground. Morning Shadow leapt up from her blanket. She clawed at the face of the man who entered, then shoved him. The two grappled. A second man entered the crowded lodge.

"Where is he?" the man demanded.

"Just kids," the other outlaw replied.

One of them grabbed Morning Shadow by the neck of the shirt she wore. "Where is he, that Fox Sumthin' gunman?"

The outlaw had his left hand around both her wrists, so she tried to bite his face instead of answering. He swung his right hand at her, the one holding the gun. The impact jolted her. She butted him in the nose with her forehead and brought her left foot up high to kick him where her father taught her. As the gunman yelled in pain, his partner, who could see almost nothing, fired at Morning Shadow point blank. The shock and force of the bullet sent her tumbling down to her blankets, where the smaller girls rose to fight off the attackers.

"Got him?" snarled Tallridge, aware that the noise was attracting attention.

"Ain't here, Tallridge."

"Soldier said he was here!"

"Not here, Tallridge."

Voices were being raised, and shapes were moving in the dimness. A running dog was barking. "We better git."

One gunman fired several blind shots at the children, who

dropped to avoid the bullets. Then he hurried out of the lodge, with his partner on his heels. Both soon caught up with the limping Tallridge. The three turned and fired one short pistol volley aimed at discouraging pursuit. As the howl of a wounded dog filled the night in anguish, they were soon swallowed up in the darkness.

It was barely dawn when Malvers was summoned to Col. Meyers's office. He found the colonel livid as Meyers outlined what had taken place at the lodge of Lame Bull, one of the most respected of all the Lakota leaders, and one of the foremost advocates of creating a lasting peace with the whites.

"When I find out how you are connected to this, Malvers, you will be driven from the army. I told you to put your private feelings aside. Look what you've done! We'll be lucky if we don't have a full-scale Indian war out of this!"

Malvers asked what had taken place.

"Don't play innocent with me," Meyers replied. "Overnight, a collection of toughs, maybe two, maybe six, attacked Lame Bull's lodge. Do you know who he is, Malvers? He is one of the men we work with to keep the peace, to ensure that hotheads on either side do not cause trouble. Is. Was. He was shot to death protecting his family. Two of his girls and his son were hurt by the men, who also shot his eldest daughter. She's probably going to die, although the Lakota will not let a single white man within a mile of her to see. Someone even shot at their dog, Malvers, but just grazed it. Do you know why this happened, Malvers?"

"No, sir!"

"They told the family to turn over Fox Running, who was not even staying there."

"He wasn't?" The answer came out too quickly. Both Malvers and Meyers knew it.

"No, he was not! Now, why would a gang go after one Cheyenne kid on a reservation full of Lakota hotheads, a lot of whom are now justifiably wound up over the lack of protection the army has given them against white men?"

"I . . . I don't know, sir." Malvers was taken aback and angry. Petengill must have been drunk, he told himself.

"We are organizing a full-fledged hunt for the men, one of whom appears to have been stabbed in the fighting."

"Yes, sir! I will—"

"You will confine yourself to your quarters until all the facts in this case are known," Meyers said. "When the facts *are* known, you will have your court martial, and you will be thrown out of this army as a lesson that whatever kind of Custer tactics you think are proper, they have no place on the frontier as long as I am the commander. Guard!" A soldier entered. "Escort this . . . officer to his quarters. Ensure that you or another guard are posted outside his door at all times. Dismissed, Malvers, and get out of my sight."

"I need my guns," Fox Running said as he entered Rides a Crow's lodge without the least ceremony or manners.

"Does my Cheyenne brother allow me the opportunity to dress myself?" she asked from her blankets.

It was not even fully light. Wrapped in a Blanket, the child Rides a Crow was raising, started to cry at being rudely awakened. Rides a Crow held her.

"You have scared the child! Now hush! Most men who spend time with the spirits emerge in a state of peace and wish to talk about what they have undergone. I can see you need more time alone on the rocks."

"Perhaps I shall do that if I return. I have no time for such things now. I must go. Morning Shadow is hurt."

"Tell me from outside the lodge," Rides a Crow instructed.

241

He complied, and went outside the skin-and-frame structure.

"Talk," she said as he waited. "I do not rise without a prayer to the spirits. I can hear you and them."

"I was on the rocks last night; the rocks that rise like a buffalo's spine. I had climbed them and spent two days there."

Climbed them? Rides a Crow was stunned. Many had vowed to climb them, but none had ever succeeded in getting past the lower ledges, so steep was the ascent.

"In the night, I dreamed of her, or had a vision of her. I do not know which. Then a black cloud came upon her, and the cloud dripped blood. I awoke, and I knew this was no dream that comes with sleep. Something has happened. I must go."

Rides a Crow emerged from the lodge holding his gun belt. "Is that all you saw?"

"No," he said. "I do not know how to say it, because there is a part of me that understands but cannot put it in words. It is about justice, that there is a path for me, and that it is what I am given to do, but then came this later vision, and now all I feel is that Morning Shadow is hurt, and I have a duty to her. I do not fully know what I am supposed to do or feel, Rides a Crow, but I know whatever I am supposed to be is within me."

"Then the spirits are with you, and you take them on your way. Ride with them, Fox Running, and return when you can."

"If what I feel within me—full where there was empty—is what you are in being a Spirit Walker, your life is blessed," he told her.

"Sometimes it is so; sometimes it is not," she replied. "Yet I know above all, I will never walk alone. Go now. You have my blessing and theirs. Do what must be done."

He had buckled on the guns and was mounting the horse she had cared for while he was off by himself. "If you have words that can help the spirits preserve a life," he said, "please say them for her. And if there are words to help punish those who did evil, please say them for me, that if she has been hurt as I fear, I can right this wrong."

He kicked the horse into a gallop.

Rides a Crow watched him ride away, wondering if the death she saw as she looked upon him was his, or that of another. Either way, he was riding toward that which the spirits set as his destiny.

For once, Fox Running was not worried about being seen as he pushed the horse as fast and long as he could. Anyone who came up against him now would wish they had not. He did not know more than his dream vision had told him, but Morning Shadow was hurt. His place was with her. No one would keep him from that.

As he rode through what he was certain were the lands bordering the Lakota reservation, he saw the patrol. There were perhaps twelve men riding at a leisurely pace. Two scouts rode ahead. Crow? No. Shoshone.

They were looking for some trace of someone or something. He found it hard to believe they were looking for him. He had been gone more than a moon from Pine Ridge. He had not even ridden this way when he went to the Tongue River. Still, he stopped and observed the soldiers. He did not want trouble now. They soon made camp. He waited until the fire was dying, and the men would be tired after a day of riding.

"Halt . . ." one sentry began, stopping when he felt the muzzle of a pistol against him and a hand covering his mouth.

"Do not speak loudly," Fox Running said. "Where are you from, and why are you here? Whom do you seek?"

He lifted his hand from the trooper's mouth. He could sense the young soldier making a decision.

"I do not choose to hurt any of you," Fox Running said. "Tell me. Do you hunt an Indian?"

The soldier shook his head.

"Who, then?"

"Gibbons? Who are you talking to?" It was the tone of an officer.

"Say nothing," whispered Fox Running, poking Gibbons with the pistol.

"Gibbons? Where are you, soldier?"

"He is here," said Fox Running as the officer's shape emerged from the darkness around him. "He is not hurt. I will hurt no one if you tell me what I need to know. I saw your patrol and want to know your purpose."

"The army does not share its business."

"I have traveled these hills. Perhaps I have seen who you are hunting. Consider this, captain. It is captain?"

"Captain Stephen Broadbent, from Fort Robinson."

"If I wished your patrol dead, Captain, you would be dead. I do not want to fight you. I am only asking a question."

"We're hunting a gang that attacked a Lakota family," Broadbent said. "There was some sign they went this way, but we lost it a day ago."

"The family of Morning Shadow?"

"If that is the girl, yes. Lame Bull's family. He was killed."

Fox Running had guessed as much. "What of her?"

"When we left the fort three days ago, she was alive. She was shot, but she didn't die right away. Now, who are you?"

"I am Fox Running, Captain. I am—"

"I know who you are. The whole world knows who you are! We have been ordered to bring you in if we find you."

"Am I being arrested or charged with a crime?"

"No. I don't know the reason. I was told only we should keep an eye out for you and bring you to the fort."

"I will not go with you, Captain. I will ride to Pine Ridge, and I will go to the family of Lame Bull. If the army wants me, it can find me there. Do not interfere. Please. I do not seek to make trouble, but I will not be delayed in going to her lodge."

"Do you point guns at us because you have peaceful intentions?"

"No, Captain, it is to ensure that you do. No men have ridden the way you are going. Do not worry about those who killed Lame Bull. I will find them. They will not bother the army."

"Army business."

"I will find them first, Captain, and it will be my business. I will go now. Do not follow. I do not wish to hurt any of you. There are times and places, Captain, when your laws cannot achieve justice. This is one of them."

The soldiers waited. After a moment, each looked at the other, silently asking if a sound had been heard. Moments later they heard a horse riding away in the night. Fox Running was gone.

"We ride back to Fort Robinson in the morning, Gibbons," Captain Broadbent said.

"Don't we need to find those men, sir?" said Gibbons.

"Sonny, you want to come between that fella and whoever it was that injured those Indians? That man is a killer. Not our fight." The captain rubbed the whiskers on his jaw. "Besides, Gibbons, if half of what I hear is true, having that Cheyenne on their trail is worse than having a whole fort full of cavalry chasing you. And, Gibbons, just to make sure you understand, we saw no one, we never spoke to anyone, and we have no idea about anything that might happen to anyone, understand that, soldier?"

Gibbons nodded and saluted. Indians doing the army's work. The world had gone upside down.

Chapter Seventeen

Two days later, Fox Running reached the village where Lame Bull's family lived. Some looked at him as though he was a ghost, for his arrival came far too soon for messengers to have found him in the Cheyenne lands.

"You are looking for her?" asked Blue Sparrow as he reached the ruined, bloodstained lodge where the family had lived. Their few possessions remained. "You are the one they sought. They came for you, and you were not here."

"I am here now to right this wrong. Who came, Grandmother, who came?"

"None saw the faces clearly. There is a man named Tallridge who does evil things for hire. He limps. One man in the night limped. If the white men pay him to kill or kidnap, he will do the thing for which he is paid. No Lakota has ever had any dealings with him, and we know of no reason why, if it is him, he would attack. Do you know this man?"

"I do not."

"Then if it was him, someone else sent him to look for you here," she said. "Morning Shadow is at the healing lodge. The spirits have not yet decided if she is to go with them or remain with us. She does not carry the bullet in her, but much blood came out of her. She was hurt also in the head, boy, and she has not woken or spoken."

"Take me to her, Blue Sparrow. I must go to the place her

246

father is buried, and I must see her family. But first I must see her."

"Why did you leave her?" the old woman asked sharply.

"To protect her," Fox Running replied. "To do that which was right."

The old woman weighed his misery and touched his arm. "There is much I know about healing, Fox Running. If she can be saved, I shall save her. The spirits will decide your fates in the way that they wish."

Morning Shadow was by herself in a lodge with a small fire. A huge bruise stood out on her right temple. A blanket covered her. Her eyes were closed. Her hand was like ice as he took it. There was breath from her mouth, and it was regular. Yet when he spoke she did not respond.

"There are times when the spirits do not know the future, my child," said Blue Sparrow. "They decide whether it is best for her to go with them or stay. I talk to them as I sit with her. You must have faith in them, child. She was hurt very badly. The body does not always recover as quickly as warriors think it should. She will be here when you return."

"How do you know I am leaving?"

Blue Sparrow patted his right arm. "I believe it would take horses and chains to make you stay. Ride safely."

Crow Rising and Lame Bull's other children were being cared for by Waiting Bear, a cousin. Crow Rising told Fox Running everything he could remember. He had seen one man's hands, and the hand looked gnarled. He believed it was the left hand, because the man held a gun in his right. One man was clean-faced; the other had a thick, black beard. The man at the edge of the lodge wore a jacket that was dark with something white at the collar. He could see nothing more. They all agreed their father had stabbed one man.

Small Deer, the youngest, said that one man called the other by a name that sounded to her like "all-rich." She also said one man said something about a soldier, which she understood to mean that a soldier had told them Fox Running would be at Lame Bull's lodge. She said the marauders were very angry that he was not.

The children also told about Morning Shadow's confrontation with Petengill. They were proud of their sister, and how she intimidated the white man who came from the place that made Fox Running sad. He shared their pride, but he wondered if something she had done or said had triggered the attack and felt a creeping sense of guilt that he had not been there to protect her.

No matter. He was here now.

Petengill was, as he expected, long gone. When Fox Running made up a story about a younger brother whom the school might benefit, the clerk at the hotel vouchsafed that the man spent a lot of time at the Boots and Saddles. Perhaps the bartender there would know. But the clerk had a warning.

"Lots of soldiers there, Son," he said. "A few toughs. Some bad men. Tallridge's gang likes to go there. Men like that. You might go in alive with all your parts, but you might not come out the same way. From what I see, you Indians are as good as anyone else, but some don't agree. Them in there don't."

Fox Running found a place to watch who came and went from the Boots and Saddles. During the day he slumped in the sun like other idlers, hat pulled down to cover much of his face. In the night, he moved closer but remained out of sight. If the others—drunks, loafers, and the like—knew or cared he was Indian, they did not show it. They exchanged gossip about those who came and went until Fox Running knew many of the secrets of Dahlgren Post and those clustered around Pine Ridge.

The men who came and went from the saloon looked rough,

but no one came in or out who resembled the picture he had in his mind of Tallridge and the men who attacked Lame Bull's family. Some soldiers came in the evening, looking furtive as though they were away from the post without permission. He spent two days there and was ready to give it up after one more day for fear someone might notice him.

Then he saw a familiar figure hurrying down the town's main street. Malvers looked up and down it before ducking into the Boots and Saddles. Before Fox Running could make up his mind about following him inside, Malvers emerged. Fox Running would need to find him later.

The army was not officially at war with the Indians, which transformed discipline at the barracks of Dahlgren Post. The gates were no longer routinely shut and locked at night, and the sentries who walked the rounds found their chief enemies were boredom and sleeplessness. This made it easy for Fox Running to slip in as soon as it was dark and find the quarters where Malvers lived. With his target selected, he waited until well into the deep of the night to act.

Malvers woke with a start, certain he'd heard a noise. "Sergeant, is that you?"

"It is not."

Wide awake now, Malvers reached for the pistol and holster at the foot of the bed, but they were not on the chair where he always left them. As he felt for the gun that was not there, he heard the click of a pistol.

"I know you were part of the attack on Lame Bull, or you were behind it. Where are the ones who killed him? Tell me, or I will kill you."

Fox Running! Malvers cursed inwardly. He had thought idly when the Indian boy was young that it might be better to end the life of a combative child then rather than face what he might become. He had been right.

"You cannot threaten an army officer. This time you will . . ."

The tip of a knife poked Malvers's neck. It drew blood. Malvers had not even heard Fox Running move.

"Your threats mean nothing," Fox Running said. "I will die when I will die. Until that day, I will walk the road that was laid for me. Tell me, or die, Captain Malvers. Those are your choices. I doubt your colonel would care about being rid of you, if the gossip of your soldiers as they drink their whiskey is correct. Where is Tallridge? I know you sent him to their lodge. You go to the saloon where he is often present. You are seen often with him. You and he scheme together."

Malvers's mind was racing. If the Indian went to find Tallridge, the outlaws would surely kill him. Even if he just sent the Indian after them, there would still be time to raise a pursuit. If Fox Running killed white men, the army could arrest him. If Fox Running was killed by an army patrol rescuing white citizens from the Cheyenne Kid, then that would be just as well. The army might even intervene and kill Tallridge's men, which meant no one would be alive to tell tales about Malvers. Yes, there was opportunity. Time. He needed time.

"Tallridge has a hideout. Near Brittle Canyon, by the Buffalo Calf Fork of the White River." Malvers's eyes shifted as he spoke, but darkness covered his expression. He doubted the savage could even guess he was being led into a trap Malvers would spring, but he tried to let the fool Indian think he held the advantage. "I speak the truth. Go ahead and kill him, for all I care."

"I shall find it. If you tell anyone of this meeting, or if you follow me, I will kill you," Fox Running threatened.

"I promise I will not."

Fox Running ordered him to lie on his stomach on the bed. Malvers thought of overpowering Fox Running but then acquiesced, expecting at any second a bullet through his head.

As he waited, he heard faint sounds. Then none.

He rolled over. The wind streamed in through the open window. Fox Running was gone. Malvers ran to his door and called for the alarm to be sounded, that an intruder was in the post. The gates were bolted immediately and extra men sent to watch the walls for anyone trying to scale them.

As the alarm spread, the order went up the chain of command to wake Colonel Meyers. To the great relief of the private dispatched to rouse the short-tempered commander, Meyers was already awake and seemed to be treating this disruption of his sleep as unimportant.

"Thank you, sir," said his uninvited guest, after the private left. "I need just a few more minutes of your time. I think I can help you with a problem you cannot solve on your own, and I think you can do the same for me."

John Dooley had been warned that the farther west he traveled, the more raw life became. What no one told him was that as the layers of civilization around him were discarded, he felt more and more alive. This West was violent and dirty, but it was honest in a way Boston never was. He saw now why men came here and never returned, for it was like filling one's lungs with freedom.

The last restraints proper society had laid upon the life Dooley led in Boston were shed in Cheyenne, Wyoming, where Dooley had to travel to connect with a coach because no trains ran to the Great Sioux Reservation. As he set down his valise at the station, easing muscles cramped from the long journey, he saw Peter Petengill waiting unhappily for an eastbound train with a group of six Indian children. He strode to the man, sudden anger flooding through him.

"Dooley!" Petengill exclaimed. "What are you doing here?"

"Finding salvation," Dooley remarked acidly. "Where are

these children from?"

"The Crow reservation, mostly, along with some Cheyenne kids whose parents didn't really know what was best for them," replied Petengill. "I tried the Sioux, but that brat Fox Running had been there and . . . stop!"

Dooley was a big man, and, although Petengill had grown bulky, he was no match for an angry Irishman.

"Peter, do you recall the day you took Foxy and jammed his head against a window he broke and told him you would gouge out his eyes with the glass? Or the day you promised you would break his legs when he kicked a bucket of cleaning water on your new suit because you told him he was a 'piece of savage scum'?"

"I . . . I acted for their betterment. Discipline breeds responsibility," Petengill said. "Now put me down, or I shall fire you!"

"Ye canna, sir," Dooley said. "I already quit."

Petengill swung one flailing arm. He hit Dooley's hat and knocked it to the dirt.

"Shouldn't ha' done that, sir."

A few moments later, Petengill lay on the ground, a moaning, pitiful wretch with a broken nose, bloody mouth, and one eye swollen shut. Dooley walked off from the station with six children in tow, saying he needed to find a sheriff to report a kidnapping.

CHAPTER EIGHTEEN

The cabin was where Malvers said it would be. Fox Running had expected perhaps a handful of men, but there were at least fifteen gathered. One man who limped was in charge. He wore a dark jacket with white on its lapels. This must be Tallridge. Two other men—one with a heavy beard and one clean-shaven—were constantly with him. The bearded one was purple-faced as though he had sustained an injury.

Armed men guarded the cabin, but they were lax, not alert. These looked like the dregs of the frontier—men who had come West with dreams that died, or who were running from the law until they thought it was safe to stop.

He had visited Morning Shadow before he left Pine Ridge. She breathed in. She breathed out. He told her everything he was planning. He told her all the spirits had told him. He hoped for some flicker of life, some sign that what he was doing was right. There was none.

He had come ready for the job he had planned. He rode with no saddle but draped saddlebags over the horse with enough ammunition to finish what he would momentarily begin. A rifle hung in a loop of leather over his left shoulder. He tied around his head a bloody strip of fabric left behind after the attack on Lame Bull's family. He closed his eyes briefly and spoke to the spirits. "I ask not for my life, but that I may avenge what was done to those whose only crime was being kind to me," he said to the sun and the wind, knowing that, beyond them, Someone would hear.

Then he mounted the horse and went to settle the score.

One single rider slowly walking his horse toward the cabin did not create any excitement for Mike Brady, who had drawn the afternoon sentry duty shift. He stepped out from under the shadow of the tree where he'd been waiting.

The rider didn't appear to be a threat, just some Indian, from the way his hair flapped in the wind. His hands were on the reins, and he bobbed and wove as he rode as though he were either drunk or not used to riding.

Brady wondered if the fool wanted to trade. They were always wanting to trade nothing to get something—sometimes liquor, sometimes guns. The rider was within earshot now.

"Go away," Brady called, sweeping his arm across his body in a gesture as clear as could be. "No want trade. No have whiskey. Go, Injun!"

The horse came closer, as if its rider could not hear or did not understand. His head lolled back and forth with the rhythm of each step the horse took.

"Git!" Brady yelled as the fool Indian rode to within fifteen feet of him. He pointed back toward the hills around the canyon, using the rifle to point at the jagged rocks. "Go away! Or I'll kill you!"

"I do not think so," came a low-voiced reply. Brady wasn't sure he'd heard right at first, but the pistol that materialized in the Indian's right hand made the young man's meaning clear. "You may drop the rifle, or I will shoot you."

Brady threw the rifle down and reached for the pistol under his coat. He never touched it.

Fox Running's gun fired twice. Brady staggered and then fell. Loungers at the cabin heard the shot, then saw some Indian on horseback riding for them.

"Take cover!" one yelled.

Fox Running had holstered the pistol. He rode with his legs guiding the horse as he emptied his rifle at the men, striking a man who had filled the cabin's doorway before he rode away out of the range of the guns that fired back at him.

Tallridge looked at Mike Brady's body as it lay in the doorway. A dead center shot. He looked at the Indian waiting on his horse just out of range, defiant as the devil himself. This must be the Cheyenne Kid, or Fox Running, or whatever he was called.

Just for a moment, Tallridge felt a sense of fear, as though the implacable hatred Fox Running felt had sent itself into Tallridge's soul. This was not some warrior out for a killing. This was a challenge. They could kill the Indian, or he would stalk them until they were dead.

Tallridge had never let anything stand in his way before. One Indian would not do so now. "Mount up, men," he called. "Ride him down!"

Six men mounted quickly; their horses were already saddled. Fox Running began to gallop away, but not as fast as those pursuing him could ride. Soon they were within range. One fired from the saddle, but the shot went wide.

Fox Running turned as he reined in the horse. His pursuers, whose mounts were going so fast they were all but out of control, frantically tried to slow their animals. Fox Running's horse stopped. His pistol fired again and again with deadly accuracy. Four saddles emptied as two men were killed outright and two others were wounded.

Tallridge was certain Fox Running cast one defiant look his way before the Indian turned his horse to the west and rode— deliberately and without any sign of panic—for the rough, rocky formations of Brittle Canyon.

The chase was on.

After finally tracking down the Indian, Tallridge's men were cold and mean as light spread across the canyon. One man had been wounded in the night by a stray long-range shot from the rocks. The intermittent gunfire had led them to douse the few fires they could kindle with the sparse wood available. There would be no food, coffee, or warmth until daylight made it safe.

Tallridge had fought in the War Between the States. He knew that to trap a man, he needed to surround him, not just charge. But first he needed to know where Fox Running was. Indians were easily outsmarted.

He limped out alone to the edge of the rocks. "Indian!" The word echoed. "Maybe we can talk this out."

Fox Running knew that to appear was to give up an advantage. But the whole game was a risk that had to be played out as it took its own twists and turns. This was about more than killing; it was his effort to find the justice the spirits said he must create, when he was uncertain what that even meant.

"Report to the fort. Have yourselves arrested. Or I kill you," he called out.

Tallridge's men heard the words and located the voice making them. Two groups began to circle up the slope, trying to find handholds and places where the rocks would not crumble under their feet.

Tallridge continued to talk, as though he were offering terms. Fox Running continued to pretend to negotiate. Tallridge's men labored up the jagged rock face, like a pair of heavily armed jaws beginning to close on unsuspecting prey.

Tallridge noted with grim satisfaction that his men would soon be within rifle range of the spot where the voice was coming from. The longer he could keep the Indian talking, the closer his men could get when they opened fire. With men on each side of him, the Indian would not last long. It was a matter of time now. Just a little longer.

Abruptly, he realized his last challenge had not received a reply. He scanned the rocks for a sign of the Indian. "Injun!" he roared.

Then he saw him, running like a crazed goat down the rocky face, almost skipping from ledge to ledge. No man could move that way!

He yelled and tried to point to his own men that were far up the rocky wall. If any of them understood, none altered their efforts to move in on the spot where Fox Running had been.

Tallridge finally understood. He had been outmaneuvered. While he sent his men for the Indian, the Indian let them get virtually out of range and came directly for him.

Tallridge pulled his pistol. Long range. Moving target. He fired. Missed. The shots alerted his men. One of the groups began trying to move down the slope, but it was much harder going in their heavy cowboy boots than it was for Fox Running in moccasins.

Tallridge reloaded after using six shells to no purpose. He glimpsed black hair behind a rock and fired. He clicked on a spent shell after again firing with no hits.

"Drop it."

Fox Running had emerged and was twenty feet away, with a pistol trained on Tallridge. The men on the rocky face, all of whom had finally turned back to climb down, might have hit the Indian, but most were doing all they could just to keep their footing. A few rifle shots went wide. Fox Running paid them no attention.

Tallridge tossed the pistol down and lifted his arms out from his sides. He needed to buy time. "We can talk this out."

"On a horse, now," Fox Running demanded. "You are going

to admit what you did and tell who hired you, because that's who I really want to kill."

"Had nothin' against anyone," Tallridge said. "Just doing a job."

"For who?"

"Can't say."

Fox Running shot Tallridge's hat off his head. There was a risk he would miss low, but he did not have time to wait forever, and he was not all that worried at the consequences of a mistake.

"Malvers! Malvers! That army captain. Crazy man. Wanted you captured. Didn't think it would go sour."

More of Tallridge's men must have decided a shot was worth the risk, because a volley erupted from the rocks. Fox Running once again did not bother turning.

"On the horse," he said, gesturing with the gun. "You are going to the post to pay for your crime."

Tallridge kept his hands wide as he moved toward the horses.

"Up."

Tallridge put his left foot in the stirrup and lashed out with his right as he mounted, spooking the horse into a sudden gallop. It kicked dirt and dust all over Fox Running. Tallridge was angry. That fool Injun kid was humiliating him. No man showed up Dirk Tallridge!

The saddle still had a rifle in its scabbard. Tallridge pulled it free. The horse didn't like being kicked and bucked. Tallridge pulled the reins hard to show the animal who was boss and kicked it again to ride down the Indian.

Tallridge put the rifle to his shoulder. It never fired. While he fought the horse, Fox Running had moved in for the kill. The bullet from Fox Running's only shot took Tallridge high in the chest, knocking him back in the saddle and sending the rifle from his arms. It struck the dirt and flipped end over end. Tallridge rocked forward in the saddle and reflexively grabbed the horse's mane. The animal tried to shake off its unwelcome load and galloped hard until, after about fifty yards, Tallridge fell.

By now, Tallridge's men were nearing the bottom of the rocky slope. The first round of shots they fired as they neared level ground went wide, but Fox Running knew that as they came closer, their aim would improve.

The sound of a cavalry bugle broke through the gunfire. Malvers rode at the head of a dozen men. All had their rifles pointed at Fox Running. Tallridge's men stopped firing. They knew who their friends were.

"You have committed the crime of killing Dirk Tallridge," Malvers said as a fine dust from the horses drifted across Tallridge's body towards Fox Running. He was pleased with the fact that Tallridge had been silenced, and Fox Running would soon be silenced permanently as well. "I am taking you back to be hung for your crime. You may surrender your guns or be killed, and I hope you do not surrender."

"I expected you yesterday," Fox Running said absently, placidly reloading his revolvers in defiant disobedience. "Did you get lost? I don't know how the trail could have been clearer, and you white men can't seem to find it! I was worried we might need to hold a tea party and wait for you, but there was no tea to be had."

"Put the guns down," said Malvers, not heeding anything Fox Running had said that might indicate the Cheyenne was not in fear for his life. "If you refuse to obey the order, I will have my men here kill you."

"I doubt that very much," said Fox Running. "I know many of your soldiers hate Indians. I know that when you have lost men in battle, it is very hard to not hate those who kill them. But some men understand it is time to bury the past and not each other. You are not one of those."

"Surrender!" Malvers roared, turning purple in the face as

this flippant brave continued to defy him.

"Sergeant!" Fox Running called. "Your colonel gave you an order?"

Paddy O'Reilly, a grizzled veteran who until this mission thought he had seen everything, looked as though he had bitten into a can of beans while they were still in the container. He grimly nodded.

"Ground arms, laddie-os," he said in the tone reserved for orders he disliked. "Ground arms."

"What is this? What are you doing?" Malvers sputtered.

"Squad dismount!" O'Reilly called. He looked at Tallridge's men. "The army is arresting all of you for kidnap and murder. Lay down your guns and submit to arrest."

No one moved. "Squad ready!" O'Reilly said. "Take aim at these scum!"

The same rifles that had been focused on Fox Running shifted to point at Tallridge's stunned men, who belatedly complied with the command.

"What is the meaning of this?" Malvers demanded.

"Colonel's orders, sir," O'Reilly replied. "Said the Injun fella was working with him to bust the Tallridge gang for attacking the Injuns and killing that Lame Bull man, which he said you been part of, sir, so respectfully, sir, would the captain mind standing with the other prisoners?"

Then he blurted out a final statement. "Makes it easier on the Irish filth ye command to know who to shoot, if ye don't mind me quotin' yourself to yourself, sir."

Malvers moved over to where Tallridge's men were standing. Fox Running followed. He wanted to deliver only death. The spirits wanted him to manufacture justice. He would try.

"At least one of you went with Tallridge a few days ago and killed Lame Bull, and shot his daughter," he said, eyes lingering on the bruised face of a heavily bearded man who looked as though his swollen nose had been smashed recently.

"You went because he," he pointed at Malvers, "hired you. The rest are the army's business. Whichever ones killed Lame Bull and harmed his family, you are mine. If I do not get what is mine, the soldiers have been instructed to turn all of you over to the Lakota police, so that a trial can be held on the Lakota lands."

One man spoke up. "They'll kill us."

"Yes," Fox Running agreed. "You are thieves, cutthroats, and killers. It would be justice if you die. The government signed a treaty that gives the Lakota power to use their justice for crimes committed on their land, and the penalty for murder is death by burning. Under the law, anyone who participates in a crime is guilty, so you will all be charged with murder to ensure that whichever among you is guilty, you do not escape your punishment. You will all die."

"You can't do that," Malvers called out.

"Your colonel believed it would be a way to reduce problems with the Lakota," said Fox Running. "Isn't that what he said, Sergeant?"

"Aye, sir," O'Reilly replied with some vigor, apparently warming to his task. "Said something about getting justice for once. Said the boys might be invited to watch the burnings as a warning."

The captives buzzed. Being burned to death was not what they signed up for.

"Now, if I can learn who attacked Lame Bull's lodge, only those involved must fear anything. The rest of you can deal with the army, which I suspect has more important things to do than send you to jail or have you roasted," Fox Running said. "Speak now, or our destination is the tribal justice circle of the Lakota."

Silence fell. Fox Running felt the taste of defeat. His bluff had failed. Dividing a group against itself must only work when the army does it to Indians, he thought.

" 'Twas Naylor," one tough said, nodding toward the outlaw with the purple bruise dominating his face. "Him and Brady and Tallridge. They went in. I held the horses, but I never set foot on the Indians' land. I never did nothing. They paid me to hold horses, and I held 'em."

"I should kill you, Peters," growled the man with the bruise. Naylor turned to Fox Running. "Do your worst, Injun. Better men than you have failed. You can't put me on trial. You're bluffing."

Fox Running felt light-headed. "You are right," he said. The smile that flashed on his face was vicious. "I am. Brady?"

"Dead," said Peters. "He's one of the ones you killed the other day."

"Sergeant, you and your men have done your duty, I believe," Fox Running said, nodding at Tallridge's men. "Take away everyone except Malvers and Naylor. The rest is my business."

" 'Tis not as I was told, sir," O'Reilly replied. "Told to stay out of it we were, but not to leave you alone. The colonel suggested things might not go according to army procedure if that were to happen, and the accounting for the dead might be more than we could handle. With respect, sir."

Fox Running wanted to argue, but he could tell O'Reilly would not leave unless shot down.

"Malvers, Naylor. You are right that the army cannot put you on trial in a Lakota court. In fact, I made all that up. Instead of a courtroom, where you might twist the truth with words, we will pass justice here. The Cheyenne believe that the spirits decide who is in the right and who is in the wrong through trial by combat. You have your choice of weapons. I have mine. You murdered a good man. You shot a good woman. I am here to hold you to account. Find weapons. Rifles, pistols, whatever you wish. Then you two and I shall determine whose side justice is on."

O'Reilly looked as though he wanted to stop the fight but did nothing.

For a moment, no one moved.

"Or I kill you where you stand," Fox Running called out.

Malvers hurried to his saddle for his rifle, checked to see if it was loaded, and stepped away from the horses. Naylor grabbed a shotgun one of Tallridge's men had dropped. The man dropped some shells into Naylor's beckoning hand as Fox Running watched stone-faced. Naylor jammed the shells into his left jacket pocket, then stood next to Malvers, who threw the man a glance of distaste.

"Orders are orders, but sure of this, are ye, lad?" O'Reilly said to Fox Running as the younger man made sure his guns were fully loaded, then settled them lightly in their holsters. "The colonel said you had a plan, and we were to take them to the fort when it was over, but this seems more like a wish for death."

Fox Running turned on the Irishman in anger.

"Can you tell me that the god of white justice, who is so very, very blind when an Indian is the victim, will suddenly see the need for action and fairness and meting out punishment to the guilty when these men go to trial? *If* they go to trial?" he barked. "Sergeant? Is that what will happen?"

O'Reilly looked down at the ground.

Fox Running touched the man's arm. "It is not your responsibility, Sergeant. This is what I want. The risk is mine. I accept it. I know of no other way to achieve justice, and I will have justice for a friend who was killed and a woman who may die. This is . . . I do not know how to say it so you can understand . . . it is what I must do."

Fox Running's intensity and the blazing light in his eyes made the Irish sergeant recall those he'd heard of who went into battle half mad.

"It is in the hands of the spirits, Sergeant. This once. We will see what they make of us all. Do not worry about getting in trouble. It could be, you know, that I did not tell the colonel this part. I forget things sometimes."

Fox Running looked up, saw Malvers and Naylor waiting. He had put his life in the lap of the spirits, as had Dead Face. They could take it or give it back as they chose.

"I shall give you two more of a chance than you gave Lame Bull," he said, then glanced at O'Reilly. "Do you know 'The Rising of the Moon,' Sergeant?" he asked. The Irishman nodded. "Then sing its first line, for it would be grand, would it not?"

"And how is it I am here with an Irish Indian?" O'Reilly asked.

"It is a long story," Fox Running replied, thinking of O'Malley and Dooley—men who reached out across the gulf of hate as friends. "I will tell you on the way home, if the spirits let me live." To Malvers and Naylor, he called, "You can begin to fire when Sergeant O'Reilly is done."

Fox Running had never felt lighter, faster, or more sure of his purpose. He was twenty-five feet from Naylor and Malvers.

"The spirits go with you, Morning Shadow, whether I see you in this life or the next," he whispered as he nodded to O'Reilly. "Dead Face . . . this is how I keep faith."

The Irish sergeant began to sing. " 'Come and tell me, Sean O'Farrell, tell me . . .' "

The shotgun boomed. The bark of a pistol shot echoed with it.

Fox Running went down.

O'Reilly was certain a haze of red droplets sprayed as the young man fell. The fool courted death and got what he wanted!

Malvers fired his first bullet as Naylor ejected his shells and began to reload the shotgun. Fox Running's left foot kicked up like a puppeteer had pulled its string, then slammed to the ground. Both men fired at the prone Cheyenne, who rolled to his left and drew one gun as a wave of buckshot ripped through the air and another shotgun shell kicked dust at his head.

"Finish him!" screamed Malvers, shoving the other man forward.

Naylor scurried toward Fox Running as he broke open the shotgun and reached into his pocket for the final two shells he carried. He looked up. The Indian had rolled to an unsteady position on both knees. No threat there. The kid had been game, but it was over. He looked down as he slammed the shells home, then snapped the gun closed, brought it to bear, and ran even closer.

His body kept moving even after a .45 slug passed through his throat and staggered until he landed at the knees of Fox Running. Blood sprayed over the Cheyenne and his victim.

The gun had grown heavier than Fox Running's arms could hold. He lifted it two-handed as he had years before as a child. As Naylor fell, he fired where Malvers should have been.

But the captain had seen his chance while Fox Running was occupied with Naylor. Malvers had been more than willing to sacrifice the outlaw to save himself. He ran forward. He fired once. Fox Running jerked.

Fox Running fired his last bullets. One hit Malvers in the thigh. Another nipped the officer's flesh as it passed through his jacket.

The first bullet threw Malvers back. He staggered as blood pumped from his wounded leg. He almost fell over Naylor, then pointed the rifle at the squirming Cheyenne. "Die, you miserable Indian!"

The next shots rang out together.

O'Reilly held a smoking cavalry pistol in a steady hand.

"Oh, lads," he called out, "me pistol discharged itself."

No one heard him. The sergeant's words were lost in the blast of the shotgun, which went off even as O'Reilly sent a bullet into Malvers. The army captain jerked into the air and toppled to the ground. Fox Running, who had grabbed the shotgun Naylor dropped, collapsed from the effort of reaching the gun and pulling its triggers. Malvers's pistol sent a bullet harmlessly into the ground near Fox Running's bloody head.

Once more, Fox Running struggled to his knees. He leaned on the shotgun to stand. He looked at the sky and raised one hand as if invoking something from beyond as the other hand shook from the effort of holding himself upright. "It is done."

He looked a challenge at Tallridge's quaking men, then collapsed to the dirt without another sound.

For a moment, everyone froze.

"Boys!" O'Reilly called. He went for Fox Running as others went to examine Naylor and Malvers. Both were dead. The squad kept rifles trained on Tallridge's men, some of whom had hoped the spectacle would divert the soldiers.

O'Reilly bent over Fox Running. "Ye got 'em, lad. Ye got 'em," he said.

"Bury me by Hat Creek Bluffs," said the bloody mess of the Cheyenne, as he slumped in the sergeant's arms.

CHAPTER NINETEEN

November 1882, Pine Ridge Agency, Dakota
Blue Sparrow, who had at first resented the intruder, wished a warm good-bye to Rides a Crow as the Cheyenne woman left the healing lodge on the day she was to return home. Together, they had worked until the pieces the soldiers brought back from Brittle Canyon were healed into a man who had finally emerged from his long sleep.

"It is like having five hundred children," Blue Sparrow remarked as they discussed warriors.

"Only on the days when they behave. On other days, it feels like a thousand! Thank you, my sister," said Rides a Crow. "They will live. We can only hope the spirits have a purpose to all of this."

"They must," Blue Sparrow replied, "but what it could be, I do not know."

"I know."

Both women turned to look at Fox Running, who would have fallen if Morning Shadow had not held him up. His face would be forever scarred by the buckshot that ripped across his cheeks. The deep wound to his left side would heal but leave him aching if he lived to be old. His left ankle was broken by one bullet, while another had cracked a bone in his left arm.

"You asked about the spirits," he said to Rides a Crow, as if a conversation that had ended weeks ago were still continuing. "They told me I am here to bring justice to these people, all these people—the white settlers, who want nothing more than a place to live and to plant things that grow, and our people, who want to worship and ride and live as we always have without killing any who do not deserve to die. There is good and bad in all; few can look past who they are to find it. This is the purpose the spirits have given me—to bring justice. I could easily have killed all the white men at the canyon, but they would have died as victims, not outcasts. The scribblers would once again have written about the Cheyenne Kid, and I would have been hunted all over again. I do not know if what the spirits want me to do will change anything—I do not even know if I understand—but I wanted you to know before you leave."

"And the justice you will get is to drop dead like a rock if you do not listen to me," Morning Shadow scolded. "Now lie down and stop bleeding on the blanket my cousin just made!"

She pushed him back into the lodge and smirked at the older women. "I believe you mean five hundred mischievous, ill-behaved, hard-of-hearing, self-willed, and disobedient children," she added.

"Who give women with nothing better to do the chance to talk about them," came a voice from the lodge as the two older women laughed.

Laughter was a welcome change. For days, Fox Running and Morning Shadow had lain next to each other, half alive. Morning Shadow had awakened one day and began preparing the lodge for Fox Running as though she were fully healed and knew he would live.

Fox Running had returned from the Brittle Canyon fight badly wounded. The army used its telegraph to reach Rides a Crow, who was famed as a healer. She brought Dooley, who had returned the Cheyenne girls taken by Petengill and learned that way of his friend's wounding. That triggered a wave of telegrams flying from Fort Keogh to Boston and back. They resumed after Dooley reached Dahlgren Post, changing dramatically in tone when it was clear that—after fourteen days without a clue whether he would live or die—Fox Running would live after all.

In the days that followed, the white soldier chief, Colonel Meyers, made a rare trip to the Indian land of the Pine Ridge Agency. The explosion he expected from Lame Bull's death was defused by the deaths of those who were guilty, and the fact that the army was part of bringing the men to justice, as Fox Running had told him would happen.

"You made a convert out of O'Reilly," Meyers admitted. "Perhaps I am one as well. I thought it might be generations before we ever work as one people. Perhaps there is hope amid all the hate. This was my last posting out here. I hope whoever comes after me can bring people together. It will never be easy, but perhaps it can happen."

Fox Running knew one incident would not change the tides that were colliding against each other, but he did not want to dash cold water on the man's hopes and said nothing.

Soon, he had reason to smile.

One day, the Lakota guards said a white man was there. He gave his name as John Dooley.

"Mr. Dooley?" Fox Running all but leapt into the Irishman's arms. "You are here! Here! How did you know? Why are you here? I am so glad to see you! Morning Shadow! Morning Shadow! This is my friend. The man who saved my life and soul in Boston!"

Dooley said he was there to talk about the future. He had waited until Morning Shadow, who he found as formidable as Katherine McGillicuddy, gave him permission to approach his friend. He'd brought with him a man named Paul Collins, whom Fox Running recalled as the man who spoke with the runaway Cheyenne at Hat Creek so long ago.

"There will be a reservation for the Northern Cheyenne in the Tongue River Valley. Somewhere in the next two years, I hope," Collins said. "Washington is . . . well, they can't make their minds up, but I know it will happen in the end. It is going to be a difficult time. Land issues. History. White men take potshots at Indians; Indians show their manhood by raiding whites. We have decided there must be someone who will work with the Cheyenne, with the army, with the government, with everyone when there are crimes so that only the guilty are punished and no war is started by one man being stupid.

"My fiancée has a cousin in Boston who knows of you—a woman named Katherine McGillicuddy." Collins paused as Fox Running registered the name of someone he had not thought of in months. "My fiancée told me to tell you, Miss McGillicuddy said your friend lies in her family garden, which she hopes will scandalize the next owners."

It hurt, but Fox Running laughed anyhow. Then Dooley took over.

"Miss McGillicuddy—and there, lad, is a lady of conviction—has decided she is starting a business. With her money—and she had lots of that, laddie—she wants to hire us to be a detective agency in Montana in this Tongue River Valley—a lovely place, lad, nothing like the city of Boston—that will solve crimes in ways neither the U.S. Army nor the Indians can because the army can't go on Indian land without a fight, and Indians trying to take the law into their own hands can spark a war. Apparently, someone from Fort Keogh has approved this and will work with the agency, a Captain Evans. There's a lass named Rides a Crow who is in this somehow, a Spirit Walker, they call her. She says you are to live with your people in the Tongue River Valley, and not here at Pine Ridge, because that is what the spirits demand. I hope ye understand that better than

I do, lad, but that was firm, and she appears to know more about your life than you do! I spoke with her. Did I tell you I broke yon Petengill's nose?"

Fox Running laughed at that. Dooley told the full story, chuckling at the encounter as he explained how he had come West in the first place. Fox Running realized it was good to have laughter back in his life; it was good to have friends.

"Your friend sent you a message to get well so she can work you to death creating justice out here, lad." Dooley was grinning. "It shall be an impossible job, but I think I shall enjoy it! Did I tell you I'm the boss? Ah, I warn ye, I brook no back talk from my employees!"

Fox Running couldn't resist smiling at Dooley. Then he looked at Morning Shadow, who was watching quietly.

"The Tongue River means moving," he said. She nodded. He turned back to Dooley. "The spirits wanted me to find justice. They have set me a challenge. I do not fully understand, but I accept. I will be bringing Morning Shadow and her brothers and sisters. When I was troubled, the Lakota sheltered me. Now, the Cheyenne can shelter a Lakota family."

They agreed the work would begin in the spring, because Fox Running was still weak from his wounds, and with the winter ready to begin any day, the world would be buried in white for weeks to come. Dooley, who said he always wanted to build something, would be going ahead of him to build a cabin. Fox Running was pleased to see the joy that radiated from his friend. The cabin would be ready in the spring, or perhaps sooner, Dooley said.

"Fall it will, lad, but I'll put it up again until it stays," Dooley said. "This building of life out here agrees with me!"

Fox Running was not worried about the time. Morning Shadow would be in mourning for her father until spring. When the snows melted, she and her family would be free to go with him to the lands of the Cheyenne, to form one more bond between the Cheyenne and the Lakota.

When Collins and Dooley had gone, Morning Shadow waited with a look of anticipation. Fox Running asked what could be on her mind.

She held his gaze. "Is there a question you wish to ask?"

"No."

"No?" Her tone was arch.

"As the oldest man in the family, it is Crow Rising I must bargain with, not his sister," he said with a grin, pointing at her brother as the boy approached. "But I fear I cannot find the two suitable cows, and he may drive too hard a bargain!"

"I believe the price has doubled," she said. "It may rise further if his sister decides to seek a better offer. Many men might wish to marry She Who Makes Men from the East Flee."

"I thought Crow Rising said it had been reduced, since no man wants his sister now that she has shown herself to be She Who Wields a Knife Freely."

She smiled. It seemed odd to feel happy, for as the world seethed around them, hate and fear were normal, not banter and hope. But as the north wind howled down, the way it had from the dawn of time and would until time ended, she knew the grim times the spirits sent were always followed by something better. The spirits sent those things, too, as a balm for torn souls.

Fox Running understood. The spirits had given him a purpose. The tangled path of his life had molded him into a man who belonged in no world and in all worlds. There would be storms and winds, brutal and deadly. Yet that was the way of things.

He watched Morning Shadow as she walked off with her brother and the rest of her family. They would be safe, now. Would he? The spirits knew the answer, perhaps. He did not.

Nor was he certain it mattered.

He had understood dimly over these past weeks that his life was no longer fully his own, that it was tied up in a purpose that went beyond him, that the winds governing his life could blow him about like the dead leaves flying before the cold gusts of approaching winter.

Morning Shadow and the rest of Lame Bull's surviving children were distant now. He was alone.

He turned into the wind and spoke.

"I do not know what will come, but I promise you who watch this day from a place I do not see that I will never surrender, until the stars leave the sky and the grass no longer grows. I shall make a path for the Cheyenne children to come that is worthy for them to walk," he said. "For all children."

He let the wind blow around him. He let it seep within him. He let it fill him.

"Or I shall die trying."

ABOUT THE AUTHOR

Rusty Davis is a freelance writer whose first four novels, *Wyoming Showdown, Black Wind Pass, Rakeheart,* and *Spirit Walker,* were published by Five Star. Rusty is currently writing the next chapters in the series of books chronicling the adventures of Fox Running and his friend John Dooley as they try to bring justice to the Tongue River Valley in a time of sorrow and strife. Rusty can be reached by emailing him at rustywork777@gmail.com.

The employees of Five Star Publishing hope you have enjoyed this book.

Our Five Star novels explore little-known chapters from America's history, stories told from unique perspectives that will entertain a broad range of readers.

Other Five Star books are available at your local library, bookstore, all major book distributors, and directly from Five Star/Gale.

<u>Connect with Five Star Publishing</u>

Visit us on Facebook:
    https://www.facebook.com/FiveStarCengage

Email:
    FiveStar@cengage.com

For information about titles and placing orders:
    (800) 223-1244
    gale.orders@cengage.com

To share your comments, write to us:
    Five Star Publishing
    Attn: Publisher
    10 Water St., Suite 310
    Waterville, ME 04901